ONE SWEET KISS

"It is perfectly acceptable for your maid to stand in for your mother," Simon said.

"I prefer to wait for Mama to come back from Europe."

"Nonsense," Simon said, dismissively. "I will not take no for an answer. Your grandfather thinks you should go into society and I have promised him to see that you do." Not quite the truth, but he was not going to let her wiggle out of the invitation. He brought her hand up and brushed his lips against her knuckles. "I can't let Lord Hamden down."

He dropped her hand and caught her chin with his fingers. "I want to see your eyes without these." He lifted her spectacles from her nose and set them on an end table. "Such a lovely violet color, a perfect complement to your dark curls."

Simon leaned over and kissed Brianna full on the mouth. He held the kiss a little longer than he meant, yet it was fairly brief.

"Until seven," he said, surprised to find himself a bit shaken by the sweetness of so fleeting a kiss . . .

—from *The Perfect Bride*, by Alice Holden

WEDDING DAY KITTENS

Jo Ann Ferguson
Alice Holden
Melynda Beth Skinner

ZEBRA BOOKS
Kensington Publishing Corp.
www.kensingtonbooks.com

CONTENTS

SOMETHING OLD, SOMETHING MEW

JO ANN FERGUSON

CHAPTER ONE

"Impossible!" Charlotte Longmuir peered over the line of freshly washed clothes. A dark-haired man was riding toward her.

Was it possible? Could Jeremy Drake be coming back to Upper Milburgh?

She bent to get another item out of the wash basket. It had been ten years since the marquess had left. He must be returning for his sister's wedding, but did he intend to stay after that?

Hanging the small shirt over the line, she watched the rider come closer. His hair was as black as Jeremy Drake's, and he must be as tall. He rode with the arrogance Jeremy Drake always had, even when he left Upper Milburgh in a cloud of shame when he was barely seventeen. Since then his father had died, and the title of Lord Milbury had come to him. Not once in those ten years had the marquess returned to Upper Milburgh. He had, it was said, been overseeing the family's shipping business, often traveling far beyond the horizon.

His hat and black coat were different because fashion had changed in the past decade, and she did not remember him having a mustache, but there might be other things different about him. Ten years could do a lot to change a man . . . or a woman.

The rider drew in his gray horse on the other side of the flint wall. He tipped his tall hat to her. "Good afternoon, miss." He smiled as he glanced at the line of clothes. "Good afternoon, *ma'am,* I should say. I trust I am not intruding on your wash day."

"Of course not." She tried to smile, but feared she had managed no more than a grimace when his eyes, which were the same silvery color as his horse, narrowed. "What can we do for you . . ."

"Jeremy Drake," he said, confirming what she found difficult to believe. His grin reappeared, as scintillating as sunshine on the stream behind the cottage. A twinkle in his eyes warned that he had not changed in the years he had been away. He still had a streak of mischief as broad as the sea. Woe be to the woman who forgot that. "Can I trouble you for some water for my horse and myself?"

"It is not far to Upper Milburgh."

"Upper Milburgh?" His eyes became ashen slits. "What makes you think that is where I am headed?"

She shrugged, hoping the motion looked nonchalant. "The road does not go much of anywhere else."

"You are right. So may I get some water, ma'am?"

She pointed toward the barn. "The well is on its far side. Help yourself."

He put his fingers to his hat. "Thank you, ma'am."

Charlotte's gaze followed as he rode toward the barn. Her hands gripped the prickly rope. Mayhap he was different if he thought of his horse before himself.

Or mayhap he did not want the poor beast to drop dead, so he would have to walk into Upper Milburgh.

Lowering her eyes before he chanced to see the accusation—and the guilt—there, she told herself she should not be judging him. She might have known him, but ten years must have made some difference in him. It had in her.

She froze as she heard a screech. A child's cry. She flung the shirt back into the basket. Gathering her skirt in one hand, she ran toward the sound.

By the barn, the horse was rearing up on its hind legs. Lord Milbury was struggling to calm the beast. Beneath it were two small creatures. A child and a calico kitten. The child was grasping for the cat, oblivious to the danger to both of them.

She ran forward and ducked beneath the horse's hoofs. Lord Milbury shouted something. She paid it no mind as she grabbed the little boy and threw herself back away from the horse. The child screeched again as they hit the ground hard, and the kitten gave a soft mew.

Charlotte gathered Hughie into her arms. He bristled with three-year-old indignity. Putting her cheek against his, she murmured nonsense phrases as she stroked his hair, which was a shade redder than hers.

"Is he hurt?"

At Lord Milbury's question, Charlotte shook her head gently as she continued the babbling sounds. The silly noises always quieted Hughie. She smiled as the anger left his pudgy limbs, and he softened against her.

"My kitty," the little boy said proudly as he held up the kitten, who was wiggling all four legs in an attempt to escape. "I catch my kitty."

"You could have been killed!" the marquess snarled.

Hughie stared up at him and burst into tears.

Lord Milbury started to apologize, but Charlotte said, "It might be better if you were silent now."

He seemed startled by her request, even though he was nodding.

"You must be more careful, Hughie," she murmured to the child. "You must never run in front of a horse."

"That big horse and that man were going to step on Patches." He glowered at Lord Milbury. "I saved him."

"And you. You must be more careful."

The little boy nodded with obvious reluctance, and he was confused why he was not being lauded for his heroics.

Kissing the top of Hughie's head, she called, "Petey?"

A tall, slender boy, teetering on the edge of manhood, peeked around the corner of the cottage. A puppy bounced along after him. "Yes?" He grinned and crowed, "So this is where she went!" He scooped up the kitten. Sitting beside

Charlotte, he put his hand on the little boy's arm. "Hughie, the kitten is all right."

"He was frightened," Charlotte said quietly. Then she smiled and tousled Petey's sleek black hair. "But you are not, I collect."

Petey chuckled. "Not me."

"Good." She stood and faced Lord Milbury, who was staring at the boys. Swallowing her sudden irritation, she told herself she should not expect him to be any different from the others in Upper Milburgh just because he had flouted their rules. "Did you find the dipper, Lord Milbury?"

"Lord Milbury? You know me?"

Knowing she must be careful, she said, "Everyone around Upper Milburgh knows you, my lord."

"I see." He wiped his water-jeweled mustache with his fingers, then rested his hand on the barn door. "Are these your sons?"

"Yes." Charlotte gave the boys a smile. Petey scowled at Lord Milbury, then, without speaking, carried the kitten into the cottage. Hughie hurried after them.

"Both of them?"

"Yes." She was not going to satisfy his curiosity. Too many times she had been asked who Petey's parents were. She had given up answering long ago. What she had to say nobody wanted to listen to, so why waste her breath?

She was about to tell him that. An excited bark interrupted her. This time, she grabbed two handfuls of her skirt and raced back to the line. The puppy was happily tearing into the laundry basket. Even as she ran, he jumped to grab the clothes on the line.

Charlotte clapped her hands sharply. The brown pup looked at her, his tail wagging. He tugged on the clothes.

"No!" she cried.

She tried to reach the tree to catch the loosening rope. It fell to the ground, inches from her fingers. The pup fled with two small shirts draped over him. She sighed. It all would have to be rewashed. Bending, she began to collect the soggy clothes.

"Wait a moment," Lord Milbury said.

"What . . . ?"

With a smile, he picked up the rope and lifted the clothes off the grass. She knew how heavy the line was and was amazed at his strength. What had he been doing while away from Upper Milburgh? Putting her hands next to his on the rope, she strained to help him.

"Hold it right there," he said through gritted teeth. "Let me wrap it around the tree."

She nodded and planted her feet against the trunk. Even so, the rope pulled her toward the tree. She held the rope up. Any slack would keep him from tying it. When he asked her to raise the rope higher, she did, leaning closer to the tree. His long coat flapped against her skirt, and a pleasing scent washed over her.

"There," he said as he knotted the rope into place. "Your laundry looks clean, save for what the pup stole."

"Thank you."

"I am pleased I could help."

She was about to step away to gather the few things that had fallen off the line, but his hand on her arm halted her. Looking over her shoulder, she said, "Lord Milbury, I have work that cannot wait." She hoped the trite words would cover her pulse's swift throbbing. She had not stood so close to a man as handsome and reckless as Lord Milbury . . . in ten years.

"Those boys are too old for diapers," he murmured. "How many youngsters do you have?"

His silver-gray eyes caught her gaze and held it. All good humor had vanished, leaving his face shadowed with a frown. She wanted to look away, but could not. Aware of the breadth of his shoulders beneath his black coat, she took a step back. Wet laundry caught her in a clammy caress.

At her gasp, Lord Milbury's easy smile returned. "You are skittish."

"I am not accustomed to people sneaking up on me."

"All I want is an answer to my question."

"What question?" Charlotte was afraid she sounded witless, but she could not recall what he had asked. Being unsettled by a man's bold stare was stupid, especially when that man was Lord Milbury, who was reputed to be the ruin of more than one young woman's reputation.

Not that she had anything to worry about. Her wicked reputation was well established in Upper Milburgh.

"How many children do you have living here?" he asked.

"Only three."

"Only?" He arched an ebony brow. "Quite a collection for a young woman like you, Mrs. . . . ?"

"Longmuir." She squared her shoulders. "*Miss* Longmuir."

His eyes widened. "Longmuir? Like Hubert Longmuir? Are you his daughter Charlotte all grown up?"

"Yes, Hubert Longmuir was my father."

"How is my old tutor?"

"Father is dead."

His smile wavered. "I am sorry."

"Thank you."

"You have changed."

She wanted to retort that he had not. He was just as dangerously charming as she remembered. She gave him a cool smile. "It has been quite a while since the last time you were dragged in for your lesson."

"I was never dragged." He walked around the wall and smiled. "I went when I knew there was no other choice."

Charlotte pulled a diaper out of the basket and hung it on the line. Mayhap if she did not answer, he would leave.

He did not. "I remember you with orange-red hair that stuck out in every direction. You were skinny and spent most of the time with your nose in a book. Did your hair turn to this lovely gold-auburn overnight, or did it take a whole decade? And I must say you have filled out very nicely." He eyed her boldly. "Very, very nicely."

"I hope the water satisfied your thirst," she said in her coldest voice, "for the rest of your journey."

"Why don't you just tell me to take my *congé*?" His fingers closed into a fist on the wall. "You were a nice little girl. I did not think you would grow up to hold a man's youthful pranks against him."

"I hold nothing against you."

He grinned. "And that is an even bigger shame. I can think of several things I would very much like you to hold against me."

Charlotte flushed, the heat scoring her face as it did when she went out for too long in the summer sun. She had hoped he was unaware of the rumors that began with, "Have you heard about Charlotte Longmuir and . . . ?" It did not matter which name was attached to hers.

The wisest thing she could do was to be quiet and hope he would leave. If it had been anyone other than the marquess, she would have gone into the cottage. She did not know if she could trust him not to steal the chickens clucking by the barn door. He had done that and worse in the year before he left.

"Youthful pranks does not describe what you did," she said, rearranging the clothes so she could fit more on the rope. "You should have known better."

"Comments like that convinced me to leave." He paused, then asked, "Aren't you curious where I have been?"

She shrugged, this time not having to pretend to be nonchalant. The conversation was going nowhere. He might have the whole day to idle away. She did not. She had bread to finish baking and tonight's supper to prepare and the baby's bottles to clean and . . . She did not want to think about what else she had to do before she tucked the children into bed.

Once she would have enjoyed a lively discussion about the places and people Lord Milbury had visited. How she had delighted in Father's tales of the people he had met during his travels when he was the marquess's age. Her father had possessed a storyteller's gift, and he made everything seem so real she felt as if she had been there herself. Now she was the storyteller to three children.

"It is not very neighborly of you to freeze up like the stream in winter," Lord Milbury said.

"We never truly were neighbors, Lord Milbury." Knowing she should not, she could not keep from asking, "Why are you back?"

His shrug mirrored hers. "It was time." His grin returned as he folded his arms on the wall. "After all this time, I thought people in Upper Milburgh might have missed me."

"If you wanted to give them someone to talk about, there was no need. They always find someone to talk about." She draped the last piece of laundry over the line. Wiping her hands on her stained apron, she said, "I hear your sister is marrying George Berringer."

"So did I." He laughed, and she could not keep from smiling. She knew too much about "the marquess's terrible son," but she had to own he still had that way of making a person feel important when he spoke to them. "When I heard about Eugenia's wedding plans, I knew I had to come home. So I left my bachelor's fare in London and—" His smile broadened. "I should not speak of such things with you, should I?"

She hefted the basket and balanced it on her hip. "You do not need to mince words with me. I am no wilting flower, Lord Milbury. We hear what London is like. Some of it might even be true."

"Some of it would singe your ears." He touched his fingers to his hat. "Thanks for the offer of some water, Charlotte."

"You—you are welcome." Her given name spoken in his deep voice sent shivers, not cold shivers, but heated ones, rippling along her skin like currents around a boulder. As he went toward his horse, she called, "Lord Milbury?"

He turned. A humorless smile pulled at his lips. Opening his coat wide to reveal his gold brocade waistcoat, he said, "I give you my word, for what it is worth, that I left everything where I found it."

"I did not mean—I was not going to accuse you of—" Taking a steadying breath, she came around the tree. "Lord Milbury—"

"You used to call me Jeremy. I would appreciate if you would call me that now." He held up his hand as she opened her mouth to protest. "I cannot call you Miss Longmuir any longer. You must address me as Jeremy so I can call you by your given name as I did when we were young."

She smiled. "That was not the only thing you called me."

"Pip, I believe, was the worst of the lot."

"You remember that?"

"My misdeeds come back during quiet times to haunt me." He grinned as he lessened the distance between them. "What happened to your freckles, Charlotte? Are you hiding them beneath rice powder?" He raised his fingers toward her cheek.

She moved back and put the basket between them, holding it with both hands. He stared at her, emotion gone from his face. Keeping her chin high, she met his stare. No matter what he might have heard, some things about Charlotte Longmuir had never changed.

For a long moment, he did not move. Then his outstretched hand lowered. She could not guess what he was thinking. His eyes were as hooded and lifeless as the big snake that came out to sun itself on a rock by the stream.

She said nothing as he swung into the saddle. He did not look back as he rode away. She clenched her hands on the basket. Too many times, she had seen Jeremy wear that expression when he was forced to attend tutoring sessions with her father. It meant trouble.

Lord Milbury's return was trouble for Upper Milburgh. She was certain of that. She wished she could be as certain if he intended to cause trouble for her and the children. She needed to learn straightaway.

CHAPTER TWO

Upper Milburgh was just as Jeremy remembered. On the stone church's square tower, roses grew higher. There was a new name on the smithy next to the market square. Otherwise, Upper Milburgh was unchanged.

He shifted in the saddle while he rode toward the great house dominating the village. Once Milburgh Hall had been a fortified house, but now it sat, complacent, on its small hill. Gardens surrounded it like necklaces around a dowager's neck. It, too, had not changed since he had left for London.

Everything was the same, even Charlotte Longmuir's soft blue eyes.

Why was *she* still in his thoughts? He should be thinking only about seeing his baby sister for the first time in ten years. Yet, he could not help being curious about what his onetime tutor's daughter was doing in a tumbledown cottage with three children.

He looked toward the church. Charlotte and her father used to live in the shadow of its tower. What had happened? Why was she now living outside of Upper Milburgh?

Jeremy stopped at the front door of Milburgh Hall. Only strangers used the ornate entrance, but he no longer felt at home here. Even in London, he often seemed an outsider. He had become too accustomed to a swaying deck beneath his feet.

He dismounted and looked around. The bushes along the walk were shorter than he recalled, but as neatly trimmed.

Mother never wanted anything to grow wild and free—not her hedges, not her son. She was about to discover she had succeeded better than she could have guessed. Ten years smoothed rough edges off a man.

He pulled his single bag off the horse and threw it over his shoulder. Climbing the steps to the door, he paused with a wry smile. Did the prodigal son knock or just walk in? He really did not want his mother to swoon. The odor of *sal volatile* was disgusting.

The door swung open. A squat, round man regarded him without expression. His gray coat gave his face a sickly hue, but his white waistcoat and breeches were spotless and his shoes shone.

"May I help you, sir?" he asked.

"Markley, don't you recognize me?"

He squinted. "No."

Taking off his hat, Jeremy grinned. "Have you really forgotten when I hid a stolen goat in the kitchen, Markley? I was sure you and Mrs. Langston would never forget how he ate half the food on the table and the tablecloth, too."

"Mr. Jeremy?" His eyes narrowed into ebony slits in his full face. "What in the name of heaven are you doing back here, my lord?"

"Heaven has nothing to do with it."

"I guessed that." The butler did not step aside to let him enter, nor did he smile.

Jeremy was saved from having to answer by a light voice calling, "Who is there, Markley? Is it Mr. Berringer?"

Although the old man looked as if he wanted to slam the door, he answered, "Lord Milbury is here, Miss Eugenia."

"Jeremy!" A flurry of white came down the stairs Jeremy could see past the door. Above the flounces and lace, a slender face bore only a hint of the child his sister had been. "Jeremy!" She pressed her hand to her mouth, then flung out her arms. "Oh, Jeremy! It *is* you. You are here."

"Yes, I am." He pushed past Markley and tossed his sack on the black marble floor. He grasped Eugenia at the waist and spun her about. When he set her on her feet, his brows lowered as she backed away, patting at her dark brown hair. She was nearly as tall as he, for the top of her head was even with his nose. Still as shapeless as a rag doll, she had apparently inherited Mother's bare bones shape. It was a shame she bedecked herself with ruffles that emphasized her spare frame, he thought, for her features were finely drawn, but he knew how important fashion was to the ladies.

Not to Charlotte Longmuir. The thought formed before he could halt it. Along with it came the image of Charlotte sitting on the ground, cuddling the child and kitten. Who would have guessed, after years of teasing Charlotte, that when he returned to Upper Milburgh, thoughts of her would taunt him? He wondered what other surprises were lying in wait for him.

"Eugenia," he added when he saw she was waiting for him to continue, "you have grown up on me."

"Ten years ago, I was only nine. And now—"

"You are marriage-high, as Father used to say."

Her smile wavered. "Is that why you are here, Jeremy? For my wedding?"

"What else do you think would bring me here? I could not have you getting wed without your big brother to weep at your wedding. Who else would be certain that you had something old and something new and something borrowed and something blue?"

Markley mumbled something under his breath as he went toward the back of the house. He did not close the front door. To make it easier for Eugenia to toss him out, Jeremy guessed.

He shut the door. He had not been thrown out of any place in more than five years. That night had changed his life by almost taking it. He had been stupid to get into that fight, and he nearly had paid with his life. If his first mate had not been there to gather up what remained of him and taken him back to the ship, Jeremy would not be alive now.

Picking up his satchel, he followed his sister up the stairs and into a parlor. It was the room where the family received guests, not the slightly more comfortable chamber where the family gathered. The room was well decorated from its painted ceiling to the pale yellow walls. A pair of rigid chairs faced a settee. A single table was set between tall windows. On it sat a sculpture of a dog amidst the aroma of beeswax and homemade soap. No doubt, Mother was determined to have everything perfect for the wedding.

Looking around, he asked, "Where is Mother?"

Eugenia drew a linen handkerchief out of her bodice and wound it around her fingers. "She is calling on the vicar. She should be home soon. I could send for her if you wish."

"There is no need to disrupt her day any sooner than necessary." He laughed as he dropped the satchel by a chair. "After all, that will give me time to unpack. Mother would never ask any guest, even her black sheep son, to leave."

"Jeremy . . ." She looked away.

"Go ahead," he urged.

"I have no wish to hurt your feelings."

"You cannot say anything to hurt me, Eugenia."

She crossed the room and sat on the settee. Raising her brown eyes, she whispered, "Mayhap you should not stay."

"I will do nothing to ruin your wedding, Eugenia."

"I know that, and even Mother will own to that once she gets over her shock." Tears bubbled at the corners of her eyes, and she dabbed her handkerchief against them. "I just do not know if Mr. Berringer will understand."

"He will understand." He laughed softly. When George Berringer had been sent away to school, it had been to prevent him from becoming involved in Jeremy's mischief . . . again. Only Jeremy and Berringer knew how many of those antics had been devised by the squire's son. "If he truly loves you, Eugenia, he will accept me just as I am. After all, I am your brother."

Jeremy sat on the white chair beside the hearth. He started to put his boots on the footstool, then halted when he saw the fancy embroidery and the pained expression on his sister's face. Nothing in this room was meant to make anyone feel at home.

"I know that." She reached forward and sandwiched his hand between hers. "Mayhap you have forgotten how long memories are in Upper Milburgh—"

"No, I have not forgotten. Nor did I expect anyone else to either."

She released his hands and turned away. "What I did not expect was for you to return for my wedding."

"Did you think I would miss it?"

"I hoped you had enough good sense to stay away." Her eyes filled with tears were reflected in the glass on the chimneypiece. "Mama will be so distressed."

"You mean she has not been pining away for her only son?" He laughed. "And here I was imagining Mother weeping into her pillow, night after night, with worry for me."

Eugenia's lips tightened into a straight line as she faced him. "This is no joking matter, Jeremy."

Slowly he came to his feet. "Do *you* want me to go?"

"Mother would—"

"No, Eugenia. Do *you* want me to go? I am not asking about Mother or George Berringer. I am asking about you. What do *you* want?"

She stared at him for a long minute. Indecision and anguish battled in her dark eyes. How different she was from Charlotte Longmuir! Charlotte had not hesitated a moment to answer his questions. He pushed aside these unbidden thoughts. Now was the wrong time to be thinking about a pretty redhead whose eyes were as heated as Eastern spices and whose heart apparently was bigger than the stack of books in her father's study. And, if those kids were hers, one thing *had* changed in Upper Milburgh. Charlotte had been as good as he had been wicked.

"Jeremy," Eugenia whispered, intruding on his thoughts again, "I would like you to stay."

"But?"

"No but. I would like you to stay."

He kissed her cheek. "I appreciate this, Eugenia, more than you can know. I have missed you."

"And I have missed you." She rested her head against his arm.

Jeremy swallowed his reply as Markley appeared in the doorway. He was carrying a tea tray with Mother's finest silver. No sign of his thoughts was on the butler's face. Jeremy struggled not to smile. Mother must have irritated Markley. Otherwise, the butler would not be risking Mother's ire by using her best silver for Jeremy.

"How lovely!" cried Eugenia, clapping her hands as Markley set the tray on the biggest table. "Thank you for being so thoughtful, Markley. Jeremy must be thirsty after his long ride."

"Mr. Berringer will be thirsty, too," Markley said grimly.

"Mr. Berringer!" Eugenia whirled to look out the window. "I forgot he was coming by this afternoon."

Leaving, Markley said only, "Humph!"

"Are you sure you wish to marry Berringer?" Jeremy asked. "I have heard one's lover is supposed to haunt your every thought."

"I can be excused in light of your unexpected arrival."

He smiled as he picked up his bag. Flinging it over his shoulder again, he went out into the hallway. He looked around the hallway, with its gallery of paintings of their ancestors.

"Don't you want some tea?" Eugenia asked, following him with the hushed swoosh of those ornate ruffles at her gown's hem.

"I should remove the road's dust before your intended arrives." He rubbed the back of his hand against his mustache. "I suppose I should get rid of this as well." He chuckled when she reluctantly smiled. "Now, little sister, let your big brother get a bath and cleaned up so I do not smell of horseflesh and dust when your beau comes to call."

"Mr. Berringer will enjoy seeing you, I am sure."

He started up the stairs, then stopped. "Are you sure about marrying him?"

"Mr. Berringer is a fine man. He has some land south along the river where he intends to build us a house."

"South? Near Charlotte Longmuir's place?"

Eugenia drew back in horror. "Charlotte Longmuir? Don't speak her name here. That harlot!"

"Harlot?" He could not keep from laughing, even as his thoughts strayed to her soft curves. And her lush, red hair—he would enjoy watching it loosened from its prim bun and falling across her shoulders . . . and his.

Eugenia's sniff halted his pleasing thoughts. "Who would have guessed your tutor's daughter would turn out to have no more morals than—?"

"Me?"

"—than a cat?" She frowned as she folded her arms. "Jeremy, how is it that you have already found the lowest of the low?"

"A special talent, I guess." He came back down the stairs. Why did Eugenia react so fiercely at the mere mention of Charlotte's name?

"That is not amusing."

He leaned his hand on the banister. "On that I agree, Eugenia. Why did you call Charlotte Longmuir a harlot?"

She gave a genteel shudder. "You saw those children."

"Yes."

"All of them?"

"I saw two boys, and I believe she mentioned she had three altogether."

"Three?" Eugenia's face blanched. "I thought it was just two."

He shrugged. "Two or three, what does it matter?"

"It matters a great deal. How many of them are hers, do you think?" Raising her chin, she smiled coolly. "Mayhap you have spent so much time among riffraff that you do not recognize decent people."

"Don't try to sound like Mother at her worst, Eugenia." He

sighed. "Are you certain it is your fiancé who will have a problem with me? Mayhap it is you."

Her stiff pose crumbled, and she pressed her hand to her bodice. "Oh, dear Jeremy, I did not mean to suggest you have done anything wrong."

"No, you meant only to suggest that Charlotte Longmuir has been corrupting the morals of Upper Milburgh while raising Cain. Cain and Abel and all their siblings, I would guess."

"Do not make a joke of her immorality."

Taking Eugenia by the shoulders, he drew her into the parlor and sat her on the settee again. "Tell me," he said, "what is so immoral about taking of children."

"If those boys are hers—"

"She would have had to have been with child before I left Upper Milburgh, and, as I recall, Charlotte is your age, Eugenia. I recall as well that usually her only companion was a book. The only miscreant in her life was Jeremy Drake."

Her eyes grew wide. "Jeremy, I did not mean—"

"I know what you meant."

"Stay away from her. She is trouble."

"Eugenia, stop talking in riddles." He readjusted the sack on his shoulder. "She is taking care of someone else's children. For that, Charlotte Longmuir should be praised, not vilified."

"I am not surprised *you* think so," said a deep voice.

Jeremy turned as Eugenia brushed past him. He had learned long ago not to make any sudden moves around strangers, especially ones with smooth voices.

He recognized George Berringer by his blond hair. Taller and stockier, Berringer had the bump on his nose where Jeremy had broken it when they were about the age of Charlotte's oldest. Brown eyes behind his spectacles narrowed as he lifted the gold rims off his nose. The sunlight glittered off the pearl buttons on the sedate black waistcoat beneath his coat of the same drab shade.

"Welcome home," Berringer said with a smile that suggested just the opposite. "Can I assume you will be staying for our wedding?"

He held out his hand. "Good to see you, Berringer." He noticed his sister was looking uneasily from him to her fiancé.

Instead of shaking his hand, Berringer put his arm around Eugenia's shoulders. "Listen to your sister and stay away from Charlotte Longmuir. You must not blacken your sister's name by connecting it with that harlot's."

"I was not planning on taking Eugenia for a call. I am curious about Charlotte Longmuir. If I had given her half a thought during the past ten years, I would have guessed she would be married to the vicar's son and teaching embroidery and music lessons. She was the most decent young woman I ever met." He rested his hand on the banister again.

Berringer gave a superior chuckle. "I collect you were wrong." He steered Eugenia into the parlor.

As he turned to climb the stairs, Jeremy caught his reflection in the glass over the hearth. Slowly his hand rose to touch the scar beneath his mustache. Two stitches had closed his lip when he had been on the wrong end of a knife. Two tiny stitches which left only the hint of a scar. Two tiny stitches sewn by Charlotte's steady fingers when he had reeled into her father's cottage, bleeding and drunk.

Not once had she chided him for being a fool. Rather she had sewn him up, warned him to watch for infection, and watched as he made his stumbling way home. Even when rumors of the fight had filtered through Upper Milburgh, she had not said a word.

Charlotte Longmuir had been a gentle, forgiving child. What had focused the town's ire on her? He intended to find out.

CHAPTER THREE

The door slammed, and Charlotte looked up from her sewing. She kept one foot on the rocker of the cradle as she turned to see Hughie giggling in the kitchen. She put her finger to her lips. He got wide-eyed and tiptoed closer to the cradle, holding the kitten with care.

"My baby is sleeping," Hughie announced in a lisping whisper.

Charlotte smiled. From the moment Dolly had joined their family, Hughie had considered the baby his. He had even chosen the baby's name. His cloth doll, also called Dolly, sat hunched in the corner, ignored since the baby's arrival.

"Yes," Charlotte murmured, "she is sleeping."

"My baby needs lots of sleep."

"Yes, she does."

"Hughie and Petey need to be quiet."

She smiled, because the little boy was so serious when he repeated back Charlotte's admonitions. "That is right."

"And she is smiling!"

Charlotte brushed Hughie's hair back from his face. It was just as stubborn as Charlotte's had been at that age. "Do you know what that means?"

"No."

"That means Dolly is listening to angels singing."

"Really?"

"Really." She smiled. "Why don't we go and get some milk for your kitten?"

"And lemonade?" Hope glowed in his eyes.

"First the kitten's treat."

Once the kitten had a bowl of milk and Hughie a glass of lemonade on the step where he could not ruin anything when he spilled it, Charlotte sat again by the cradle and worked on the small shirt she was mending. When she had these wonderful moments with the children, she no longer wanted to change her life. When she had first come here, she had missed her life in the village. Now she liked the quiet.

She chuckled softly. Quiet? She could not remember what that was. Even at night, when she tried to escape for a short while into a book, she had one or more of the youngsters snuggled up with her.

The door crashed closed again. Charlotte smiled when Hughie came in, putting his finger to his lips at the same time she did.

"Do you want more lemonade, Hughie?" she asked.

"Want him to have some, too?" he asked.

"Him?"

"The man in the yard."

"There is a man in the yard?" She stood. "What man?"

He shook his head. "Don't know. Man."

"Have you seen him before?"

"Yes."

"When did you see him before, Hughie?"

"Ago."

She smiled and patted his shoulder. Everything that was not now was "ago" or "tomorrow" to him. Gathering up the sleeping baby, she held out her hand to the toddler. She led them outside.

With a frown, she scanned the yard. It was empty. Hughie always told the truth, something she wished she could be as sure of with Petey, who sometimes stretched the truth to unbelievable lengths to keep himself out of trouble.

Trouble . . . The word lingered in her head as she stared at the gray horse tied to a tree. Lord Milbury! What was he doing back here?

Voices drew her toward the barn. Walking beneath the row of trees at its side, she started to step out of the shadows, but stopped when she heard Petey laugh. The sound astonished her. The boy was usually shy with strangers.

The marquess's laughter drew her gaze to him. His dark green coat had clearly been made by a skilled tailor. Above his now-polished boots, buckskin breeches followed the contours of his strong legs. His cravat was perfectly tied, and he looked every inch a marquess, even though his dark hair fell toward his gray eyes. She had held her own in their conversation yesterday, except when those incredible eyes focused on her. Hints of emotions best left unexplored had tempted her too much.

"So you are named Petey?" Lord Milbury was asking.

"Yes, sir." Guilt flashed across the boy's face. "I mean, yes, my lord."

"There is no need to look so abashed by a simple slip of the tongue."

"Charlotte says we need to speak better than others in the village if we want to make something of ourselves."

Lord Milbury's eyebrows rose. "She is right. A man is judged by the first words out of his mouth. So, what do you want to make of yourself, Petey?"

"A teacher mayhap." He grinned. "Or mayhap a sailor."

Charlotte's smile vanished as she heard admiration in Petey's voice. Lord Milbury was certain to make an impression on a boy Petey's age, but most likely the wrong kind. Without a family name as respected as the marquess's, one mistake could ruin Petey's life.

Lord Milbury's chuckle added to her irritation. "Petey the sailor? Or would you prefer Peter?"

"No." She heard the boy's pride. "Petey is what Charlotte calls me. My real name is Pitri Jahnu Dhumavarna."

Amusement filled Lord Milbury's voice. "That is quite a name."

"It was given to me by my mother before . . ."

"Before what?"

Charlotte had heard enough. "Petey, will you gather the eggs? The hens are hiding them again."

He grinned and with a shout ran around the barn. Hughie followed.

"What are you doing here?" she asked as she met Lord Milbury's eyes evenly. She must not allow those broad shoulders and that easy grin to beguile her. She had not slept most of the night because she could not rid her mind of him.

"I was merely talking with the boy."

"Interrogating him it sounded like."

Running his fingers through his black hair, he grinned. That curious warmth undulated through her again, but she tried to ignore it.

"You cannot blame me," said Lord Milbury, "for being curious about what is taking place here."

"Nothing is taking place. We are trying to live our lives." She looked down at the baby stirring in her arms. As she turned to go back to the cottage, she added over her shoulder, "And we could, if people would leave us alone."

"They will not."

Charlotte looked at him. "What have you heard?"

"Heard?" He shook his head. "Nothing, but I do not need rumors to know that your neighbors are not happy about what you are doing here."

"I told you. I am not *doing* anything."

"You are doing something genuinely kind by taking in children who are not yours." He gave her a cool smile. "Or are they not yours?"

"It is not like you to repeat gossip."

He hooked a thumb toward the well. "I stopped for a drink of water, but the boy said something about lemonade. That sounds delicious."

"Yes, it does."

"From your tone, I can see you have no interest in sharing some lemonade with me while we enjoy some poker talk."

"I told you that I have no use for gossip."

"I should think not when your name is the main topic of

conversation in Upper Milburgh." He sat on the edge of the well.

"All the more reason why you should leave. We do not need your kind of trouble here, Lord Milbury."

"*Lord Milbury?* I thought we were going to treat each other like friends again."

She shook her head. "No, I do not think so."

"Even your father gave me a chance to reform my ways."

"Father had that luxury. I do not." As the baby began to whimper, she rocked it gently. "Good afternoon, Lord Milbury. I hope you enjoy your visit in Upper Milburgh."

Jeremy smiled as Charlotte carried the baby toward the cottage. A most pleasing sight, for her exasperation added to the enticing sway of her skirt. When he had been talking to Petey, he had noticed her coming around the barn. He had wondered how long she would lurk in the shadows listening.

That conversation had been a surprise. If the boy had a name like Pitri Jahnu Dhumavarna, he must have at least one parent from India. His mother, Petey said, had given him that name. Although Jeremy had been certain that Charlotte could not be the boy's mother because the boy had been born before Jeremy left Upper Milburgh, he wondered about the other children. Hughie had hair that matched Charlotte's. The baby had been hidden in the blanket. Even if she had given birth to Hughie and the baby, why did Petey live with them?

Jeremy strolled toward the cottage. When the door closed quietly behind Charlotte, he sighed. He had hoped to get some answers, but she had kept her tongue firmly behind her teeth.

He leaned one shoulder against a tree. How could anyone consider her a light-skirt? She was the same Charlotte he had known ten years ago. Prim one minute and plainspeaking the next. Her quiet resolve and the certainty that she was doing what she must—a trait she had inherited from her father— was unaltered.

Yet, Eugenia believed that, unlike the rest of Upper Milburgh, Charlotte Longmuir had changed. And his sister was right. The bookish girl had become a beauty. Her rail-thin form had filled out in a way sure to get a man's attention.

He sat on the step and whistled a tune he had heard on some dock in the Far East. The words would turn even his ears red, but the melody was cheerful and perfect for a sunny day.

When Petey squatted next to him, his shirt loosened to hold a half dozen eggs, Jeremy waited for the boy to speak. Charlotte was right. He had been asking the boy probing questions, hoping to find out more about him and Charlotte and her unexpected family.

"Are you really a sailor?" the boy asked.

"I have been." He guessed Petey had asked Charlotte about *him*.

"I wish I could sail away." Setting the eggs by the step, Petey drew up one leg and propped his chin on his skinny knee. "I would go to where there are people like me. There are none around here."

"That is because you are special." Charlotte held a cup out to Jeremy.

He took it and sniffed.

"It is lemonade," she said stiffly as she set a basket holding the baby on the step. "I did not have time to brew up any hemlock."

"Lucky for me." He drained the cup in one gulp. "Thank you, Charlotte. You have been very kind. You must be accustomed to being very kind to passersby out here."

She flushed and motioned for Petey to go into the cottage.

Jeremy said nothing as the boy, confusion stealing his smile, gathered up the eggs and obeyed. Jeremy stood as Charlotte folded her arms in front of her. He recognized that stern scowl, because he had seen it on her father's face too many times.

"I have no idea what you are trying to do," she said in a stiff whisper, "but I will not have you making lascivious suggestions in front of the children."

"Lascivious? I was just trying to thank you."

"Were you?" Charlotte struggled to keep from raising her voice. "Or were you hoping to discover which rumors are true? You were pumping Petey like a dry well. You gave him a couple of compliments as a primer, then pumped and pumped and pumped to learn what you could from him."

"Do you think I am trying to be friendly only for that?"

"Of course you are." She jammed her hands into her apron pockets. "I don't know how long you will be staying in Upper Milburgh, but do not become friendly with my children."

"Because they might miss me when I leave?"

"Because they may get the wrong ideas about what is right and wrong."

"Just because I talked to them?" He gave a terse laugh. "You give me more credit than I deserve."

"I have never given you more credit than you deserve." She pointed toward his horse. "Have a pleasant ride back to Upper Milburgh, Lord Milbury."

He shook his head. "I'm not leaving until you stop calling me Lord Milbury. Charlotte, you always called me Jeremy. You were nice to me when no one else was."

"So be nice to me now and leave."

When he did not fire back a quick answer, Charlotte dared to look at him. He wore an expression as sad as Hughie's when the little boy was about to cry.

"And who else have you been nice to?" he asked.

She squared her shoulders and lifted her chin. Feeling sorry for him had been silly. "I think you should leave."

"Not until you tell me the truth. Which of those kids are yours?"

"All of them."

"Petey told me about his mother."

"I heard that."

"So which kids are yours?"

"I told you. All of them." She came down off the step and walked toward his horse. Cackling chickens surrounded her as she untied his horse from the tree. Holding the reins out to him, she said, "Good afternoon."

He grasped the reins and her hand. Pulling her toward him, he said, "Mayhap *you* will miss me when I leave."

"Don't flatter yourself."

"I would rather flatter you."

She tried to draw her hand out of his grip, but it was impossible. She could have jerked one of the trees out of the ground more easily. "Save your pretty words for your high-flying ladies in London."

"I hear you could teach them a trick or two."

Lowering her eyes, she shivered even as heat climbed her cheeks. "You wasted no time listening to rumors."

"I have not been here for ten years. It was kind of you to give them someone else to talk about."

She saw he was grinning. Knowing she was a fool, she smiled back. Jeremy had too much charm. She should be resistant, but she could not help liking how he countered everything she said with a quick answer.

Quietly she said, "Giving them someone to talk about was not intentional."

"This is."

Before she could speak, he released her hand. His arm encircled her waist.

She held up her hands as he leaned toward her. "Stop, Jeremy!"

"Now that sounds like the Pip I used to see with her nose in a book."

"Let me go. If someone were to see . . ." She shuddered at the very idea.

"You are right. There is already too much talk about you, but you cannot fault a man for being curious about what is true and what is not."

Exasperated, she tried to squirm out of his arms. They tightened around her. "Let me go!"

"Not until you tell me the truth. You are acting like a little girl still, abashed at the idea I might kiss you."

"You should not say things like that." She knew she was blushing when her face became hot and his smile grew tight.

"I suspect you do not get kissed often, other than by the children." He framed her face with his broad hands. "To be honest, I suspect you have not been kissed at all." He tilted her face closer to his. "What is the truth, Charlotte? It is time you tell me."

CHAPTER FOUR

"The truth is simple," Charlotte whispered as she gazed up into Jeremy's amazing gray eyes. So many emotions had flashed through them, but now she dared to believe she was seeing honest curiosity. And why shouldn't he be curious? "The many tales that swirl through Upper Milburgh have very little resemblance to the truth."

"Which is?"

"That I am the mother of all these children."

"Charlotte . . ." he growled.

"I am their mother *now*."

He stepped back, drawing his arm from around her waist. She wanted to ask him to hold her again, but she would not be so witless. If someone had happened to see her in Jeremy's arms, new tales would fly through the village.

Leaning against the tree, he lashed the reins around it again. He looked back at her. "Who was their mother before?"

"Their *mothers*. Petey has different parents from the younger two."

"So the younger ones are related?"

She nodded. "Their mother is my cousin Sylvia." Blinking to keep back the tears that came too easily when she thought of her cousin, she whispered, "Their mother *was* my cousin Sylvia Passmore. She died when Dolly was born.

"I guessed that." He frowned as he glanced in the direction of the village. "But why would everyone fault you for taking in your cousin's children? Such things are done often by people with good hearts like yours."

"Not everyone in Upper Milburgh faults me. Some like the vicar and Mrs. Croft at the butcher shop have never flagged in their faith in me and the truth."

"But why have others changed their minds about you?"

She plucked a long piece of grass and ran her fingers along it as she walked back toward the house. "Before Hughie was born, my father sent me to help Sylvia because she was ill. I stayed with her and her husband Lionel at their house on Lord Williard's estate where Lionel serves as the earl's estate manager. I was there until Hughie was born. Not once did I come back to Upper Milburgh, not even when my father died."

"You did not come home for your father's funeral?"

She understood his astonishment. He must have seen that she and her father had been so close. How many of their conversations about the books they read had Jeremy interrupted when he came for his lessons?

"Sylvia needed me," she said quietly, "and I knew Father would have understood."

He picked up the kitten that was peering into the basket and set it where it would not risk being trampled again. Sitting on the step, he folded his arms over his knees.

She could not keep from staring at his hands. She had always admired strong hands, and Jeremy's were lined with sinews and covered with soft, dark hair and rough skin that bespoke a life far from the gaming hells and brothels of London.

"Is the baby your cousin's, too?"

"Yes." When her eyes filled with tears, his hands blurred in front of her. "Sylvia did not survive that birth, and her husband could not bear the sight of the baby, so I offered to take Dolly." She looked at the basket and smiled sadly. "Lionel used to come and visit Hughie regularly when he could take time from Lord Williard's estate. He has not been here since Dolly was born three months ago because he has been busy overseeing the planting and preparing the estate for the earl upon his return from the Season in London."

"Your cousin's husband would call and remain here overnight?"

"He *is* family, Jeremy!"

Holding up his hands in surrender, a pose she suspected he seldom took, he grinned. "Do not aim that glare at someone who is not accusing you of anything but having too generous a heart. You must realize that Passmore's visits are what gave rise to the rumors about you having a lover."

"Oh." She knew she should say something more intelligent, but no words came into her head. She had not given any thought to where that rumor had arisen.

"And what about Petey?" Jeremy asked.

"My cousin's husband had served for several years in India. A friend there, who had an Indian mistress, asked Lionel to bring Petey back to England where he could be educated and eventually serve as his father had."

"Why didn't the friend bring the boy here himself?"

"He was married well, and he knew the family would never accept the boy. Lionel has no title. As well, he owed his friend for saving his life, so he assumed Petey's care."

"And then he gave the task of raising the boy to you?"

Charlotte shook her head, smiling as she recalled the conversation at the Passmore house. "I offered, Jeremy. I was healthy, and I could take care of two boys as easily as one while my cousin regained her vigor." Her smile faded. "Or so I thought."

"Until you returned to Upper Milburgh."

"Where the assumption was that Hughie was mine." She smiled as she glanced at the two boys running along the stream. "He really is mine now."

"But if you refuted the rumors—"

Her mouth tightened. "Don't you think I tried? Each time I thought I had the rumors halted, they would begin anew. Finally I decided defending myself was not worth the effort."

"Your reputation—"

"Is not worth the children's unhappiness. Even though Petey is quite young, he is well aware of the stares and the whispered asides. I chose to move here where they could live without a shadow over them." Her fierce expression eased into another smile. "And, to own the truth, I have enjoyed being here."

"You always enjoyed being able to spend time by yourself." His nose wrinkled as he gave her a wry grin. "And here I thought you were wasting your life."

"Isn't that a coincidence? I thought the same about you."

"It seems neither of us have turned out exactly as we—or anyone else—assumed we would."

Her reply was halted by shrill laughter from near the stream. It was followed by splashing and more laughter.

When Jeremy looked at Charlotte, he was amazed to see an expression he had seen often on her face ten years ago. Then he had not understood what it was. Now he did. It was a longing to throw off her obligations of being the well-behaved daughter and to delight in some childish fun.

Standing, he grabbed her hand and tugged. "Come with me."

"What?" Her expression now belonged to a woman.

That realization halted him from pulling her toward the stream. The longing still remained on her face, but it was unlike the childlike craving he had seen moments ago. Her lips had softened with the single word and remained parted, an invitation for him to satisfy the yearning in her eyes. An answering need surged through him, an exquisite ache that had plagued him from the moment he had seen her doing her chores. When he lowered his mouth toward hers, her eyes closed, her ruddy lashes curling against her skin.

"No! Me first!" came a cry from the stream.

She pushed away from him and ran toward the back of the cottage. He wondered what the children were about to attempt that they should not.

Picking up the basket, Jeremy followed. The slope was gentle, and he took care not to jostle the basket. Hearing a bark, he saw the pup that had pulled down the laundry was now splashing along the stream toward the boys. Hughie was standing on the shore while Petey hung upside down from a branch hanging over the water.

The boy inched back toward shore when Charlotte called to him. He looked down at the pup, which was leaping up to grab his shirt. With a surprised cry, Petey tumbled from the tree into the water. The pup raced away, terrified.

Jeremy was not a bit surprised that Charlotte began to laugh. She had been very willing to overlook his misdeeds, and, as much as she loved these children, she was sure to forgive them for even more.

"Are you hurt?" she called from the bank.

The boy sat in the slow-moving water and rubbed his head. "That was fun."

"Me next!" cried Hughie. "I want to jump down from the tree."

Jeremy laughed as he came to stand beside Charlotte. Handing her the basket, he bent toward Hughie, who was hopping up and down in excitement.

"Falling out of a tree headfirst is not always a good idea," he said.

"I want to fly!" Hughie insisted.

"That is easy enough to do." He grasped the boy by the arms and swung him gently in a circle.

"Faster!"

He turned a bit more quickly.

"Higher!"

Raising his arms, he lifted the boy farther off the ground. Hughie chortled with excitement, but Jeremy looked past him toward Charlotte.

She sat on the ground, and she was smiling that indulgent smile he had seen each time she looked at the children. It was the same expression he had witnessed when she had spoken with excitement about a new book her father had brought her to read. He wondered if she had time for reading now.

As Petey clamored for a turn, Jeremy set the littler boy on

the ground. He spun the older one around, taking care that Petey's longer legs did not strike anyone or anything. Then he found himself giving Hughie another turn. Petey waited patiently before holding out his hands again.

Jeremy grasped them, but his eyes were caught by an unexpected expression on Charlotte's face. He spun the boy as he tried to keep his eyes focused on her. Why did she look as if she were about to cry?

"Petey," he said as he lowered the boy to the ground, "your turn to spin Hughie. Be careful with him."

"I will!" He motioned to the younger boy. "Give me your hands."

Paying no attention to Hughie's squeals of delight, Jeremy went to where Charlotte sat. He squatted beside her and asked, "What is wrong?"

"Wrong?" She looked up at him with glittering eyes. He wondered if anyone had ever seen such a vivid shade of blue as her eyes. Not even the sky over a calm sea on a cloudless day could aspire to such a perfect blue.

"You look as if you want to cry."

"There is nothing wrong," she whispered. "I am simply amazed how Petey put his hands out to you. He seldom trusts any man. I think it is because his own father abandoned him and Lionel seldom is here."

"You are raising them well."

"I hope so."

"So they don't end up in trouble all the time as I did."

She laughed. "You were not in trouble *all* the time."

"Most of it."

"Yes, most of it. I cannot imagine what you might have done while hanging upside down from a tree."

"No need to imagine. I can tell you." He sat beside her. It took every ounce of his self-will to keep from reaching out and tucking one of her auburn curls back behind her ear. If he touched her, he doubted he would be satisfied with such a chaste pleasure. Realizing he was staring at her lips, he forced his gaze to the sparkling stream. "George Berringer lashed me up one time and left me hanging there overnight."

"Mr. Berringer? The man who is marrying your sister?"

"He was not always the pattern card of propriety."

"I know."

Charlotte looked away from Jeremy's frown. She did not want to be reminded how Mr. Berringer had teased her often when they were children. The past was in the past, and she did not want to revisit it.

When the boys rushed forward, grasping Jeremy's hands and urging him to twirl them around again, she laughed as he pretended to be reluctant to come to his feet. He wrapped an arm around each boy and lifted them into the air. They shrieked with anticipation of what he might do next.

She watched as he set both boys on their feet and sat again. They tugged on his sleeves until he motioned for them to sit beside him. Quickly he loosened Hughie's shoes, pulling them off. Petey undid his own and needed no invitation to jump into the water.

"Wait for me," Jeremy said to Hughie, who rocked from one foot to the other with impatience.

Pulling off his boots, he tossed them onto the grass. He picked up the little boy and jumped with both feet into the water. Water rose around him, speckling all of them. As she jumped to her feet with a gasp, he put Hughie down in the water. He did not let go of the little boy's hand.

"You next, Charlotte!" he called, waving for her to join them.

"I cannot leave the baby alone for—"

"She will be fine in the basket, and you can hear if she wakes."

"I have so much to do." Her excuse sounded lame, even to her.

"I would say you do, and the first thing on your list should be to join us for some fun." He handed Hughie's fingers to Petey, then waded toward her.

When she hastily stepped back, unsure what he planned

to do, she was not quick enough. He grasped her foot. As she tried to shake it loose, she leaped about, waving her hands wildly as she fought for her balance. The boys crowed with laughter, shouting to Jeremy.

He did not reply as he slowly drew her foot toward him. Sliding down the slight slope toward the water, she tried to keep from falling. It was useless. She dropped to the ground with a thump.

Even though the children laughed, she was about to lambaste Jeremy until her gaze was caught by his as he pulled off her shoe. The stream at flood tide could not douse the fires within his storm gray eyes. His fingers boldly uncurled along her ankle. She needed to tell him to stop. No, that was not what she needed, for a quiver rippled outward from where he touched her, proving that her real need was his touch.

Had she lost every bit of sense she had ever possessed? How many other women had he caressed as brazenly? She did not care about the answer to either question when he cupped her other ankle. As gently as if she had no more substance than dandelion seeds floating on the breeze, he drew off her other shoe. He did not let her eyes evade his as he set the shoe carefully in the grass. Stepping back, he held out his hand.

She wondered if she could move her fingers to put on his hand. Every inch of her was tingling with the memory of his touch. She had been wrong when she believed Jeremy had not changed. He still had that powerful charm, but now it was a man's charm, a dangerous mixture of desire and mischief. Any woman who allowed herself to be caught up in it was want-witted.

Her hand settled on his. Everyone thought Charlotte Longmuir was a fool, so why not exult in proving them right? Just for a few minutes.

"Shall I jump and splash everyone as you did?" she teased.

A mistake, because the boys called for her to splatter them. She gave them a smile as she stepped carefully into the water. It was still cool, perfect for the day.

Laughing as the children played, Charlotte sat on the edge of the bank. Her feet dangled in the water while the boys cupped handfuls of water and tossed them at each other. When she sprayed water toward them with her feet, they crowed with happiness and begged her to do it again. She did, and they giggled.

When Jeremy sat beside her, he said, "I will watch them if you want some quiet time to yourself."

"What?" She had not thought he would want to rid himself of her so quickly.

"I know how you love to read, Pip, and I doubt you get much time with a baby and two boisterous boys."

He slid his arm behind her, but did not touch her. Even so, she was aware of each inch of his brawny arm so close to her. Was it jeweled with water like his other, the droplets clinging to the hair along it?

"You want me to go?" she whispered, unable to halt the words from slipping past her lips.

"When is the last time you had a moment to yourself?"

"I don't remember."

"I thought as much. I will watch over them. Go ahead. You will not hurt my feelings."

Awed by his generosity when she had been icy to him less than an hour ago, she let amusement drift into her voice. "There are those who say you don't have any feelings."

"You never believed that."

"No." She could not use humor as a shield when he remained serious.

"Then believe me now when I say I do not mind watching the children while you have some time alone to read—"

"I don't have any books except ones for the children to study. My father's books were sold along with the cottage in the village."

"Then I must bring you some to read. I think I saw the latest collection of poetry by the French poet Marquis de la Cour on my sister's table. Do you like his poetry?"

"I prefer prose. That way I can become lost in the story or the theory proposed by the author."

"I shall bring you books next time I call. You do want me to call, don't you?" His voice became a husky whisper. "Unless you truly want to be alone . . ."

As his breath warmed her cheek, she turned her head to see his face close to hers. Her gaze flicked down to his sensual mouth, but she quickly raised it. Not fast enough, she realized when the silver flames in his eyes deepened.

"It is difficult," he whispered, "to imagine Pip with her freckles and her unruly red hair has become such a beautiful woman."

"You are just as I imagined you would be."

"Does that mean you have thought about me in the past ten years?"

She smiled. "I doubt anyone in Upper Milburgh has forgotten you."

"I was not talking about anyone else. Just you."

"I did think about you. I have to own that I wondered, on more than one occasion, if you were in a foreign prison somewhere."

He picked up a strand of her hair and twirled it around his finger. "Since I left, I have been most of the way around the world, and I learned to obey the laws of whatever land I was visiting."

"Even Upper Milburgh?"

He laughed. "Especially Upper Milburgh."

As the boys ran toward them, he brought her to her feet. He picked up his boots and the basket with the still-sleeping baby. Looking from his filled hands to her, he smiled and held out his elbow.

She gathered up her shoes and the children's before putting her hand on his arm. The day had become wonderful, especially because she knew how unique it was. Jeremy had not mentioned how long he would be staying in Upper Milburgh, and she did not ask. She did not want to know how long it would be before he left her alone—really alone—again.

CHAPTER FIVE

The sideboard in the breakfast room was loaded with food, and as Jeremy looked over the variety of food, he could not help wondering what Charlotte would be eating this morning. He heard the clock from the hallway chime the midmorning hour, and he guessed she probably had already eaten and fed the children and was busy with her chores.

He hoped she would find time to read the books he had stacked in the book room. That chamber had been his father's favorite place in the old house. He doubted anyone had been within its walls, save to clear away the dust, since his father's death. The stacks of papers on his father's desk, accounts that were months overdue even though there were funds to pay them, had been handled by the butler whenever he could steal time from his other work. Learning that nobody had taken over Smythe's work after the estate manager had retired last year, Jeremy knew he must get the accounts back in order himself, a task he usually would have anticipated with glee because he enjoyed seeing a column of numbers making perfect sense.

Instead he had spent his time choosing books for Charlotte from the untouched shelves. Mother preferred reading the newspapers to see if she discovered a friend's name in one of the columns. Eugenia had not been much of a reader as a child, and he had seen no sign that had changed, for the only book he had seen her open was the book of sickish sweet French poetry.

As if she were answering his thoughts, Eugenia walked into the room. She gave him a joyous smile and a good morning, and he guessed she was thinking of her wedding breakfast, which would be held in two days. Or was she thinking of being in her husband's arms the night after they spoke their vows?

The picture in his mind of Berringer kissing Eugenia metamorphosed into himself holding Charlotte. He thought of her soft lips parting as he sampled them. They would be sweet. He was certain of that.

"Good morning, Jeremy," his sister repeated firmly, and he guessed he had been lost in his imagination long enough for her to grow impatient.

He kissed her cheek. "Good morning, Eugenia. Are you finished with that book of poetry I saw you reading?" He spooned steaming eggs onto his plate. There was enough food for a dozen people. Mayhap there was to be a gathering at the house. If so, no one had mentioned it to him.

"Do you want to read it? You called the poems mawkish, I believe." She regarded him with amazement while she put much less food on her plate than on his.

"I have a friend who would be interested in reading it."

"In Upper Milburgh?"

"I *do* have friends." He carried his plate past the tall window with its ivory draperies. He sat across from her at the mahogany table and poured himself some coffee. When he held up the pot in her direction, she shook her head. "If you are done with it, I would like to share the book."

"You are welcome to it." Her nose wrinkled. "To own the truth, Mr. Berringer agrees with you about the poetry. He does not like me to read such insipid verse."

He laughed. "Insipid? The marquis is quite the talk of London. As usual, if I understand poker talk correctly."

"You? Listening to gossip?" She trilled a laugh. "You never had use for gossip before."

"Not when it was about me."

Color flashed up her face, and he apologized. He had not

meant to put her to the blush. Eugenia had not minded straightforward conversation when they were younger. Now she seemed shocked by too much he said.

Changing the subject, he asked, "Are you expecting guests for breakfast?"

"No." She turned, the spoon halfway between her plate and mouth. "Why?"

"There is enough food on that sideboard to feed half the crew of a ship."

"Cook wishes to make sure her assistants know how to make enough food for the wedding breakfast, so she has been having them practice." She reached for a muffin from the basket on the table. "There must not be any lack of food that day. We do not want anyone going away hungry, for that would be a bad omen for my life with Mr. Berringer."

Jeremy chuckled. The guests at the wedding breakfast! Why hadn't he thought of it before now? Picking up his cup, he took a sip before saying, "I trust it will be no problem if I invite a guest or two more." He grinned over his cup. "Or three or four."

"Just let Markley know so there are enough settings."

"I shall do that."

"May I ask whom you plan to invite?"

"Charlotte Longmuir and the children she cares for."

"What?" Eugenia's face had become as colorless as the draperies behind her. "What did you say?"

"I wish to invite Charlotte to the wedding."

"How could you even suggest that!" She set the spoon on the table with a crash. Putting her hands up to her face, she cried as her shoulders shook, "You will ruin everything, Jeremy!"

He stood and, walking around the table, gently drew her hands down. "I had hoped you would be willing to help someone who needs your help so badly."

"*She* does not deserve—"

"To be banished from Upper Milburgh. Eugenia, your wedding is the most important event in this village in years.

If others see that you are willing to welcome Charlotte, the rest of the village will follow suit."

She rolled her glistening eyes, and a single tear flowed down her cheek. "Jeremy, you are asking me to tarnish my reputation and my wedding for a woman who has disgraced herself and the village."

"You know I would do nothing to hurt you."

Her eyes widened. "Is this an attempt to infuriate Mother?"

"Why would I wish to do that? Mayhap exasperating her was my goal when I was younger, but I have learned what a waste of time such pranks are."

"You seem to be gaining some wisdom at last," said his mother from behind him.

Jeremy smiled as Lady Milbury entered the sunny breakfast room. She was the picture of what Eugenia would look like in thirty years. Tall, but spare, she wore her graying hair beneath a cap with a ruffle that framed her face perfectly. Her morning gown was a sedate color, even though his father had died not too long after Jeremy left Upper Milburgh.

"Mama!" beseeched Eugenia as she rushed to Lady Milbury's side. "Do ask him to be sensible."

"It sounds as if he is."

"Not when he intends to invite Charlotte Longmuir to my wedding!"

"Is that so?" She turned to her son. "I assume you have a reason for such an out-of-hand action."

"I do have a reason," he replied, clasping his hands behind his back. He shifted when he realized that was the same posture he had assumed as a youngster when his mother was about to scold him.

"Which is?"

For a moment, he was tempted to tell her the truth. The idea had come to him upon seeing the feast waiting on the sideboard. Charlotte and her children needed a chance to have a day without any worries, a day when the children could scamper about with the children from the village and when Charlotte could join in with the dancing they would enjoy at the wedding breakfast. Dancing *with him,* for the idea of holding her close and swaying to the music was as heady as the finest Jamaica rum.

Instead, he repeated what he had told his sister about the wedding being a chance to mend the chasm that had grown between Charlotte and those who believed the stories about her. It was the truth, as well, but not the complete truth.

"Jeremy, you are Lord Milbury," his mother said, "and it behooves us to listen to your requests, but you must try to see the situation from your sister's point of view."

"I do, Mother. I see how the situation has estranged once-good friends in the village. The few who side, albeit not openly, with Charlotte are taunted as widgeons. The others who repeat in any willing ear the gossip about her and the children do so only because they believe, for the most part, that they are uttering fact. They believe the lies are true because no one in this family has done anything to countermand them."

"Are you asking us to lie?" choked out his sister.

He motioned for his mother to sit. Once she had, he answered, "You know I would never ask that of you, Eugenia. Nor would I ask that of you, Mother. I have long seen how you value the truth. That is why I never spoke anything but the truth to you."

"When you could not avoid my questions of what mischief you had embarked upon." His mother smiled and wagged a finger at him. "My dear boy, you were cursed with your father's charm and your mother's brains, and you learned to use both at a very early age."

"I had excellent teachers." He bowed his head toward her before adding, "Including Mr. Longmuir."

"And his daughter?"

"What could a child have taught me?" He did not add that there were a few things he would greatly enjoy studying with his tutor's daughter now. A study of pleasure, both giving and taking.

"I have no idea, but I know you, Jeremy. You have always

had, in spite of your rambunctious nature, a great sense of honor. Even though you were willing to sully your own reputation whenever you wished, you have chanced besmirching your family's on very few occasions. Each time, it was because you believed most sincerely that a great wrong must be righted."

He nodded, recalling both times he had dared to risk his parent's ire *and* the title's honor. Once, it had been to protest a plan to put a dam across the stream that ran through the village, so a mill could be built. Several families, including the Berringers, would have lost their homes, but not building the mill was an embarrassment to his family and kept much gold out of their coffers. The second time had involved the village's vicar, whose living belonged to the marquess. He could not recall the details of what he and Berringer had attempted, but he remembered the discouraged look on his father's face when he was called to task for the prank.

"So why are you willing to risk our family's honor now?" continued his mother. "What about Miss Longmuir has persuaded you that she needs a knight in shining armor to save her?"

Eugenia had remained surprisingly silent throughout the exchange, so Jeremy was not astonished when she burst out with, "She has a rare charm of her own. I have not ever seen it myself, but she works her spells over the men coming to call on her at the oddest hours and staying beyond the length of decency."

"You are speaking of Charlotte's late cousin's husband," Jeremy said quietly.

Too quietly, he discovered when his sister raged on. "Now she has cast Jeremy in some of her dark magic." Her eyes grew wide. "Do you think that she was studying evil magic all those years she spent doing little but reading?"

"Unlikely." Mother folded her hands in her lap as she aimed a scolding glance at Eugenia. "Mr. Longmuir was a man of unquestionable integrity. He would not allow his daughter to do anything out of hand."

"You do not believe the rumors about Charlotte!" Jeremy gasped.

"Not with certainty, and your explanation that her late cousin's husband came to call and was granted the privilege of sleeping under her roof with her and her children—"

"*His* children. The youngest two were born of his wife, and he is the guardian of the oldest."

His mother nodded. "You have no idea how pleased I am to hear that, Jeremy. I never could understand how such a fine girl could go so bad so quickly."

"But why have you allowed the rumors to continue?"

"I have not *allowed* them to continue. Any attempt to silence them seems futile. Like weeds, they simply sprout in a new place."

"Then, mayhap, having her and the children attend Eugenia's wedding will put the rumors to rest once and for all." He looked at his sister, who was regarding both of them with shock as if she believed they both had gone mad. "You agree, don't you, Eugenia?"

"Mother!" she moaned.

"I must concur with Jeremy on this, Eugenia, but it would be pleasant to have your agreement as well before he extends an invitation to Miss Longmuir and the children."

Eugenia turned on her heels and ran from the room. Loud sobs came in her wake.

Lady Milbury stood and wiped her hands of some unseen dust. "Well, that matter is set."

"What?" he asked.

"You may invite Miss Longmuir to attend the wedding."

"And the wedding breakfast?"

His mother smiled. "You are never satisfied with a small victory, are you, son? Very well, you may extend her an invitation to the wedding and the wedding breakfast." She went to the sideboard and picked up a plate.

He started to walk back to his seat, then paused. Helping Charlotte was uppermost in his mind, but he did not want to hurt his sister at the same time.

"Mother, I thought you wished Eugenia to agree before an invitation was extended."

He was astounded when she winked at him, and he wondered if his mischievousness had been a legacy from his mother instead of his father.

Laughing, she said, "But, my son, she did not say no."

"No."

Jeremy wondered what he had said to cause Charlotte to misunderstand him. In his mind, the words had been simple and to the point. She and the children were welcome to come to the wedding at the village church and the wedding breakfast at Milburgh Hall.

Charlotte looked exhausted, her red hair loose around her face and her blue eyes dim, so mayhap she *had* misunderstood him. He would try again.

"Mother and Eugenia are willing to have you attend," he said, stretching the truth only a bit, "and I think it would put an end to the rumors when the rest of the village sees that the marquess's daughter welcomes you."

"Thank you."

He had expected more than those two chill words. Uneasy and uncertain, sensations he was barely familiar with and did not appreciate, he stumbled on. "Don't you see, Charlotte? Once you are seen to be in good pax with Eugenia, who can denounce you?"

"It is kind of you to make this offer, Jeremy, but no."

"No?"

Charlotte might have found Jeremy's boyish bafflement charming under other circumstances. His wide eyes and raised brows reminded her of the lad he had been, full of devilment and yet so kind to a quiet girl who saw him as brave as one of the heroes in the books she loved.

"Please thank your mother and your sister for the invitation, but I cannot chance what might happen. The children—"

He frowned. "Children can weather far more than you give

them credit for. Hughie and Dolly are too young to take note of any slights, assuming there are some. Petey has already endured them."

"Too many."

She thought he might argue more, but he nodded. That startled her. The Jeremy she had known would never accept defeat. Had he changed more than any of them had guessed?

When he walked toward his carriage that looked out of place in her simple garden, she almost called him back, almost shouted that she would do whatever he wished her to do if it meant spending another minute with him. Last night, her dreams had been filled with scenes by the stream, but these had not included the children. Only Jeremy, who gathered her to him and kissed her with the fire she saw in his eyes.

She said nothing as she heard Petey calling to Hughie to catch the ball. Her promises to her cousin must never be forgotten . . . no matter how much she wished otherwise.

"I brought these for you," said Jeremy, startling her again, for she had not heard him return. He held out five books.

Her fingers trembled when she reached for them. Of all she had sold when she moved to the farm, she had regretted the loss of her books the most. When his finger grazed her cheek, gentle yet tempting, she basked in his smile.

"You helped me so many times," he murmured. "I thought I would repay the favor."

"Thank you," she whispered, wishing she could put all her joy into words. She did not know where to begin. With this kindness? With how easily he had taken to the children? With the truth of how her life had been fuller when he was about sharing tales of his adventures with her?

She looked hastily away before she blurted out her thoughts. Telling herself to think only of his gift, she tilted the books on their sides to try to read the titles. Her hands quaked so much she could make out barely the letters stamped with gold into the leather.

When she gasped to see the title was *The Midnight Groan, or, The Spectre of the Chapel,* he chuckled and said, "I remember you like stories of the greatest derring-do. I pilfered these books from a shelf in my father's book room." He laughed again. "I doubt Mother would approve of such splendid tales of abduction and dangerous locations and doomed love."

"Not all the loves are doomed." She opened the cover of the topmost book. "Some are intended to have a happy-ever-after ending."

His finger beneath her chin tilted her head back so that she looked up into his gray eyes. The storms within them were wild, unlike any she had ever seen. When he spoke, his voice was low, yet was as untamed as the heat from his eyes.

"Is that what you want, Pip? A happy-ever-after ending?"

"I have one."

"With the children?"

She started to nod, but his finger kept her head back. When his thumb coursed across her lower lip, she could not keep her breath from flowing out to caress it.

"Don't you want more?" he whispered.

"I am not like you, Jeremy," she answered as softly. "You would never be complacent. You always want more."

"You are right." His finger edged along her upper lip as his arm slipped around her waist. When he drew her closer, the books halted him. He reached to pluck them from her arm, but he paused when the two boys came running to greet him. "Why don't you go and read for a while, Charlotte?"

"What?" That was the last thing she had expected him to say. Even though she should be accustomed to being surprised by him, she had guessed his thoughts matched hers when he touched her.

"I will watch the children while you relish a moment to yourself."

As the boys cheered, she wanted to join in . . . and to weep. She was thrilled Jeremy was granting her such a wondrous boon, but at the same time she did not want to share a single moment of her time with him. Not even with the children.

"Thank you," she said again, for there was nothing else she

could say. If she spoke of her longing to be back in his arms, she would reveal the tremulous state of her heart. Not once had Jeremy said anything about staying in Upper Milburgh. To offer him her heart and then have him leave again would be more than she could bear.

CHAPTER SIX

So this was what misery was. Being surrounded by happy people and having every reason to be happy himself, but unable to be.

Jeremy watched the wedding ceremony as his sister and Berringer spoke their vows of love and devotion and fidelity. He had worn a well-practiced smile while he stood in his late father's stead and gave his sister away. That smile still clung to his lips, but its hold was growing more precarious by the minute.

Never had any wedding ceremony taken so long. He was sure of that. When his sister kissed Berringer to seal their vows, the music from the pipe organ swelled through the church. His smile became genuine for the length of time it took for the newlyweds to walk back up the aisle of the ancient church, past the bellpull and the carved wooden font. He did not doubt the cover of it would be lifted off within the next year to baptize the first child born of the marriage consecrated today. Eugenia was the devoted daughter, and she would be a willing wife, doing as Berringer asked.

Unlike Charlotte.

His smile disappeared and refused to return. Why hadn't Charlotte seen that he was trying to help her? He had not rejected her assistance in years past. Why would she turn away from his offer now? Even if she had not been willing to face possible scorn for herself, he had been sure she would attend the wedding in order to give the children some excitement beyond their own garden.

A hand clapping on his shoulder and the call of congratulations gave him a lifeline out of his dismals. He struggled to smile and must have been successful because nobody seemed to notice he was thinking of anything but his sister's nuptials and the blending of the village's two most prestigious families.

Letting the crowd of guests sweep him out of the church, he took a deep breath of the rainwashed afternoon. Spring was at its most abundant, filling the trees with leaves and scattering flowers in every direction. In the field beyond the churchyard, sheep grazed while lambs bounced about on stiff legs.

Jeremy's eye was caught by a motion near the gravestones by the back wall. For a moment, he thought he had seen only the slow movement of one of the sheep; then he saw the motion again. It was the arm of a youngster clearly having trouble sitting still and out of sight while the guests filed out of the church.

He threaded his way among the stones to the shadows draped in green from the trees along the flint wall, keeping several yards between him and the stone, where the arm peeked out again. Inching toward the stone, he smiled, quite sincerely this time, when he saw slender fingers gently pulling the arm back out of the guests' view.

He said nothing until he put one hand on the tall stone and the other on the wall. Looking down at a straw bonnet and a basket where a baby wiggled, he grinned when the two boys, one with sleek black hair and the other with bright red, giggled while pointing to someone among the guests emptying out of the churchyard. A parade walked toward the village green while carriages were steered toward Milburgh Hall.

"What is so funny?" he asked.

The boys spun about and let out a happy shout. He hugged the boys, who threw their arms around his legs, but he looked at Charlotte. She sat on a well-worn blanket next to the baby's basket. Instead of the simple gown she usually wore, she was dressed in sprigged linen. The flowers printed on it exactly matched her eyes' warm blue, but he noticed her hand pressed to the intriguing curves above the blue ribbon on her gown's high waistline. He wanted to peel the boys from his legs, send them on their way, and show Charlotte how he ached for a kiss and so much more.

"You frightened nigh to a year from my life," she gasped. "Why are you skulking about the churchyard?"

"I thought you might try to flee like pixies."

"Doing that would be the very best way to call attention to ourselves."

Her commonsensical words shredded his fantasies. While he could think solely of her, she must always keep the children foremost in her mind. If he had stayed in Upper Milburgh . . . He could not think of that, because she had been not much older than Petey when he left. Yet he could not keep from imagining what her life might have been like if he had been in the village to denounce the rumors. And what his life might have been like.

"Why did you come?" Jeremy asked bluntly, trying to shove those compelling thoughts aside.

Charlotte took Jeremy's hand as he brought her to her feet. She was astounded by how perfectly her fingers fit into his.

Forcing her heart to slow its frantic beat, she said in what she hoped was a normal voice, "The children love music, and Mrs. Plant always does her very best playing at the organ when there is a wedding or baptism."

"But not for funerals." He leaned one arm on a stone and looked back at the church his family had endowed so many years before. "I believed she did not play two notes in a row right during my father's funeral."

She was taken aback. "You came here for his funeral?"

He nodded.

"But nobody ever said—That is, I assumed—"

"That the wayward son did not attend his father's memorial service? I came, staying at the back of the church where I would not be noticed among the crowd of mourners." He smiled gamely. "Such dreary talk for such a joyous day. I would rather say how pleased I am that you decided to accept my invitation after all."

"I am sorry, Jeremy."

"That you came?" His eyes were wide.

She put her hand over his on the stone, knowing that she was being bold and that the single action could curse her in the eyes of those who loathed her. She did not care. How could she have missed the sorrow within the man who had learned to conceal his feelings behind a cocky smile?

"No. I am sorry that nobody realizes what a good son you have become."

"It was a long, circuitous journey." A hint of his smile returned.

"But you have reached your destination."

"Egads, I hope not!" He chuckled. "I would hate to think of myself as a priggish peer who never does anything unexpected."

"I doubt anyone would accuse you of that." Bending, she reached for the basket.

When he grasped her arms and drew her up against him, he whispered, "Let's make sure *you* never will."

His kiss was as dangerous and sensual as she had imagined. Even more so, because it seemed to send a soul-deep craving careening through her. She clasped his arms as his tongue traced her lips as his finger had when he brought her the books. Slowly her hands climbed his strong arms to slide along his nape. When her fingers combed up through his ebony hair, he teased her lips to soften and grant him a welcome within her mouth.

Her heart thudded against her chest as if trying to escape in order to lie beside his. She seemed to have forgotten how to breathe. Not that it mattered, because his own breath pulsed into her throat, giving life to every dream she had ever dared to lose herself in.

When he lifted his mouth away, she did not move. If she

did, all of the joy and the eager need within her might be proved to be nothing more than another dream.

"Charlotte . . . Pip," he whispered.

At the nickname she shared only with him, she opened her eyes. Her fingers rose to trace his face's stern angles, which shifted when he smiled. He tilted his head to brush his lips against her fingers; then, with a groan, he grasped her wrist and pressed his mouth to her palm. Her head spun with the strength of her yearning to have his lips on hers again.

With obvious reluctance, he released her. "I must go to toast my sister's marriage."

"I know."

"Will you come with me?"

She shook her head, although her heart cried out for her to agree to anything to be with him. "I need to take the children home before I tend to my chores."

"Then come to the wedding breakfast on the morrow." Before she could say anything, he smiled at the boys who, she realized belatedly, had been watching the kiss with uncharacteristic silence. "I know these two fine gentlemen would enjoy the grand repast Cook has planned for the breakfast. I can come by to pick you up in my carriage and bring all of you in prime style to Milburgh Hall."

"Say yes, Charlotte!" begged Petey as Hughie hopped about like a maddened rabbit.

"Yes, say yes, Charlotte," Jeremy repeated, his smile warming every inch of her.

On his face, she saw the naughty boy he had been and the exciting man he had become, and she knew there was only one answer she could give.

"Yes."

The wedding breakfast was already underway. In Jeremy's ears still echoed the music from the orchestra set in one recently dusted corner of the ballroom at Milburgh Hall. He had waited for his new brother-in-law to escort Eugenia into the ballroom, where their guests anticipated the generous feast to be brought from the kitchen. He had lingered even while the first dishes were brought for the guests.

Only then had he slipped away and called for his carriage. Because the celebrations were well underway, nobody would note his disappearance or his reappearance with Charlotte and the children. He hoped that by the time the other guests discovered she had joined the festivities, they would have to acknowledge, as well, that she was not the epitome of wickedness.

When he drew in the horses near Charlotte's cottage, he was astonished to see another carriage in the garden. Not a fast phaeton like he drove, but a closed carriage that showed signs of a long trip because there was mud and dirt caked on the wheels and its sides. Yet, even that filth could not disguise how well the vehicle had been made, and he could see the fine seats within it. The boot was open, but like the interior of the carriage, was empty.

As he slowed his own carriage, a trio of men came out of the cottage. They all wore simple livery of a dusty black. No doubt, they had traveled in the carriage to obtain that layer of dirt. Each man carried a wooden case. They glanced at him and then away as they each placed a box with care in the boot. Without another look in his direction, they went back into the cottage.

Jeremy jumped out of his phaeton even before it had come to a complete stop. Curiosity spurred his feet. Who was calling on Charlotte in such a grand carriage and with three servants? Why were crates being removed from Charlotte's cottage? What was in those wooden boxes?

He heard a furious mew. Looking down, he saw that he had almost stepped on the children's kitten. He scooped it up. Its tiny claws clamped onto his waistcoat, and he could feel the kitten's rapid heartbeat. Something had scared it, something more than his feet, which must seem monstrous to such a tiny creature.

Carrying the kitten, he walked toward the cottage. The clatter and voices grew louder on every step. Easily he picked out the children's voices and Charlotte's, but he heard another voice. A deeper voice, where he had not heard a man's voice other than his own.

The front door was wide open, giving a good view of the entry and the stairs rising along one side. Amazed to realize he had never been inside the cottage, Jeremy walked in as pain exploded within him. He struggled to control the irrational hurt. There was no sense in being wounded because she had never invited him in, but clearly had let this other man and his retinue into her home.

Seeing a few pieces of furniture he recognized from his tutor's house, he noticed how most of the legs on the chairs had been repaired. The single table tilted at a sharp angle. Yet, the sole upholstered piece, a settee, held, in addition to some unfolded laundry, a stuffed doll and two books. One book had been among those he brought to Charlotte, but the other was homemade.

Awkwardly he picked it up while trying to keep the kitten from falling on the floor. The book's pages had been stitched together and were decorated with brightly drawn pictures. He guessed Charlotte had made it and was trying to instill her love of books in the boys.

A shadow appeared in the doorway leading to what must be the only other room on the cottage's ground floor. His heart leaped as wildly as the kitten's before he saw the shadow could not belong to Charlotte or the children. It was too tall and too broad-shouldered.

A man stepped into the room and demanded, "Who in perdition are you?"

"Milbury," he replied in the same sharp voice. No man on land or aboard one of his ships had ever spoken to him with such a tone and not come to regret it. "Sixth marquess." As he had hoped, the announcement of his title took some of the bluster from the man, who was walking about Charlotte's house as if he were master of the cottage and all within it.

Letting a cold smile curl along his lips, he asked coolly, "And who in perdition are you?"

"Lionel Passmore." He paused a moment, then added, "Estate manager for Lord Williard."

Both names seemed familiar, but he was unsure from where. "That tells me nothing. What are you doing running tame through Charlotte's cottage?"

"I could ask you the same, my lord."

Jeremy had to admire how quickly Passmore regained his aplomb and seemingly self-righteous outrage. Hearing footfalls behind him, he did not turn. They were too heavy for Charlotte's light steps. Guessing they belonged to the liveried servants, he silenced his curiosity about what they were taking out of the house. He needed to know more about Passmore first.

"You could ask me the same," he answered, "but I posed the question first, Passmore, and I believe you owe me the courtesy of an answer before I respond to your question."

"There she is!" cried Petey as he rushed into the room and held out his hands. "You found her, Jeremy. Thank you so much!"

Plucking the clinging kitten off his waistcoat, Jeremy placed it on the boy's hands. "You should keep a closer eye on her. She was wandering through the garden, and she nearly got stepped on."

"I will put her in a box."

He thought of the wooden boxes the men had been carrying. "What?"

"One with holes so she can breathe." Petey gave him a condescending glance. "I know better than to put her in a box without holes."

Passmore said quietly, "Put the cat in your room and close the door." He watched the boy hurry away before turning back to Jeremy. His voice hardened again. "What business do you have in this house, my lord? Whatever it is, you should finish it quickly because—"

"Hughie, are you in here?" Charlotte hurried down the

stairs and into the room. She held a small shirt open as though she were about to put it on the child. She came to a stop so swiftly that she stumbled forward a step. Squaring her shoulders, she smiled. "Oh, I see you have met."

"We have exchanged names, nothing more." Jeremy knew his voice was too honed when she looked at him in abrupt dismay. "I still have no idea why this man is in your cottage."

"Jeremy, Lionel is Hughie and Dolly's father."

"I see." No wonder the name had seemed familiar, but why was Passmore at the cottage now? Blurting out that question could add to the other man's vexation, and that anger might be re-aimed at Charlotte, for Passmore was looking daggers at her, clearly appalled that she had allowed Jeremy to enter her cottage.

Jeremy was unsure what else to say. Unsure? He had never been unsure about anything before his return to Upper Milburgh. No, it had nothing to do with Upper Milburgh and his family. This unsettled feeling focused on Charlotte and her assemblage of children.

"It is good of you to pay the children a call, Passmore," he finally said into the silence, glad, for once, to fall back on commonplaces.

Charlotte glanced from Jeremy at Lionel. Both men's faces were taut. She wondered why they were glowering at each other like two bulls in the same field, but she suspected any attempt to calm them would have to wait until the two men were separated.

Quietly, she asked, "Lionel, would you check on Dolly? She should be waking just about now."

"I would rather you called her by her real name," he replied.

"I am sorry. We simply have become accustomed to calling her Dolly instead of Sylvia." She looked back at Jeremy. "Sylvia was my cousin's given name, and Lionel wished to have his daughter share her mother's name."

Jeremy began, "Dolly—"

"Is what Hughie calls her," she hurried to explain. Letting

the conversation continue would give Lionel an excuse not to leave the room. She was guiltily pleased when the baby let out a cry, and Lionel hurried to check on his daughter.

"I assume," Jeremy said, looking her up and down, "because you are dressed in your work clothes that you do not plan to attend my sister's wedding breakfast."

"Not now."

"Passmore is welcome to attend, too." He grinned wryly. "We will find a place for him among the rest of the guests, I am sure."

Joy filled her at his kindness after Lionel had been so icy to him. Her arms begged to be thrown around his shoulders as she pressed close to him. Their kiss yesterday had been so wondrous, but now . . .

Walking to the settee, she folded the small shirt she held. She put it atop the other clothes on the settee before she said, "Thank you, Jeremy, but we cannot go."

"Why not?"

"We are packing. Lionel wishes for us to return with him to his house."

"For how long?"

"Forever." She folded another small garment and placed it on the pile. Working gave her an excuse not to look at Jeremy. She doubted she could bear seeing sorrow in his expressive eyes. "He misses his children."

"He should have thought about that before he sent them away with you and ruined your life."

Raising her head, she blinked back tears. "Is that what you think? You think the children have ruined my life? I thought, by now, you understood that they *are* my life."

"Your whole life?"

"I don't understand what you are asking."

"I think you do."

"Let's assume I don't. Tell me what you are asking."

She *did* understand what he was asking, or she thought she did. Was he asking if there was room for him in her life? That was a silly question, because there had always been room for

him in her life, but now she must think of the children and
their future. His was assured, for he was now Lord Milbury,
a respected marquess. And her own . . . She could not guess.
She did not want to guess.

"You simply do not want to own up to the fact that you are
fleeing from Upper Milburgh," he replied.

She laughed icily. "If I had intended to flee, don't you think
I would have done so before this? I did not let the rumors
chase me away."

"But now the rumors are going to be put to rest, and you
would be welcome to return to Upper Milburgh." He took the
shirt from her and grasped her arms. "Charlotte, have you
been fleeing all your life? Is that why you clung to the corners
like a frightened kitten? If your nose was in a book, you could
not be lured out into the real world."

Shaking his hands off her, she retorted, "The real world
where you were so bored and unhappy that you wasted your
whole youth causing mischief?"

"I am not saying I did everything right then, Charlotte, but
I have learned that hiding behind pranks is no way to live.
Why can't you see that hiding behind old excuses is no way
to live either?"

"You make it sound so easy."

"It is not easy, but all the struggle is worth what you win in
the end."

"And what is that? Lies and rude looks and assumptions
that one is more wicked than anyone else in the world? More
wicked even than the marquess's heir?" She put her hand over
her mouth to halt more bitter words from spewing forth.

When he laughed, she was astounded. He put his crooked
finger beneath her chin and tilted her face toward his. "Pip,
nobody could ever believe you are as wicked as I was believed to be. By Jove, even *I* was not that wicked!" His eyes
softened as he bent toward her. "But touching you gives me
the most wicked thoughts ever."

"Jeremy . . ." She breathed his name in the moment before
his mouth found hers.

His kiss was both sweet and desperate, pleading with her to change her mind. Such a proud man, he could not speak the words, but she knew what he was asking.

Stepping back, she drew his arms from around her. Her hands lingered for a long moment on his sleeves before she forced them to lift away. Even so, she was unsure if she could have resisted edging back into his embrace, save for Hughie running into the room, crying as he held up his right forefinger.

Jeremy watched as Charlotte knelt and soothed the little boy. The mark on his finger was hardly visible once she drew a splinter from it. Letting him lean on her shoulder, she patted his back as he wept.

He looked away, unable to watch any longer. Even if he had not heard Charlotte speak the words, he knew the children were her life. He might have changed, but Charlotte had not. She still opened her heart and her home to those who needed her most. What he had taken for granted as a boy—that she would always be there to patch him up and listen to his misadventures and give him courage to face what he must when the truth became known—these children now did.

How could he deny them what he had treasured?

When she stood to let one of the servants go to the settee to put the stack of clothes in another box, she lifted Hughie into her arms. But her eyes focused on Jeremy, and he saw the pain he had tasted on her lips.

He had no idea how long they stood there. He had no idea how much longer they would have stood there if Passmore had not come to the door and, standing with his hands behind his back, cleared his throat.

"Yes?" Charlotte asked, still gazing into Jeremy's eyes.

What was she seeking? The man she had hoped he would become? He almost laughed, but there would be no humor in it. She deserved a man who would love her first and foremost, a man who would understand that the children held a very special place in her heart. Had he become such a man?

"Everything we are taking with us," Passmore said, "has been loaded. It is time to leave."

"I must get my bonnet."

Passmore held it out, and Jeremy saw Petey stood behind him, gripping the handles of the baby's basket tightly. "Here it is."

Setting Hughie on his feet, she took the straw bonnet and tied it beneath her chin. She took the little boy's hand and took a step toward the door.

Jeremy wondered if she was going to leave without another word, but she turned to him. He had never seen such sorrow on her face, not even when she spoke of the rumors spread about her.

"Jeremy?"

"Yes?"

"Could you do something for me?"

He hesitated on his answer, although he wanted to shout he would do anything for her. He owed her so much, and he wanted to give her even more. Aware of Passmore standing not much more than an arm's length away, he wondered how he could say what he needed to say without looking foolish. Mayhap there was no way. Mayhap because he *was* a fool.

So he said only, "Of course, Charlotte."

"Will you make sure the animals are cared for until they can be sold?"

"You are selling my kitty?" cried Hughie, bursting into tears again.

Squatting in front of the child, Jeremy put his hand on Hughie's hair. He ruffled it as he spoke with a serenity he hoped the child would believe. He doubted anyone else would.

"Charlotte sold it to me." He reached beneath his coat and pulled out a small gold coin. Putting it in the child's hand, he said, "This is what I paid for your kitty."

"Jeremy, that is too much," she protested.

He looked up at her as he said, "Hughie, you can come and visit your kitty whenever you wish."

The little boy was now too fascinated with the shiny coin to pay attention to anything else.

Slowly coming to his feet, Jeremy added, "That invitation is for all of you."

Petey blinked back tears. "Come and visit us, Jeremy."

"I just may." Again he looked at Charlotte, but her face was shadowed by the brim of her bonnet.

He did not need to see it, for he heard grief in her voice as she thanked him for watching over the animals and bid him good-bye. He remained where he was as she went out of the room, Passmore putting a protective arm around her shoulders while they walked out. He was still standing in that spot when, minutes later, the closed carriage drove out of the garden and onto the road.

CHAPTER SEVEN

"How long are you going to mope around here?" demanded Eugenia.

Jeremy looked over the top of his book. "Did you come to Milburgh Hall simply to chide me anew?"

She laughed as she drew off her shawl and draped it over the back of the nearest chair in the book room. "I came to speak to Mother about what to do with that hideous vase her aunt sent to George and me as a wedding gift, but scolding you is always an added bonus. I have had so few chances to give you sisterly guidance."

He closed the book and placed it on the table beside him as he came to his feet. He had not put a marker in it to save his place. It did not matter because, although he had been staring at the pages for the past hour, not a single word had lodged in his brain. He had tried to do some of the estate's accounts, but those numbers, which usually filed into his mind in a logical progression, had been as recalcitrant as the words.

"I suppose I would be no gentleman if I did not give you a chance to give me a sisterly dressing-down."

Her smile faded. "Jeremy, you cannot continue to hide yourself away as you have."

"How would you know what I have been doing? You have been away for your honeymoon and are just back."

"You know Upper Milburgh. How everyone likes to talk about everyone else's business, and the favorite topic is you."

Into his mind came Charlotte's voice on the day he had ridden back home: *If you wanted to give them someone to talk about, there was no need. They always find someone to talk about.*

I have not been here for ten years. It was kind of you to give them someone else to talk about. Those had been his own teasing words.

She had replied, *Giving them someone to talk about was not intentional.*

And then he had wanted to kiss her. Just as he wanted to kiss her now.

"Let them talk," Jeremy grumbled. "Such talk has never bothered me before."

"I don't expect it to bother you now, not when you are pining away for Charlotte Longmuir." Eugenia folded her arms in front of her and gave him a frown she had borrowed from their mother. "Why don't you do something about that?"

"Do something? I thought you despised Charlotte."

"I did, but you don't, and you are my brother, so I have to respect your opinions."

"Really? That is something new."

A hint of a smile touched her lips at his teasing. "You have changed, Jeremy. Mayhap I can as well. So why aren't you doing something about your infatuation with Charlotte Longmuir? Something that will encourage you to leave the house and regain your life?"

"Something like forgetting her?"

"I would guess that is impossible from seeing you moon about the house. It is not like you, Jeremy, to give up so easily."

"What would you have me do? Ask her to choose between the children and me?"

Sorrow filled her eyes. "There must be some other solution."

He sank to the settee. "If there is, I have not found it in a month of searching."

"If anyone can, you will." His sister kissed him on the cheek before going to speak with their mother.

He wished he had Eugenia's faith in him, and he wished he had an answer to the dilemma that had haunted him for a month. Somehow he had to find a way to bring Charlotte back to Upper Milburgh.

Reaching for his book, his eye was caught by the papers still piled on his father's desk. A smile edged along his lips as it had not in a month.

"Impossible!" Charlotte peered over the line of freshly washed clothes spread across the hedges on the comfortable estate manager's house on Lord Williard's estate. A dark-haired man was riding toward her.

Was it possible? Could that rider be Jeremy?

She bent down to get another item out of the washbasket. At the same time, she warned her silly heart to stop beating like a tattoo. She could not let it continue to leap within her breast each time a dark-haired man rode past the cottage in the center of the village.

Not that many passed by. The village was smaller than Upper Milburgh, and it was half a day's ride to the nearest market town. Anyone who traveled through probably gave no thought to the dozen houses edging the road. No magnificent house rose on the hill to loom over the cottages. Very little reminded her of the place that had been her home for most of her life.

In the month since she had departed from Upper Milburgh, she had waited to hear a very special knock set upon the door. She had heard that assertive rap seldom, but whether it had come when she was little more than a child or recently, she had known Jeremy stood on the other side of the door. It had not come, and she wondered if she had done what nobody else had ever done. Had she hurt him so deeply that he could not hide that pain behind the reputation he had built for himself, both the bad of his past and now the good?

The garment fell out of her numb fingers as the rider drew even with where she was standing. As he swung down out of the saddle, where a basket was tied, and brushed dust from his dark coat, she could not speak. She could only stare, hoping this was not another of the dreams she had endured, each one filled with a happy reunion, each one raising her hopes, only to dash them with the coming of dawn.

"Good afternoon, Miss Longmuir." Jeremy smiled as he glanced at the clothes. "I trust I am not intruding on your wash day."

"Jeremy." She gasped out his name as if she spoke with her last breath.

He came around the hedge and pulled her into his arms. As his mouth claimed hers, she surrendered to her heart, which already belonged to him. Just as it had for more years than she could recall.

Raising his lips, he whispered, "Is Passmore in?"

"Yes." She could not keep from blurting out, "Did you come to see him?"

"Yes. I have business to discuss with him." He turned, his smile remaining as he called, "Passmore! Just the man I wanted to see."

"My lord?" Lionel asked, clearly baffled.

"I have a business proposition for you." He winked at Charlotte, but she was as confused as her cousin's husband. "I came home to discover Upper Milburgh has been without an estate manager for more than a year. I have asked about, and I hear you are a very competent one. If you are willing to come to work for me, I would be glad to pay you double whatever Williard pays you."

Lionel's eyes grew so wide she thought they would pop out of his head. "My lord, that is a generous offer."

"Not so much generous as paying you what you should be earning if you worked for anyone other than that pinchpenny. He did not pay you enough to bring a doctor in when your wife was giving birth." He looked back at Charlotte. "I know you tried your best, Pip, but she needed more than even you could give."

Her heart was doing somersaults at the precious nickname.

Touching his arm with quivering fingers, she blinked back tears at how he had understood what she could not say, that she owed Lionel so much because she had failed him and Sylvia.

"What do you say, Passmore?" Jeremy's smile broadened. "Know that I will not take no for an answer."

Lionel did not hesitate. "It is a generous offer, and I would be stupid not to accept it. Thank you."

"One matter taken care of. Next—"

"Jeremy!" cried Petey as he ran toward them. As always, Hughie was as close on his heels as his pudgy legs allowed.

Both boys flung their arms around him, and Charlotte stepped back before she was pushed aside. She smiled as she watched the boys greeting Jeremy. Hughie was bouncing around as if he had springs in his legs. Petey was gesturing wildly while trying to tell Jeremy everything that had happened since they arrived here.

Jeremy held up his hands. "Business first." He knelt in front of Hughie. "Do you still have that coin I gave you?"

"Charlotte has it," the little boy said, his eyes as round as his father's.

"Do you think you can get it back from her?" He stood and went to the horse. Unhooking the basket from his saddle, he leaned down in front of Hughie. He opened the top just enough for the kitten to peer out. "As you can see, the tiny kitten I bought from you is now well on its way to becoming a cat, and I paid for a kitten, not a cat. Do you think I can sell it back to you? I will not take no for an answer on this either, Hughie, so you need to say yes."

The little boy dimpled as he patted the kitten's head. "Yes!"

Standing, Jeremy turned to Charlotte. "I believe you have something of mine."

"I will go and get the coin for you straightaway." She lowered her voice. "Thank you for bringing the kitten here, Jeremy. Hughie has missed it so much." She took a step toward the house, but paused when he put his hand on her arm.

He drew her back to him and framed her face with his

hands. "Pip, I know all about loneliness. I cannot believe I have let so many years of my life go by without you in them. Come back to Milburgh Hall with me, and keep me out of trouble."

"I don't know if that is possible," she whispered, her heart bursting with happiness and love.

"Then be there for me when I get into trouble."

"And listen to your adventures?"

"All my adventures I want to share with you from this point forward, Pip." He dropped to one knee and took her left hand. Sliding a sparkling ring on it, he said, "Marry me." That devilish glint returned to his eyes. "And you should realize that this is another question to which I will not accept any answer other than yes."

"That is good, because there is no other answer I want to give you but yes."

He stood to kiss her, but suddenly they were enveloped by children chasing the kitten that had escaped from the basket. He reached out to grab the kitten just as Charlotte caught Hughie before he could fall face-first onto the ground. Yelping as the kitten scratched him, he put it back into the basket and secured the top.

"It seems we have all we need for our wedding," he said as he came back to where she was brushing dirt off Hughie.

She released the little boy and took Jeremy's outstretched hands. "Everything. Something old." She looked down at the ring on her finger. When a yowl came from the basket, she laughed. "And something mew."

Her laughter met his as he brought her into his arms and kissed her, one in what she knew would be a lifetime of kisses.

THE PERFECT BRIDE

ALICE HOLDEN

CHAPTER ONE

Simon Whitten, the Viscount Glynden, settled into a chair beside his friend Robinson Fitch in the theater box directly in line with the center of the stage.

"Has she been on yet, Robby?" Simon asked as he glanced at the risqué comedic scene taking place in front of him. Some in the audience tittered at the sexual innuendoes embedded in the snappy dialogue; others were immersed in their own conversations.

"No, maybe she will sing next," Robby said.

Parker's London Theater was warm and crowded. Hugh Parker had filled every row of his five-hundred-seat playhouse and had even sold out the standing room at the back and the sides.

Most of the better-dressed gentlemen in the audience tonight habitually patronized Covent Garden or Haymarket or the three-thousand-plus-seat Drury Lane Theater, not Parker's second-rate playhouse.

The sole attraction for them this evening was Hugh Parker's new discovery, Yvette la Roche, a beautiful young French singer.

"I thought I might have missed her," Simon said to the young baron, whose formal title was Lord Cragg.

Robinson Fitch was as dark as Simon was fair. He was thin, but wiry, and shorter than his viscount friend, who was tall and fit, his long legs lean, his stomach flat. The two gentlemen had been born within three months of each other twenty-six years before and had been friends since early childhood.

"What kept you?" Robby asked. Simon's valet had secured a box for the Season by paying a premium, insuring that the two young men would have seats for the three nights a week that the lovely Yvette performed.

"A paternal command," Simon said, dryly. His father was Oliver Whitten, the Earl of Breede. "His lordship put on the pressure again."

"Ah, Lord Breede wants you to find a bride. Have you convinced him to give you more time?"

"I did not want to miss Yvette's performance. I made him the promise he required, or he would have kept me imprisoned all night."

"What promise?"

"I consented to wed no later than June."

Robby blinked. "This coming June?"

Simon nodded. "Seems my father promised my mother on her deathbed that he would see me married before my twenty-seventh birthday," he drawled. "My birthday is on the eighteenth of June, as you know. The earl would not dismiss me until I agreed. So I did, even though the deathbed scene was all a hum, but I could not miss seeing Yvette."

Robby chuckled. "Rather short-sighted of you, Simon. A marriage is for a lifetime. Yvette will perform again on Thursday."

Simon sighed. "I know, but lately I have been seriously thinking about doing my duty and getting it over with."

"Huh," Robby muttered. Simon knew he had rendered his baby-faced friend nearly speechless.

On the stage a mime in harlequin garb, his cheeks and chin painted white below his black half-mask, had replaced the comedic actors. The buzz of many inattentive patrons droned on. The pantomime required only the use of their eyes not their ears, and few were sufficiently mesmerized to apply their minds to the silent performance. Now and then, polite applause broke out, but for the most part, the mime played to a detached audience, most of whom were here to see and hear the gifted French singer.

Lord Cragg gazed at Simon. "You are not hoaxing me, Simon, are you?"

Viscount Glynden, splendid in black-and-white evening attire, shook his head.

"But why give in to emotional blackmail?" His friend, not surprisingly, seemed truly perplexed. After all, marriage could change the carefree existence of a bachelor into an endless odious agenda of marital duties, leaving scant time for pleasure. But Simon had no intention of allowing the wedded state to ruin his life. He had not gone into this as impetuously as Robby might believe. He would handle the whole unpleasant matter successfully by finding the perfect bride.

"I will tell you the why of it," Simon said. "I am an only child, Robby. You have older brothers who are top of the trees. Your family is destined to survive whether you succumb to parson's mousetrap or not. But next in line to me is that popinjay cousin of mine, Cecil Whitten, who will get the title and a large number of properties if I stick my spoon in the wall before I produce an heir."

"Upon my soul! I can see why the thought of the lackwit Cecil inheriting would send any gentleman into the doldrums. I suppose there is no help for it, your marrying that is. You must offer for somebody if you are to get an heir. Though finding a willing girl should not be difficult; after all you are what is called a 'catch.'"

"True," Simon replied without arrogance, "there are any number of sophisticated eligible females whom I can turn up sweet and of whom my father would approve, but I will seek a young biddable girl, someone who will be in awe of me and let me go my own way. I am determined that no wife of mine will require me to live in her pocket."

The harlequin mime bowed to scattered applause and left the stage. Hugh Parker stepped from the wings and replaced the mime's card on a stand with the one that announced Yvette la Roche.

Both young gentlemen fixed their eyes on the stage in anticipation of the opening of the curtain and the appearance of the luscious singer.

Robby smiled slyly. "You don't mean to give up the good life, then. You mean to take a mistress, Simon. Perchance, the lovely la Roche?"

Simon's mouth quirked. "No one can get near her. Parker has kept Yvette under wraps and away from visitors to the greenroom." He put a hand onto Robby's blue serge coat sleeve. "Don't tell me, my little friend, that the same thought has not entered your head."

Lord Cragg guffawed. "No doubt, every man in this audience has dreamed of bedding the chit to no avail."

"More's the pity, for I intend to be successful," Simon crowed as the curtains opened and the songstress stepped onto the proscenium. The crowd stilled and then broke into sustained applause.

High-lustered pearls decorated the bodice of Yvette la Roche's pale pink satin gown. Simon noticed a little white ruffle on the hem. Except for the oddity, the fashionable evening dress looked to be a knockoff of a Parisian creation.

Mademoiselle raised a small gloved hand to the orchestra leader in the pit.

The five musicians began to play a heartbreakingly sad melody, and Yvette sang, her voice low and sweet. The lyrics spoke of unconsummated love.

Simon reached for the opera glasses on a small table beside his chair. He brought Yvette's face into focus; she was stunningly beautiful. Her eyes shimmered with unshed tears. Only someone who felt the music in her heart could sing like that, Simon thought. The ballad ended, and the room was still for a long moment before the applause broke out.

The orchestra did not wait for the ovation to stop, but immediately broke into a lively tune. Simon recognized the music as Italian, a tarantella, but the words were in English. Yvette sang and did a little dance to the spirited melody, snapping her fingers. She smiled brightly, her perfect teeth white against the red stage makeup on her full lips.

Her long blond hair, a darker shade than Simon's own, swayed with her agile moves in the folk dance. Her eyes, a dark violet, a most unusual color for a blonde, sparkled. She was plainly enjoying herself. Simon lowered the opera glasses.

The people clapped in time to the gay music, smiling and laughing good-naturedly. She breathed hard as the song ended and curtsied deeply to her admirers and glanced in Simon's direction, a bright smile on her red, red lips.

The orchestra played a refrain from an operetta as Yvette regained her breath. Simon could not take his eyes off her, although some of the audience returned to their conversations and the house buzzed with talk. She met Simon's eyes for a long moment before looking away.

Simon placed the opera glasses on the table. He sighed and sat back and listened to her rendition of "The Merry Boatman." Yvette sang like an angel. He wondered about her trained voice. Lessons were expensive. Could she already have a protector who was financing her career? A lover? Simon did not want to think so. His wispy notion to make the songstress his mistress had quickly energized into gripping resolve. He applauded the light operatic solo and leaned his elbows across the front of the box.

Yvette's next selection was an Irish air. Again, she seemed to be looking right at Simon, singing for him. Only for him. He had become thoroughly obsessed with her, and she knew it.

Her eyes left his, and she did not gaze at him again. She sang another mournful ballad and finished with "Greensleeves," familiar to the audience.

The singer lowered her head in gracious acknowledgment of the applause. But a cluster of rowdy dandies near the stage yelled and whistled and shouted suggestive offers of a sexual nature. Simon was not surprised, for he had witnessed such displays many times, even in the better theaters, but he saw anger flash in her eyes. She spun around, lifted her skirts, and dashed into the wings.

The heavy blue curtains closed. The young bucks kept up the bawdy shouts and stamped their feet and called her name and yelled, "Encore! Encore! Encore!"

Hugh Parker appeared through the parted curtain and held up his hand to quiet the crowd. "Gentlemen! Gentlemen!" the stage manager cried. "*Mademoiselle* is overcome. Give her a brief respite to collect herself. If she is able, she will perform another song at the end of the evening." He removed Yvette's card from the stand and replaced it with the notice of Parker's Shakespearean Players.

As Hugh Parker slipped back through the curtain, many in the crowd booed. The stage manager's words passed from the front to the back and all around the theater, but most of the patrons saw the announcement for what it was; appeasement with no teeth. Some of the audience began to leave, but even the worst offenders quieted down when the Shakespearean ensemble began performing a scene from *Much Ado About Nothing*.

Simon and Robby remained in their chairs, ignoring the bard's play. The street in front of the theater would be mobbed with people hailing hackneys or waiting for their private carriages. During the pushing and shoving, people were prime targets for pickpockets. But tonight both men had other reasons for lingering.

"Yvette doesn't sound French when she sings," Robby said, taking a silver flask from his coat pocket. He unscrewed the cap and poured a finger of brandy into the top, which served as a cup. "Want some?" he asked Lord Glynden.

Simon shook his head. "It is common for an accent to disappear when a person sings in another language," he said, indifferently.

"Are you thinking of checking out the greenroom?" Robby asked.

"No point," Simon answered. "She won't be there. You?"

"Yvette may decide to greet her public at last. I believe I

shall give it a try." He smiled a boyishly lecherous smile. "A sweet little creature in the line of dancers during the opening act caught my eye. I would not mind taking the delicious little morsel for a late supper and see what develops."

Like the three main London theaters, Parker's evening show started at seven. The performances ran until midnight. Yvette had come on at ten, and the Shakespearean play ended the night just before twelve o'clock.

"Good luck, Robby, with your opera dancer," Simon said, getting up from his chair. "I shall see if I can sneak in back and get past Cavendish and find la Roche's dressing room."

Simon knew his way around every inch of Covent Garden, Haymarket, and Drury Lane, but had only been in the seating area of Parker's Theater. He had heard that Sean Cavendish kept anyone without an invitation from the back rooms. Cavendish was a brute of a man who had been a formidable pugilist during his days in the ring. He and Simon were sometimes friends. But even if friendship failed, money spoke. Sean was not above a bribe, which was the reason he had been barred from boxing.

CHAPTER TWO

Lady Brianna Mansfield, alias Yvette la Roche, rushed down the dimly lit hallway. The dandies had let loose an indecent deluge, and their vulgar remarks had rained down on her. She burst through the dressing room door and slammed it shut.

The black kitten in Mary Moore's lap raised his head at the commotion.

"Go back to your nap, Gilbert," Mary, Brianna's maid and companion of three years, said to the cat. "It's just your mistress about to drag some rude fellows over the coals . . . again."

Mary Moore was small of stature, with dark hair and brown eyes. She was five years older than Brianna and had been with her since Brianna was fifteen.

The songstress frowned at her friend and kicked off her black high-heeled pumps. "Those witless bounders would not dare hurl such lewd suggestions at me if I met them in a London ballroom."

"I daresay, my lady," Mary said dryly, "the clodpoles would do even worse to you if they discovered that the properly brought-up Lady Brianna Mansfield is masquerading as the divine Yvette la Roche. You will face certain ruination for singing in public if even one of them should get wind of your true identity."

Brianna wrinkled her nose. "As you have drummed into me daily since I conceived the plan to go on the stage."

But despite her flippancy, Brianna was not unaware that she was playing a dangerous game or that she was putting Mary at risk.

Settling in a chair before a mirrored vanity, she leaned over and pulled a thread and stripped off the ruffle basted to the hem of her costly gown and worked her feet into the low-heeled satin evening slippers which Mary had laid out for her.

Gilbert lifted his feline head and blinked his yellow eyes before he stood up and jumped from Mary's lap to the floor. Landing on his feet, he walked with a comical gait over to Brianna and rubbed against her leg.

The singer's expression softened. She smiled at the little cat with the crooked back leg that she had rescued from being put down. Out of necessity, she brought him to the theater whenever she performed. She could not leave him in her bedroom at her grandfather's house. Gilbert might have mewled continually until some member of the household, drawn by his cries, discovered that Brianna was not in her room or anywhere else in the house.

Mary rose from the comfortable chair and covered Brianna's shoulders with a makeup cape. She unscrewed the cap on a jar of cold cream and smeared the greasy emollient onto Brianna's face to cleanse her fair skin of the thick layer of cosmetics. Neither woman talked while executing the familiar ritual.

Brianna let herself think of the fair-haired gentleman in the center box as Mary toweled off her stage makeup. She had noticed him the last time she had performed, and he was here again tonight. He leaned his arms on the rail, listened attentively, and never talked during the singing, as some patrons did.

A dark-haired younger looking gentleman sat beside him, but the blond was the one who drew her eyes. Unlike the rude bucks in the pit, he did not hoot or whistle, but showed his appreciation with spirited applause.

Brianna sighed. No time for daydreaming about the handsome stranger. Cabs were plentiful before the show ended, but sparse afterward.

Mary finished cleansing her friend's face. Brianna stood up and quickly and deftly the two women donned their cloaks and bonnets, and Mary picked up the canvas bags which held Brianna's theatrical paraphernalia.

"I'll carry Gilbert," Brianna said, and consigned the kitten to a lidded basket.

Mary opened the door and stepped into the hallway lined with dressing rooms. A few performers whom she knew by sight were coming from the stage. She signaled Brianna that it was safe to depart, as no visitors who might be Quality were about.

Sean Cavendish, Parker's guard, opened the outside door for the two women, and they stepped into the cool night air.

The alley was empty, for this was not the main stage door, but used by porters who cleaned the theater to take out trash, and by Hugh Parker to avoid creditors.

On the street, Mary gave the driver of a hackney waiting for fares their direction and the two women climbed into the cab.

The vehicle moved into the traffic. Brianna put the kitten's basket on the seat beside her and removed her bonnet. She pulled out the pins that secured a blond wig to her own short black curls. The well-crafted hairpiece had been commissioned from the best wig maker in England and easily passed for Yvette la Roche's own hair. She stored the wig in a canvas sack and replaced her bonnet.

In the dark cab, Brianna laid a gloved hand on Mary's arm. "Only four more performances, Mary. My parents will be back from Europe in three weeks' time. Then, Yvette will disappear forever."

Mary grunted. Brianna knew that her subterfuge weighed heavily on her companion's mind. The maid could lose her position and be dismissed without a character, never to work again, no matter how much Brianna pleaded for her. Brianna was grateful for Mary's loyalty, for she could not have pulled off the masquerade without her companion's help.

The hansom eventually stopped beneath one of the newly installed gas lights in a respectable residential area of the city, and Mary pushed the fare up through the opening in the roof to the jarvey. Brianna leaped down to the ground and reached for Gilbert's basket, which Mary handed her before the maid herself alighted with the canvas bags. The cab door rattled as Mary slammed it shut.

The two women waited until the horses drawing the cab clopped around the corner before they walked to the gate in the brick wall of Lord Hamden's back garden.

Brianna inserted a key into the lock and opened the well-oiled gate. She and Mary stepped onto her grandfather's property, and Brianna locked the gate after them. The swish of their skirts and the soft tread of their slippers on the graveled path were the only sounds not of nature in the starlit night.

Brianna used a key she had filched from the housekeeper's office to gain entry to the house by a back door. Once inside, she made her way silently up the servants' stairs to her bedchamber, with Mary close on her heels.

The maid stored the canvas bags in a deep drawer while Brianna lifted the black kitten from his basket and set him on the floor. The tension in her stomach eased as she hung up her cape and bonnet; her secret was safe for another night.

Simon Whitten skulked behind the curtain and waited like a common thief in the shadows for an opportunity to creep down the passageway to Yvette la Roche's dressing room. The last performers of the night were rushing from the stage to change from their costumes to street clothes. Simon was at a disadvantage, for he was not at all certain which room belonged to the songstress. But when the corridor emptied of players, he stepped, hat in hand, into the light and walked purposefully to the nearest door and knocked. A young man in the garb of a clown opened the door while dabbing at the white makeup on his cheeks with a flannel rag.

"Sorry, old fellow," Simon said, affecting a drawl. "I thought this dressing room was Yvette la Roche's."

The clown pointed to the portal opposite to his own. "That's the prima donna's," he grumbled and shut the door resolutely.

Simon stepped across the hall and rapped softly with the gold head of his cane and waited. No one answered, so he put his ear to the door panel. Hearing no movement within, he turned the knob and pushed. The room was empty. He flinched when a firm hand grasped his shoulder from behind.

"Lord Glynden, I believe." Simon turned to face Sean Cavendish, Parker's beefy doorkeeper.

Simon grinned in relief. "I believe? What stuff! You know me well enough, Sean."

The giant of a man did not return the viscount's cheeky smile. "These premises are not to be entered by anyone but the performers, my lord, unless one is invited backstage with Mr. Hugh Parker's express approval. You are not on my list of eligibles who are so designated."

Not the least intimidated, Simon raised a brow and poked Sean in the chest with the tip of his cane. "Is that so? Did the divine Yvette la Roche leave with such a preferred caller tonight?"

Sean pushed the cane aside. "I am not at liberty to reveal that information," he said, his expression stoic, his flowery language at odds with his street accent.

Simon reached into the inner pocket of his evening coat, removed a leather purse, and had just peeled off a pound note when he noticed Hugh Parker standing in the doorway of a darkened room a few feet away, observing him.

"Put away your money, Lord Glynden." The theater manager's steely voice halted Simon's subversive activity.

The viscount shrugged, pushed the bill back into his purse, and tucked the wallet into his coat.

The fortyish Hugh Parker, a man of medium height and

build with piercing brown eyes and a large nose, stepped from his shelter into the lighted hall. A shabby brown toupee covered his bald pate.

"No need to grease anyone's palm for you to meet our performers, my lord," he said. "You are welcome to visit our greenroom on any night to make their acquaintances and express your admiration for their talents."

Embarrassed to be caught in devious behavior unworthy of a gentleman, Simon said, "Please accept my pardon, Parker."

"Nor is there a need to apologize, Lord Glynden. I appreciate your patronage, but please avail yourself of the greenroom in the future."

"Is Yvette la Roche in attendance this evening?" Simon asked, although he anticipated a negative answer.

Parker smiled, no illumination behind his brown eyes.

"Alas, my lord, the songstress has chosen to forgo meeting her public. I do not press my performers to mingle."

Simon knew better. Parker was protecting his French singer, treating her differently. Why? Could she be his mistress? Was that the reason she was performing in a mediocre playhouse when she had a unique voice that belonged in the better theaters, where she could command a decent fee?

"I'll see his lordship out, Mr. Parker," Sean Cavendish said, preempting Simon's thoughts.

Simon caught the look in Sean's eyes. He was not sure what the faint signal meant, but he followed the burly guard to the back exit without protest.

Sean held the door open for Simon, his back to where his employer stood backlit by the hall lights behind him, watching them.

Cavendish mumbled, "Be at the Gray Goose Tavern in an hour," his voice almost inaudible.

Simon said nothing to indicate that he had heard. He donned his hat, tucked his cane under his arm, and melted away into the night.

CHAPTER THREE

Hugh Parker sat behind his desk in the theater's dingy office after all the performers had left, the door open, looking over a ledger with a breakdown of the night's receipts.

Sean Cavendish knocked on the door jamb. "I'm leaving now, Mr. Parker, if you don't want me for anything else," the burly guard said.

"Go ahead, Sean. I'll lock up," Hugh replied.

"Well, good night, then," Sean said.

"'Night." The theater manager raised his hand in a negligent wave and went back to studying the numbers.

Yvette la Roche was a gold mine. He still marveled that she had come to him rather than going to one of his competitors. Yet, Hugh had no illusions that he would be able to keep her. She had refused to sign a contract and would be gone once a manager from a major playhouse made her an offer too good for her to turn down and which Hugh could not match. But he had sold out his two-dozen boxes at nonrefundable prices for the remainder of the Season for the first time ever. The rich aristocrats who had bought them would complain if Yvette was singing somewhere else, but let them. He had their money, and if the swells left the boxes empty, he could make even more of a profit by selling the seats to lesser mortals on a nightly basis at a reduced rate.

Hugh removed a bottle of rather good brandy from a drawer and poured a generous amount into the tin cup on his desk. He leaned back in his chair with a smile on his face, sipped the liquor judiciously, and relived the afternoon that Yvette la Roche had walked into this office two weeks ago.

His first impression had been that she was Quality. Her bright navy spencer was of the finest wool and her black boots were of the softest leather. Her blond curls peaked from beneath a shovel bonnet. She had brought a maid as chaperone. A society minx on a lark had been Hugh's initial guess.

She introduced herself in a fake French accent and said, "I am a songstress and am applying for a . . . ah, how you say, position with your company, *s'il vous plaît.*"

Females of her class did not apply for jobs in the theater. Slightly amused at her brass, Hugh had said, "Young woman, you are laboring under a misconception; I do not hire untalented amateurs."

"But, *monsieur,* I have talent," she replied, completely poised and confident.

Hugh could not contain a smile. "What exactly do you do?" She was an enchanting creature, the kind of girl that audiences would take to immediately.

"Perhaps, I could demonstrate, *mais oui?"*

The little minx did not wait for permission. She straightened up and folded her hands around her reticule at her waist. The gesture was familiar to Hugh as customary for a trained vocalist. He decided she was an upper-class young woman who had been coached to sing in the drawing rooms of the *ton* before her own kind. She would be technically perfect with a mediocre voice.

Hugh's assumption took a sharp turn as she began to sing. He leaned forward, mesmerized by the sweet, plaintive melody of lost love, the timbre of her voice exquisite.

"Sing something else," he said.

She complied without urging. A lively vocal rendition filled the small room, followed by an impromptu dance.

Visions of his small enterprise attracting the cream of London society night after night immediately bounced into Hugh's brain.

For a long moment, he did not speak. "Is this a practical

joke?" During his twenty years in the theater business, good fortune had eluded him time and time again, making him chronically suspicious.

Her violet eyes grew big. "No, I want to be on the stage." She raised a gloved hand in the air. "I would never make game of you."

Hugh had believed her. "If I hire you, you must tell me who you really are."

"No!" the maid warned loudly.

"Hush, Mary," the girl cautioned in unaccented English. "Mr. Parker, you must accept me as Yvette la Roche, a French songstress, if I am to work for you."

Hugh shrugged. Stage names were common in the theater. "Here are my terms," he said.

She was shaking her head even before he finished.

"I fear your rules are unacceptable to me," she said. "Come, Mary, we will look elsewhere."

Hugh's heart dropped. "Wait," he cried as she walked to the door. She turned around and took two steps back toward his desk.

"Dash it all, what do you want, girl? More money?" She was a prize, but he could not afford to pay her more. Yet, Hugh knew that she would be working for a competitor if he did not do something.

"No, sir, the money is not important. I can only work three nights a week. And our agreement must be verbal and based on trust, no written contract. Moreover, I will not appear in the greenroom, but must leave the theater directly after my performance."

Hugh was flabbergasted at her sheer gall, but he was no fool. Her demands could work to his purpose, too. He could be wrong, and she might not prove to be the sensation he imagined. But he did not think so.

"Agreed," he said. "But you must rehearse the morning of your appearance and provide your own sheet music for the five-piece orchestra and the director."

She had cocked her pretty blond head and concurred.

* * *

Hugh lifted his cup in a salute to that day when the gods of the theater had smiled on him. Yvette la Roche had turned out to be even more valuable than he had believed she would be. Obviously, he was wrong about her being of the privileged class. Viscount Glynden did not recognize her, nor did any of the other pinks of the *ton*. Of one thing he was sure—the *ton* knew their own. Yvette was not one of them. She was probably the pampered mistress of an old reprobate who indulged her with voice lessons and humored her desire to go on the stage as long as she kept his name out of it. Hugh had not stopped smiling since the first night she sang for an audience, for he had already made more money from her few performances than he would have made for months without her.

While Hugh Parker drank to his own good fortune, Simon Whitten sat at a scarred wooden table in the Gray Goose Inn, his hands around a tankard of ale. Even though it was past midnight, the room was crowded with sailors in dark knit caps, sportsmen, called the fancy, who had been to a boxing match, and the usual array of male denizens from the adjacent neighborhoods.

The smell of turtle soup and fried eels drifted from the lofted tray of a barmaid who passed by Simon's table. She was setting out the bowls and platters nearby, for the pleasure of a pair of old salts, when Simon noticed Sean Cavendish across the room near the door, scanning the customers.

Sean gave a small nod when his eyes met Simon's. The big man wended his way down the room through the numerous tables to where Simon sat in a far corner against the wall.

Sean Cavendish's large body filled the chair on Simon's left. He raised his hand to a passing barmaid and pointed to Simon's ale and said, "I'll have the same."

When the young woman walked off, Sean said, "So, my lord, you have an interest in the lovely Yvette."

Neither man seemed inclined to waste time on small talk. "If you know who she is and where she lives, I will pay liberally," Simon told him.

"More's the pity. I don't," Sean said. "Don't look so skeptical, Simon. I could use the blunt. All I know is that the chit leaves by the alley and hails a cab on the street, but never the same one."

"You have never followed her?"

"I'm on duty, then, and I wouldn't trust anyone else to do the job. Parker has made all kinds of concessions to her, treated her different. I admit I flirted with the idea of finding her protector, for I'd wager a sack of guineas that she is a kept woman. But I can't afford to rub Parker the wrong way."

Simon raised a brow. "Knowing you, I find it hard to believe."

"Believe it because it is the honest truth. I can't afford to lose the job."

Sean waited while the barmaid set a tankard of ale on the table in front of him, before he said more.

Simon tossed some coins for the drink and a generous gratuity onto her tray, and she smiled her thanks and left.

Sean quaffed his ale and wiped his mouth on his sleeve. "You have to understand my position, Simon. I need to keep my nose clean. Parker hired me when no one else would touch me. I owe him. My name is poison in all but shady circles, and I was not offered the honest work I sought by anyone else after being locked up."

Simon toyed with his tankard. Sean could be telling the truth. Prison could change a man. But the ex-pugilist had always been a shrewd manipulator. "For the sake of argument, say I believe you, Sean. Still, you're the one who wanted this meeting. You apparently think you have something to sell so spit it out."

"Same old Simon. No nattering on with you, is there? All right. I can get you close to the divine *mademoiselle* without Parker being wise."

"How?" Simon watched him with narrowed eyes.

"Thursday night Parker is leaving the theater early for a business appointment. I can be busy somewhere else, if you want to rap on Yvette's dressing room door. Whether you gain entry or not, is up to your own charming self. I can't be tied to your being there. It's the best I can do."

Simon took a swallow of his ale. Yvette had already left the theater tonight when he went backstage. He mentioned this to Sean.

"She goes home right after her stint," Sean explained. "As I said before, Parker treats her different. No greenroom. You have to leave your box before she finishes singing since she never goes back for an encore. You can stand in the shadows and wait for her to come off the stage."

The ex-pugilist tipped the rest of the ale down his throat and set down the tankard. "No need to pay me, Simon," he said, disingenuously. "I know it ain't much."

Simon motioned to a barmaid to bring Sean another drink, but put his palm over the opening in his own pewter mug to show that he did not want a refill. It was only when the tavern girl came back with Sean's drink, and Simon had paid her, that he reached into an inner pocket and took out his purse. Sean was down on his luck. Simon could not bring himself to be clutchfisted. He drew out a couple of pounds and handed them to Sean.

"I'm counting on you to make yourself scarce on Thursday night," he said.

The brawny doorkeeper nodded, took the money, and slipped the notes into the pocket of his worn black coat. "You won't see hide nor hair of me, Simon."

Simon stood up and put a heavy hand on the big man's shoulder. "Don't cross me, Sean," he cautioned and left.

CHAPTER FOUR

The morning after her performance at Parker's Theater, Brianna sat staring into the fire, stroking the napping kitten in her lap. Mary was holding up a blue brocade gown on a silk padded hanger.

"Instead of adding a white flounce, I think a dark yellow ribbon basted to the hem would look best since the trim is already gold," she said, returning the evening dress to the mahogany armoire.

To disguise her height, Brianna wore heels which had been out of fashion for years to make her seem taller. Her own perfectly designed gowns were made to be worn with the popular low-heeled evening slippers. The modiste who sewed her fine dresses would have been horrified to see the mutilation to the lines of the fashionable gowns, but the alteration to the hem was as necessary as were the blond wig and the heavy stage makeup to mask her visage.

Although Brianna was not known in London society, there was always the slight chance that without a disguise she would be recognized by one of her grandparents' friends or acquaintances.

Mary shut the door of the armoire and said, "I know it is not my place to chide, my lady."

Brianna laughed. "When did that impropriety ever stop you, dear Mary? What is it now?"

"For two performances now you have played to a packed house, a different sort of clientele than Parker's playhouse usually attracts. Word has gotten around not only to the rich cits, but polite society who frequent the larger theaters that Hugh Parker has a star worthy of their patronage."

"What is your point, Mary?"

"The boxes have been filled with gentlemen of the *ton*. Soon the ladies of the *beau monde* will insist on being taken to see the new sensation. Some of those women may have met you when you came to London when you were younger."

Brianna made a face. "You fret too much, Mary. Who would suspect that the blond French singer is Lady Brianna Mansfield? I do not go to afternoon musicales where I may be invited to sing. Moreover I have not gone to any social events at night at all, as you know. Besides, no one of that ilk sees me up close while I am at the theater."

Mary knelt down beside Brianna's chair and ran her hand over Gilbert's soft black fur. The kitten continued to purr gently.

"Lady Hamden has been pressing me to get you to accept some evening invitations that came in the post, Lady Brie. She thinks you should be among young people your own age, not visiting museums and the library and shops and taking rides during the day with me."

"Grandmother understands that I want to forsake the social scene until my parents return from abroad and Mama can chaperone me," Brianna said, casting Mary a sideways glance. "If you are getting cold feet, you can remain here when I go to the theater. Then, if I am caught, you can say you knew nothing of my prank."

Mary got up and gave Brianna a withering glance. "As if I would," she said. "I'm going to the kitchen to get some hot chocolate for us and a dish of milk for Gilbert."

The black kitten lifted his small head and mewed at the sound of the door closing.

"Patience, little man, Mary has gone to get your breakfast," Brianna said and sighed. "You know, Gilbert, my head was filled with pretty notions of how it would be. I will share a secret with you." She lifted the kitten and looked into his yellow eyes. "I will not be sorry to leave the theater. I find the innuendoes and suggestive remarks uncivil."

Gilbert let out a loud meow. Brianna laughed and lowered him back onto her lap. "You don't know what those big words mean, do you? Uncivil is having a gaggle of louts propositioning me."

The black kitten jumped from her lap and wandered over to his bed in the corner and curled onto his cushion. Brianna stared into the fire.

Her love of the theater had been born when she was taken at the age of fifteen to see the opera dancer known as Vestris, who performed at Drury Lane. The beautiful Italian singer and dancer was the toast of London.

Brianna had thought Vestris's life must be the most exciting in the entire world. She herself had a fine singing voice and was taking lessons at her home in the green hills of Somerset from a French emigré, a renowned soprano, who had spent years touring the Continent.

Vestris had inspired Brianna to hatch a plan for the future. Someday, she decided at fifteen, when the opportunity presented itself, she would find a way to sing on the London stage under the noses of the *ton* without divulging her true identity. The moment came when her parents, the Earl of Wisbach and his countess, embarked on a month's tour of Europe and left their only child with her London grandparents.

Mary came through the door, carrying a tray with hot chocolate, sweet buns, and Gilbert's dish of milk balanced against her hip. She set her burden on the table between the two fireside chairs and spread an old newspaper on the rug nearby for the kitten's breakfast. The small cat jumped from his bed and trotted to the dish she set out and began to lap up the milk fastidiously.

Mary sat down, and the two women partook of the morning meal in silence.

After a time, Mary dabbed her mouth with a white linen

napkin. "Lady Brie," she said, "you must promise me that you will give up the theater when Lord and Lady Wisbach return from Europe."

"Of course, I am not a complete ninny, Mary. My mother would not be easy to fool."

"You do not belong in the theater, my lady. I know you admire that Vestris, but you never saw her when she wears breeches and men ogle her limbs. Lascivious behavior, I call it."

"She does have hordes of admirers, though, Mary."

"As if that makes it right."

To each his own, Brianna thought. Making a living on the stage had its moments, but it was not as fabulous as she had thought it would be.

"I do wonder, my lady, why you don't put an end to the nonsense right now instead of waiting until the earl and countess return. Why risk soiling your reputation? You know if your grandfather hears of it, you will be in disgrace. And your very proper mama will be scandalized and fall into a swoon from which she might never recover. And your earl father will send you to a nunnery."

Brianna grinned at the dire predictions. "We are not Roman Catholics and Mama never faints."

Yet Mary was right. If she intended to leave Parker's in two weeks, why not now? She despised the odious attention. The money certainly meant nothing to her. Her allowance for mere fripperies was more generous.

She suspected it was the handsome blond gentleman in the center box. She was curious about him and wanted to see him again, wanted to see if he came back. He did not bray or bellow like the dolts in the pit. He behaved as if the music meant something to him, which intrigued her. There was something exhilarating about the idea of meeting a man who felt the magic of the music as much as she did.

"You know, Mary, if I had found that the stage was my destiny, I would have gone to war against anyone who tried to keep me from performing. After all, women like Dorothea Jordan have been accepted in first circles."

Mary gasped. "Lady Brie! She is the mistress of the Duke of Cumberland, and the mother of ten bastard children."

Brianna gave her an impish grin. "I did not intend to emulate Mrs. Jordan in all things."

"I should hope not," Mary said, clearly appalled.

Brianna adored the theater, but from the other side of the stage. She loved music. Yet whether she sang in drawing rooms for a few people, or in amateur theatricals at a house party, as she had back home, or to herself in the privacy of her room, the melodies and lyrics would still touch her feelings.

"You know, Mary, I don't need the stage to be fulfilled. I can take as much pleasure in private performances."

"At last you are saying something sensible," Mary said.

CHAPTER FIVE

Thursday evening, as Brianna got ready to leave her grandfather's house for her performance at Parker's Theater, the fair-haired gentlemen in the center box was very much on her mind. Would he be there again tonight? Music was her great love, and he seemed to genuinely share her passion.

"Don't pay attention to the codheads in the audience, Lady Brie," Mary said, breaking into her dreamy reverie and reminding Brianna of the unpleasant side of her stage appearances. "If you get all puffed up, you'll only court even more insufferable behavior."

Mary made adjustments to her mistress's person, smoothing down Brianna's blue gown and straightening the blond wig over her midnight black hair as Brianna observed the last-minute primping in the tilted cheval glass.

"The antics of the tulips are beyond endurance, Mary. But not every gentlemen is prone to ramshackle excesses. I found at least one who is not only urbane and elegant, but a paragon of decorum."

"Oh?" the maid questioned, but Brianna turned from the glass and said no more, leaving Mary to wonder who the gentleman might be.

Brianna donned her navy blue cloak and lifted the basket in which the maimed kitten napped. Mary picked up the canvas sacks with their theatrical impedimenta and followed her mistress into the hall and down the stairs to the side door.

The house of elderly occupants was quiet. Jonas Mansfield, the Marquess of Hamden, and his marchioness did not keep town hours. Dinner was promptly at six, not at the more fashionable hour of eight, and directly after the meal Brianna's septuagenarian grandparents retired to their upstairs apartments, rather than linger at the table, which worked in Brianna's favor. She could slip from the house in the evening with only the slightest fear of being discovered.

Outside, the night was cool; the sky filled with stars. Brianna and Mary stuck close to the house to prevent anyone who might gaze from an upstairs window from seeing them. The phantom figures traversed the shadowy perimeter of the garden wall to the gate that led to the street. Once on the sidewalk, they hurried to the corner, where Mary hailed a hackney to take them to the alley behind the theater.

Sean Cavendish, as usual, let them into the building. Once inside the dressing room, Mary prepared Brianna for the stage with practiced efficiency, finishing just as a stagehand came to summon her. She followed him to the wings, where the mime came off the stage in his white makeup and brushed past her. In Mr. Parker's absence, a fellow actor traded the mime's card for Brianna's.

She put on her public smile as the curtain opened, and she stepped forward to robust applause and shrill whistles.

Brianna sang a song about love and heartbreak and then a witty tune that made the people laugh. Her lips curved into a satisfied smile when her eyes met her blond admirer's, and he nodded his respect and esteem.

Brianna moved on to an aria that showed off the power and clarity of her voice. The blond gentleman stood up and applauded her rendition enthusiastically. Her eyes sparkled with pleasure. Whether she sang poignantly, wistfully, spiritedly, or whatever the lyric and melody demanded, she ignored the miscreants and sang only for him.

Before the final number, Brianna rose from a deep curtsy, and her heart plummeted. Her admirer had left the box. Her disenchantment was palatable, but she pulled herself together and sang the last song, fittingly an ode to unattainable love.

Simon was huddled in a dark corner within sight of Yvette's dressing room when pandemonium exploded in the playhouse, signaling to him the end of Yvette's performance. A few seconds later, the object of his vigil came rushing down the corridor, teetering on black high heels, the skirt of her blue gown clutched in her hand, the gold hem raised from the floor.

Although she forcefully shut the dressing room door, it did not close completely. Simon left his hiding place, but before he could step across the hall, he saw a coal black kitten squeeze through the opening left by Yvette. The feline mewed and walked with a curious gait to where Simon stood and looked up at him. He noticed the deformed hind leg and gently picked up the kitten by its rump and stared into its tawny eyes.

"You are a friendly fellow," he said, very softly, "but do you belong to the theater or to the heavenly Yvette? Can't say, eh? Cat got your tongue?" He chuckled at his own little joke. "Let's find out who owns you."

Simon pushed open the dressing room door with the toe of his black evening pump. A squeaky hinge abruptly halted the conversation between the two female occupants, drawing their gazes to Simon.

Brianna turned around in the chair, where she had sat down, intending to remove her shoes. Her eyes were riveted on the fair-haired gentleman for a long moment. Her heart gave a joyous leap, although his sudden appearance stole every coherent thought from her brain.

"I caught this little fellow sneaking from your dressing room, *mademoiselle*," the blond gentleman said. "Is he the theater cat or yours?" It was only then that Brianna noticed Gilbert nestled in the gentleman's strong arms.

Mary was the one who responded. "He is ours, sir," she said, reaching for Gilbert. "*Mademoiselle* must have left the door ajar when she came offstage and Gilbert decided to explore."

Brianna's admirer handed the kitten to Mary. The exchange served as a reminder to Brianna that she was Yvette and allowed her to pull herself together.

"*Merci beaucoup, monsieur,*" she said, having regained her composure. "We might never have found Gilbert if he had lost himself in the bowels of the theater."

"My pleasure, *mademoiselle.*" His smile was perfection.

Brianna got up from the chair and walked over to him. She tilted her face up toward his handsome one.

"You have the advantage of me, *monsieur,*" she said, keeping to her French accent. "How are you called?"

"Simon, dear lady."

"Simon? Just Simon?" she said.

"Just Simon," he repeated with a smile.

She shrugged.

Simon felt something electric pass between them. The stage makeup gave her the countenance of a child playing grown-up. From his perspective from the box, he had expected her to be older. Her French was bogus. No one would ever mistake her for a Parisienne. She was English, but no less enchanting.

"It is my good fortune that Gilbert, is it? decided to go for a stroll," he said. "I can now pay my compliments to you in person, my dearest wish. You sing exquisitely, *mademoiselle.* Your marvelous voice touches my very soul." He put his hand on his heart, dramatically.

The maid grunted at his excessive sentimentality. "Yvette, it is getting late," she said, but Simon was gratified to see that the songstress paid no heed to her companion.

"Are you a musician, Meester Simon? You seem quite charmed by my songs." She cocked her head, her brow quizzical.

He gave her a rueful smile. "Sadly, I cannot produce music of any kind. I appreciate real talent, such as yours, but I, myself, possess no musical skills. I seem to end up as the designated page turner at social events." He hung his head and pouted boyishly. "Alas, dear lady, my own poor musical abilities will never grace a drawing room."

She giggled, a delightful sound. "The world is in need of willing page turners, Meester Simon, particularly those who know the exact moment to, well, turn the page."

"A dubious accomplishment, but one I grasp wholeheartedly since I seem to have gained your approbation in admitting to it."

Simon smiled down into her lovely violet eyes. He must have her. She would be a stunning mistress. He would be the envy of every man in London to have such a prime article in his keeping.

Simon's blood grew warm in his veins. He longed to be private with her. Just thinking about making love to her made him ache with desire. With seduction in mind, he said, "*Mademoiselle,* would you do me the honor to take supper with me?"

The maid uttered a choking sound. A definite warning, for the object of his lust shook her blond head. "*Mais non,*" she told him. "*Ce n'est pas possible.*"

Impatience prickled Simon. "I am not suggesting an intimate meal," he said falsely, "but supper in a public venue. You may select the restaurant." He knew he sounded waspish.

Yvette shook her head again. "*Ma grand-père* is very strict. I must go home directly after the performance."

Simon almost sneered. Grandfather, folderol. She had a protector. Yvette was already someone's mistress. His heart sank. But paramours could be lured away. He brightened at the thought. It was damned inconvenient, poaching on someone else's territory, but in her case it would be worth the effort. Changing his tactics, Simon forced a gracious smile onto his lips.

"I bow to your wishes, *mademoiselle*," he said. "But would you permit me to pay my respects here in your dressing room after your next performance?"

Brianna thought a moment, but she saw no harm in seeing him again after Saturday's show. "I think that would be acceptable," she said.

The gentleman called Simon caught her hand in his and brought it to his lips. "Until then," he said. Brianna felt a flutter in her midriff. She had all she could do to keep from leaning in to him.

He left through the open door, and Mary ran over to it and looked down the hall to be sure he was gone.

Brianna smeared cold cream onto her face and began to remove all traces of her makeup.

"He went into the theater," the maid said, coming back into the room. "He is the polite one you mentioned before, isn't he? But what are you thinking, Lady Brie? Why did you encourage him?"

"I did not *encourage* him," Brianna said indignantly. "I refused his invitation to dine, didn't I?"

Mary rolled her eyes. "But you agreed for him to visit you again here on Saturday."

Brianna continued to towel the cold cream from her face. "Oh, what harm is that? He was here tonight and was pretty-behaved. If truth be told, I like him. He does not act up like the shameless scapegraces in the pit. He is most respectful of me."

Mary shook her head in disgust. "Lady Brie, that man Simon is up to no good. Gentlemen who make overtures toward actresses have one thing in mind and it is not a brotherly affection. He intends to offer you a slip on the shoulder."

Brianna frowned in perplexity. "A slip on the shoulder? Is that what I think it is?"

Mary just stared at her.

"He will catch cold at that," Brianna said halfheartedly, not wanting to believe Simon was a rake. Yet could Mary be right? Brianna had not thought beyond the interplay between them when she performed. She had flattered herself into believing that he shared some deep and enduring love of music with her, that somehow made him admire her beyond her talent.

"Your Simon has made us late," Mary said. "We must hurry. Change your shoes, my lady, and I will collect the bags, and put Gilbert in his basket." The kitten meowed from where he sat on the floor, looking up at them.

During the entire trip home, Mary stared out the back window of the cab. Brianna guessed that her friend worried that Simon might follow them home. She found herself looking back nervously as well. But the street was empty of other vehicles when she unlocked the garden gate.

CHAPTER SIX

Jonas Mansfield, the Marquess of Hamden, was tall and slightly stooped. His hair was gray and his eyes a watery brown. But Brianna's grandfather was still quick of mind. He leaned on a stout cane and motioned her to a ladder-back chair. She had come after breakfast at his request to the intimate sitting room, a favorite of both his and her grandmother's, where he often read while Lady Hamden did needlework.

From a settee beneath the window, the marchioness, a tiny woman, her eyes blue, her hair snow white, greeted Brianna with pleasantries concerning her granddaughter's night's sleep and the condition of her breakfast.

"I slept through the night, Grandmother, and my eggs and ham were perfectly cooked and the chocolate sweetened to an inch," Brianna replied cheerily to the routine questions.

Lady Hamden's companion maid Chiltern (Brianna had never heard her given name) smiled her good morning from beside her employer.

"You sound positively sprightly, Lady Brianna," the thin, long-faced woman with salt and pepper hair declared.

Brianna supposed she was a little giddy this morning. Ever since last night, her head had been filled with reflections on her encounter with Simon in her dressing room at Parker's Theater. Despite Mary's warning that he was in the petticoat line, she could hardly wait to see him again.

Before she could make some polite reply to the older

woman, Lord Hamden said in his direct manner, "I had a courtesy call yesterday from the Earl of Breede, the son of an old friend."

His gaze favored Brianna, but it was his wife who commented. "I remember Lord Breede's father, the old earl, such lovely manners. Assist my memory, Jonas. Doesn't this Lord Breede also have a son?"

"Quite right, my dear," he said, "which brings me to my reason for asking Brianna to join us. In the course of our conversation, I mentioned to Breede that Brianna was newly arrived in town, and he offered the services of his son Viscount Glynden as her escort."

Brianna's face pruned. "Grandfather, do not tell me that you acquiesced."

"Making faces is most unbecoming, Brianna, and decidedly childish to boot," Lady Hamden said, shaking her head in disapproval.

Brianna resisted rolling her eyes. "I can't like Grandfather soliciting escorts for me," she said, concentrating on a curio shelf with a collection of music boxes in order to avoid looking reproachfully at the grandparents she loved.

"Nonsense," Lord Hamden said, his tone lofty. "No reason to pull a Friday face, Brianna. Bringing together young people of good families is a perfectly acceptable practice. The Whittens are an old and distinguished family and highly regarded in first circles, and I have heard that Lord Glynden is a personable young man. I trust you shall receive him with all the courtesy due his position."

Brianna could see that her grandfather was not in a flexible state of mind and found it more prudent to capitulate than to engage in an argument that she was sure to lose. Besides, she did not want to hurt his feelings, and what harm could come of receiving the viscount for a proper fifteen minutes? She would make short work of the call.

"As you will, Grandfather," she said, mastering the impulse to sound saucy.

As if to maintain the harmony of the morning, Lady Hamden smiled at both her husband and Brianna. "You need say no more, Jonas. Brianna may be high-spirited at times, but she knows how to make herself agreeable to callers of either persuasion."

Chiltern, too, acknowledged that Lady Brianna's manners were quite polished in company.

Brianna, however, had no wish to prolong the discussion and asked to be excused, giving the impression she was satisfied with the situation.

Late that same afternoon she curled up on a sofa in the parlor, put on her spectacles, and picked up the Gothic novel she had checked out from Hookham's lending library on Bond Street. But before she could open to the page where she had left off reading earlier, Boulton, the household's staid elderly butler, appeared at the door.

"Lady Brianna, are you receiving visitors?" he asked. "The Viscount Glynden is calling."

Brianna's initial annoyance gave way to curiosity. "Show his lordship in, Boulton," she said, leaning over to pick up her shoes.

"I shall call your maid to join you, my lady," the butler said, in the interest of propriety.

"No, that will not be necessary, Boulton. Lord Hamden has endorsed Lord Glynden's visit. Just leave the door open."

"Very good, my lady," the butler said and bowed himself out.

Brianna slipped her shoes over her silk stockings and removed her eyeglasses and put them down on the sofa table beside her library book. She stood up and shook out the skirts of her yellow poplin day dress and faced the door, prepared to receive her visitor.

Within seconds, Boulton was back, and Brianna gasped at the sight of the tall, all-too familiar figure trailing behind him. Her color mounted, and her heart bounced against her chest.

"The Viscount Glynden, Lady Brianna," the butler announced in a sonorous tone and withdrew.

Simon was Lord Glynden! Brianna's anxiety level soared.

He bowed low and said in the full, rich voice etched in Brianna's memory from the previous night, "Your obedient servant, my lady."

During that lull, Brianna snatched up her spectacles and slammed them onto her face, hoping he wouldn't see the panic pouring through her, and froze.

Simon came to stand before Lady Brianna and saw the look of shocked dismay on her face and wondered about it. But since he had no notion what could have caused such a severe reaction, he waited for her to speak.

His father had assured him that Lord Hamden welcomed the earl's offer to have his son squire Lady Brianna around town. Ordinarily Simon would have resented such blatant interference on his father's part. But since he had very specific qualifications in mind for the perfect bride, rather than a particular young lady, he was open to investigating any leads provided.

"May we sit down, my lady?" Simon asked, pointing to the sofa.

Lady Brianna's cheeks reddened. "Oh, I beg your pardon, my lord. Please," she said, her voice slightly tremulous.

She lowered herself down onto one end of the sofa. Simon followed, sitting on the other end, a cushion between them.

"You are new to the London social scene, I understand," he said. His smile was wasted since Lady Brianna was staring straight ahead.

"Yes, my lord," she said and cast a cursory glance in his direction, but quickly averted her eyes.

Simon stared intently at her. "Is something amiss, my lady?"

"Amiss? Good gracious no," she said with feeling. She appeared to concentrate on the book on the sofa table. "My sensibilities are often affected by horror tales. Mrs. Radcliffe's vivid writing about ghosts and such can positively set my heart to beating erratically."

Simon stared at the book on the table and lifted an amused brow. Tame fare. Was she truly such a timid soul? He really had no polite response for her strange confession and held his tongue.

"Have you been to any of the balls since coming to Town?" he asked instead. She shook her head, a cloud of short dark curls. Simon had never seen the new style adopted by a shy young woman before. It took a somewhat free spirit to get her hair cut in that fashion and to stand up to the tabbies who considered it racy.

"Why not?" he asked. "The Season is in full swing. Are you not out yet?"

"Of course, I am out. I have been for a year," she said with one of her sideways glances. "I am restricting my entertainments until my mother returns from her trip to the Continent and is able to chaperone me."

Her explanation sounded promising to Simon. Obviously, Lady Brianna was fearful of going into society without having the authority of the Countess of Wisbach standing between her and the *ton*. This spoke well for her fulfilling one of his requirements to take an insecure creature to wife.

Encouraged by the promise of this initial foray into finding the perfect bride, Simon quickly decided that Lady Brianna was worth further study. He could see that she was pretty behind the wire-rimmed spectacles. His father already approved of her by virtue of her family's place in society. Should she prove to be biddable, he might be able to end his search and resume the more important task of seducing Yvette, but he had learned the folly of jumping to conclusions. Further investigation was essential to avoid a serious mistake.

"It is a fine day, my lady," Simon said, keeping that in mind. "Would you consent to take a turn in the park? I came in my curricle."

Once again Lady Brianna gave him her odd sideways look.

She seemed to think about it for a while, but finally agreed to it, saying, "I will fetch my cape and bonnet. Would you like some refreshment, my lord, while you wait for me to get ready?"

Simon declined and she left the room.

Upstairs, Brianna took her time getting ready for her outing with Simon. From her window, she could see Mary sitting on an iron bench in the garden, watching Gilbert, her warrior cat with his battle-scarred leg, leaping in the air after some bright elusive flying insects.

She turned from the scene and walked to the armoire and removed a navy merino cloak and matching shovel bonnet. Downstairs in the parlor, she had felt as though she were acting in a play, except that Simon had not read the script.

Should she be going for a drive with Simon? Doubts flitted through her mind. She had been face-to-face with him last night. Would he see anything of the blond, heavily madeup Yvette in Lady Brianna? Not likely.

Yet she must not underestimate Simon's intelligence. The wisest course would be to avoid his company. But with both their families approving of his squiring her, this might not be possible. She needed to employ a persona which was different from her own and keep her glasses in place so that he could not get a good look at her eyes.

Brianna fastened the cape by the frogs near the neckline and placed the bonnet over her dark curls. By what type of female would Simon be put off? she asked herself, her finger on her chin.

Hadn't he looked a bit scornful when she had pretended to be agitated by a horror story? The very thing! A shy mouse!

Brianna removed a pair of butter-soft calfskin gloves from a drawer and smiled as she plied the gloves over her fingers. She would play the milk-and-water miss to the hilt. Such timid behavior should send him running from her. Modern gentlemen did not admire lackwits who had no notion of how to go on.

Brianna took the hand Simon gave her and mounted the sporty curricle nimbly. His tiger released the horses and hopped onto the rear of the gig.

Simon was obviously concentrating on his driving as he moved into the traffic and headed for the park. He had gone only a block when Brianna began to whimper, her face averted and her finger on the bridge of her spectacles. The odious things kept slipping down to the end of her nose.

"Are you all right, my lady?" Simon asked. To Brianna's disappointment he did not sound annoyed.

Her voice trembling as if she might burst into tears, Brianna replied, "Riding in an unstable vehicle frightens me a little, my lord."

"Rest assured, Lady Brianna, you are safe with me. I have the horses well in hand."

Although not a proficient judge of horseflesh, Brianna sensed that Lord Glynden's stallions were pedigreed and expensive. She loved riding in the fine vehicle, particularly since the man was a dab hand with horses, but she had to play her part.

"I am such a silly goose. Of course I am safe in your capable hands. I can already see that you ply the ribbons with such skill that we shall not overturn."

Brianna kept her voice low and throaty.

"Your confidence is not misplaced, dear lady."

Brianna gave him her sideways glance. He had a smug smile on his lips. She would not have thought that Simon would be pleased with such a hen-hearted female.

Brianna did not want to overdo her attempts to get him to show a disgust of her and waited until they were in the middle of the crowded park before she tried another ploy.

Sounding almost hysterical, she cried, "Oh, my lord, the carriages here in the park are crowding against us so precariously. I am used to driving in the country where one hardly sees another vehicle for miles."

Brianna clung to the side of the curricle.

"Don't worry, my lady, I shall take care of you," Simon said and patted her shoulder.

He took the first exit he came to from the park and slowed the horses to a slower pace on the street.

Brianna had expected Simon to be prickly, but he was being gallant. She gave up her ruse, fell silent, and sat back and enjoyed the rest of the ride.

Brianna hung up her cloak, with Gilbert curling around her legs and mewling his feline greeting. She was in trouble. Her efforts to discourage Simon had clearly failed. He had not minced words. He plainly intended to call on her again. She could not turn him away without incurring the wrath of her family. She removed her hat and put it on the top shelf of the armoire.

When Simon had stopped for ices at Gunter's, Brianna had revived her biddable act by deferring to his choice of the flavor of their treats, an uninspired lemon. Afterward, she glanced at him only from the corner of her eye. Still, she had held up her end of a discussion of the merits of the Elgin Marbles newly installed at the British Museum, although she was careful not to trample on his opinions.

Brianna closed the armoire's door. Only this morning, she had yearned to see Simon again. However, not like this. She had been so intent on hiding her true self that she had not been able to enjoy his company.

Simon was too astute for her to fool him for long with her shy act. Sooner or later she was bound to slip up. But there was even greater danger.

Brianna patted the spectacles in her pocket, which had been a barrier kept in place to keep Simon from seeing her eyes and raising a question in his mind, as it surely would, if he remembered that they were the exact same violet hue as Yvette's.

Scooping up the kitten that rubbed against her ankle, she stared into his yellow eyes and nuzzled her face in his silken black fur. "Oh, Gilbert, Grandpa will never allow me to keep Simon away from Lady Brianna, so I must find a way to keep him away from Yvette la Roche or I am doomed, but how?" she lamented.

CHAPTER SEVEN

Brianna sat on the window seat in her bedroom in her silk robe and looked out at her grandfather's garden. The spring flowers—red tulips and yellow daffodils—nodded in the faint breeze. Some shrub that she did not know was a profusion of pink clusters.

She had agonized during sleepless periods throughout the night over what to do about Simon's interest in Yvette. There was but one answer for it: She must give up her stage career and allow Yvette to vanish forever.

According to the terms of her verbal contract with Hugh Parker, she had three more performances to complete her run. She felt she owed the theater manger some loyalty for giving her a chance to fulfill her long-held dream. She would have liked to have kept her word to him, but she knew that it would be dangerous for her to come face-to-face with Simon again.

As soon as Mary returned from taking their breakfast trays back to the kitchen, Brianna informed her that she was quitting the theater, since Simon had turned out to be Lord Glynden.

Mary had a lot to say on the subject, but Brianna tuned out her maid, who was laying out clothes suitable for her charge's call on Mr. Parker, and instead thought about what she would say to the theater manager.

* * *

Hugh Parker was alone early in the morning as Brianna had expected, his office door open. She had put on her blond wig with Mary's assistance in the hackney for the last time.

She stood on the threshold for a moment, her maid behind her, until the theater manager looked up from the papers on his desk and smiled.

"Good morning, *mademoiselle*. What can I do for you?"

His brown badly fitting toupee as usual was slightly askew.

"I find I cannot complete our contract, Mr. Parker. Some unresolvable problems have come up that force me to give up singing in public," Brianna said.

"So," he replied, not seeming especially surprised, "Yvette la Roche will be no more. I am pained to hear it, but the news is not totally unforeseen."

Not wanting to acknowledge that Yvette was a bogus name, Brianna said, "Let us say rather that Yvette will go back to her former life."

The theater manager nodded. "The truth is that I never expected to hold you without a binding contract. I did think, though, that you would go to Covent Garden or Drury Lane, enticed away by Kemble or Elliston for more money. There is some solace in knowing that you are not leaving to enrich some other theater's coffers."

"Money never mattered," Brianna said honestly. "I am grateful to you for hiring me and for keeping your word and abiding by the conditions I laid down. You are a kind and decent man, Mr. Parker."

Hugh Parker pulled a face. "What stuff, child, are you trying to ruin my reputation? Please do not repeat such fustian to the world at large. I am neither kind nor decent. You plumped my pockets with the hefty profit I earned from your performances; if you had not, I would have shown you the door long ago. Now go away. I have work to do."

But his words did not match his pacific tone, nor his heavy sigh. Although she herself did not regret leaving his employ, she could not dislike the theater manager. Yet, the whole affair had been a mad scheme. She had considered only herself.

Her family would have been mortified if she had been exposed and would have suffered malicious gossip. It would have been terrible for her grandparents at their advanced age. The *ton* could be vicious. A good deal of undeserved blame for her folly would have fallen on the two old people, since **she** had been given into their care by her parents.

Brianna was waiting for Mary to bring her tea and cakes on a tray that afternoon. The weather had turned cloudy and drizzly. Mr. Parker had taken her resignation really well. Of course, there was still a slight chance that Simon would experience an epiphany and see a link between her and Yvette. But she wasn't really worried. People tended to see what they expected to see.

Mary came through the open door with the laden tray and set out Brianna's refreshments for her and pulled a straight-backed chair to the table.

"Where is Gilbert?" she asked the maid.

"In the kitchen," Mary said. "Cook gave him a dish of tidbits and a saucer of milk."

While Brianna ate, Mary straightened the miscellanea on the lady's desk, where her mistress had been composing letters to some of her friends in Somerset. The maid kept talking as she filled an ink pot and evened the edges on a stack of vellum stationery.

"You better get that smug look off your face, Lady Brie. What do you think Lord Glynden is going to do when he learns from Mr. Parker that Yvette is gone? Gone for good."

Brianna paused with a dainty cake in midair. She put the tiny pink pastry back down onto her plate and bit her lip.

"The man was clearly besotted with Yvette la Roche," Mary went on. "I never saw a gentleman look so sappy. I tell you he had more than a platonic little supper in mind there in your dressing room. There was seduction written on his handsome face and runaway passion in those blue eyes."

"Runaway passion? You can be so poetic at times, Mary,"

Brianna said dryly. She took a sip of tea and wiped her mouth on a linen napkin. "Do you think Simon is in love with Yvette la Roche?"

Mary stacked the letters to be taken below stairs for the mail carrier and turned from the cherrywood desk, her hands on her hips. "Love, infatuation, lust. It's all of a piece. That man was going to get what he wanted and nothing was going to get in his way. Mark my words, my lady. Lord Glynden is going to turn London town upside down looking for Yvette."

Brianna pushed aside her cup of tea. She would be in danger if Simon began to question the theater people about Yvette la Roche. She could not be certain that she had not left some sort of trail or clue to her identity. Although she had taken a different cab every night, Simon might find a jarvey who remembered that she had hired his hack. A greased palm could often do much to revive a lapsed memory of two women from the theater traveling alone late at night to a better part of the city.

Brianna shivered a little. She had taken some awful chances. But would Simon go to such lengths to find Yvette? Was Mary right? She knew the answer. Simon was not a man to be denied. Her fear of his stalwart determination was the prime reason that she had left Hugh Parker's.

Despite the security provided by Sean Cavendish, Simon had gotten past the guard to visit her in her dressing room. Gilbert had given him a sound excuse for barging in on her, but Simon had not been in front of her door by accident.

Mary had been chattering, but Brianna had not been listening. She did not lament leaving Parker's, but she was beginning to rue ever having performed in public at all. The cost might prove to be too high.

Brianna came out of her room, headed for another boring afternoon of reading in the drawing room. She had run out of new places to visit in London. Since the day had turned gloomy, even a late drive in the park was out. She wished that her parents would return from abroad, for she was ready to partake of some evening entertainments.

She heard the front door open, and she looked over the rail. She recognized Simon and was about to hail him when she saw that Boulton was taking him down the hall toward her grandfather's library. Her hand went to her mouth; her breath accelerated. Could he have found out about the charade already? Was he about to expose her folly? She reversed her destination and decided to visit her grandmother in her apartments.

Lady Hamden was a clever raconteur. Her stories of London society in the late seventeen hundreds never ceased to amuse Brianna. She counted on the marchioness's compelling tales to keep her mind from bootless speculation about Simon's reason for calling on her grandfather.

Leaning on his cane, Jonas Mansfield stood up and came forward to greet Simon. "I knew your grandfather," he said in his clear voice, "and have met your father on several occasions."

Simon made some proper response and took the chair the elderly man indicated. Lord Hamden sat down across from him and propped his polished wooden cane against the side of the chair.

"I heard that you called on my granddaughter yesterday and took her for a drive in the park. I was pleased to see that she was getting out with someone other than that maid of hers. You would think a young girl would welcome the opportunity to attend a ball or rout or a performance at the theater. Both Lady Hamden and I have encouraged Brianna to accept one of the many evening invitations she has received, but she insists on waiting until my daughter-in-law returns from abroad."

Simon smiled a little. "Perhaps it is because Lady Brianna is shy."

Simon thought Lord Hamden looked at him rather strangely.

"Nonsense," he said. "The girl has been out for a year. She is of marriageable age, not some schoolroom miss."

"Yes, my lord, and that is precisely my reason for calling today. I know it is early days in my friendship with Lady Brianna, but I would like to have your permission to call on her in a sort of, well, precourtship for the lack of a better word. Quite honestly, sir, I think she is the exact type of young lady I would like to marry."

Lord Hamden said nothing for a moment. "I don't indulge in spirits much these days, but I can offer you some or perhaps tea or coffee?"

"No, thank you, my lord. I just had tea at White's."

Lord Hamden nodded. "Just so. Then, let us return to your reason for this visit." The faintest smile tugged at his lips. "Just a few hours spent with my granddaughter and you already know that you are well-disposed toward her."

It was a statement not a question, but Simon said, "Sometimes, my lord, it only takes a moment to know one's mind, but I have given it some thought since yesterday. You see I believe that in Lady Brianna I have found the attributes of the perfect bride."

Simon would rather have spent his life with Yvette la Roche, but a gentleman did not choose his wife from Covent Garden or Parker's Theater. Yvette would be his, but in a different way, while he was sure Lady Brianna Mansfield would do quite nicely as the Viscountess Glynden and a fitting mother for his children.

Simon leaned forward a little in his chair, his large hands clasped in front of him. Lord Hamden was an aristocrat. He knew the accepted qualities a gentleman of their station sought in a wife and of polite society's expectations. He felt confident he could speak frankly.

"Lady Brianna is a comely young woman," Simon said, but he thought it prudent not to add that at least she would be once he rid her of the ugly spectacles. "Your family is above reproach, no scandals and of the highest lineage. She commands a respectable dowry which I can assure you will be kept intact for our children or for her personal use."

Lord Hamden nodded as if in approval, but he said nothing and Simon went on. "Lady Brianna has shown herself to be modest." He did not want to say shy again. "I see that she is the sort of female who will defer to my judgment in all things as is proper for a wife. She is quite a biddable young lady."

Lord Hamden's thick white brows leaped up in surprise. "You speak of Brianna?" he said, a question in his voice.

Simon frowned. Had the old gentleman somehow lost his train of thought? After all, he was nearly eighty. "Yes, my lord."

"Hmm," Lord Hamden uttered. He chuckled, inappropriately, Simon thought. "Well, young man," he said, "you may call on my granddaughter, of course, since you indicate it is . . ." He paused. "What did you call it? Yes, a precourtship. I, however, am not the one for you to petition if you decide to take your friendship to the next level and ask for Brianna's hand. It is her father's prerogative to say yeah or nay."

Simon hoped he did not sound pompous, but said, "I know the protocol, my lord. Thank you for your courtesy."

He got up and made to take his leave with a few polite parting words.

Lord Hamden reached for his cane and struggled to get up.

Simon raised a hand and begged the elderly gentleman to remain seated. "I can see myself out, my lord."

As Simon traversed the hall to the front door, he thought the poor old man must have addled wits after all, for he could hear him start to laugh in a slap-kneed sort of way. Looking down the hall toward the kitchen wing, Simon saw the butler coming toward him, a coal black cat with a strange gait, running alongside him.

The confusion that strikes people who are completely disoriented overcame Simon. Gilbert? But how? It was impossible! He could accept as coincidence two coal black kittens with glowing golden eyes, but not two identical little cats with the same malformed limbs. Simon felt a chill.

The butler picked up the viscount's gold-headed cane and his tall hat from the hall table and handed them to Simon.

"Where did you get this kitten, Boulton?" Simon asked. The cat arched his back and rubbed against Simon's tight-fitting beige trousers.

"Why, my lord, Gilbert, as he is called, was born right here in our own mews, but when he had a run-in with one of the older toms and ended up with a twisted leg, Lady Brianna rescued him from being put down. Most cats are independent creatures, but our Gilbert is a friendly fellow who loves company. Lady Brianna and her maid Mary Moore simply dote on him."

With a sudden dawning, Simon felt his temper rise. Brianna had to be Yvette, damn her hide.

"Tell me, Boulton, does Lady Brianna sing?"

The butler looked as confused as Simon had felt earlier at the non sequitur, but he responded. "Why, indeed, my lord, my lady sings like an angel. When she entertains Lord and Lady Hamden at the pianoforte, all of the servants stop what they are doing and listen. She is that talented."

Simon was churned up inside. He thanked the butler, in a barely civil tone, and stormed from the house.

Leaping onto the curricle's seat, Simon snapped the reins in anger. His hapless tiger, who had been walking the horses, barely had time to jump on the back and grab hold before his master went careening down the avenue, heedless of the traffic.

Simon seethed. A maid called Mary! A unique cat named Gilbert! A voice like an angel! Lady Brianna, alias Yvette la Roche, had made a fool of him. He could feel his face heat up in embarrassment. Her grandfather had known that she was not the docile, malleable creature Simon was describing to him. That is the reason Lord Hamden had seemed to be laughing up his sleeve at him during the interview. No wonder the old gentleman had indulged in a horse laugh when Simon had left the room.

What a fribble I have been, bamboozled and made to look the complete idiot.

Simon had been so pleased with himself, thinking he had found his perfect bride. Lady Brianna was pretty and well-behaved. She would never jabber his ear off. She might not like his having a mistress, particularly someone as attractive and talented as Yvette la Roche, but being a good wife, she would pretend indifference. After all, she was too well-bred to make a scene.

Now he knew that Lady Brianna was no innocent, but a wily, sneaky female. Marriage to her was not such a brainy notion after all.

Simon slowed the horses to a safe pace in the heavy London traffic. He smiled evilly, contemplating his revenge. He would marry Brianna and make her life a living hell. Or he'd ruin her so that no decent man would have her. He saw himself circling a ballroom, dropping a word in every ear about her scandalous conduct. The *ton* would stare and point as monstrous tears trailed down her cheeks.

Yet, Simon knew he would never do any of it. He would keep the lady's secret. He was an honorable man. Drat his proper upbringing. Sometimes it took all the fun out of life.

Yvette la Roche was singing tonight at Parker's and had given him leave to come to her dressing room after her performance. Simon was thinking of how he could humiliate her when he pulled up to the curb of his town house and saw that Robby Fitch's sporty conveyance was parked close by, the baron's diminutive tiger attending his team.

"Dreadful news," Robby said when Simon met him in the visitor's parlor, where Simon's butler had seated his friend. "I passed Parker's Theater on the way here, and the poster advertising Yvette la Roche's performances had a banner across it. All of her appearances have been permanently canceled."

Simon gritted his teeth. The jade had foiled him again, but not for long. He had the upper hand now, with complete access to Lord Hamden's house and her grandfather's permission to court her.

CHAPTER EIGHT

Simon did not reveal to his friend that he had learned Yvette la Roche's true identity. As a result, Robby was surprised when Simon was not as devastated as he was by the news that Yvette was no longer at Parker's Theater.

"You don't seem the least bit blue-deviled by the bad tidings I bring you," young Lord Cragg said, raising a well-formed brow.

Simon improvised. "I always suspected that Yvette had a protector. Her secret lover must have become jealous of her notoriety and did not like the smutty talk about her in the gentlemen's clubs." His smile was neutral. "You know, I had not exactly bestowed my heart on the chit, Robby."

"You did, however, consider making her your mistress," his friend pointed out.

"So?" Simon shrugged. "Gad, Robby, Yvette was a passing fancy. You make too much of it. I would have a harem by now if every ladybird I lusted after had become my mistress."

Robinson Fitch nodded. "Just so; it's the truth."

The two young men looked at each other and laughed.

After some conversation of conquests made and conquests missed, Robby sat forward in his chair and said, "Edmund Kean is doing *King Lear* at Drury Lane. Now that there is no point in your going to Parker's since la Roche is gone, do you want to make a party of it for tomorrow night? I am taking Norah Cunningham."

"In fact I do," Simon said in a sudden inspiration. "My father has asked me to provide escort to the daughter of a family friend new to London as a favor to him. She is quite a pretty little thing."

"Who is she?" Robby asked, his eyes questioning.

"Lady Brianna Mansfield," Simon said. "Lord Hamden's granddaughter. Her father is the Earl of Wisbach."

"Young?"

"Eighteen, I believe."

"Just what you are looking for. Someone to mold to your liking." Lord Cragg took out his pocket watch. "I have an appointment at Weston's in twenty minutes, so I must be off."

The two young gentlemen quickly made their plans for the next evening's outing, and Robby got up and left to see his tailor, London's leading arbiter of sartorial tastes.

A little later, Simon called on Hugh Parker to determine if he knew that Yvette la Roche was Lady Brianna. He left the theater manager's office convinced that he did not.

Simon felt relieved not for the little fraud's sake, he told himself, but for the sake of the Mansfields. None of those upstanding people deserved to have the deceitful Brianna's sins tainting them.

But as Simon drove along streets lined with shops, he wondered at his deepest feelings, for he could not deny the attraction that flickered between them. More fool he for being drawn to a devious female of impeachable behavior.

Yet the next day, Simon called on the vixen, determined to make her pay for gulling him. He sympathized with Brianna's desire to keep her theatricals a secret, but he smarted from her making a cake of him by pretending that she was a missish innocent.

The fog which had rolled in during the night had not dissipated, although a weak afternoon sun was trying to break through the dense vapor as Simon lifted the brass knocker on the street door of Lord Hamden's house.

Boulton showed him into the drawing room. "I shall see if Lady Brianna is at home, my lord," the butler said and withdrew.

Simon stood at the window, looking out at the well-kept yard shrouded in mist. Birds called from the branches of the trees that rose to the roof line of the house, their newly sprung green leaves glistening with drops of moisture.

Yesterday he had told Lord Hamden that sometimes it takes only a moment to know one's mind. And Simon had believed it, for it had seemed to him that Yvette would have made a splendid mistress while Lady Brianna would have been a perfect wife. He had thought that he had discovered the formula for an ideal existence. Now he had neither a beautiful light-o'-love nor a sweet domestic partner, but some amalgamation that had his head zigzagging.

Simon turned from the window when Lady Brianna's cambric gown, a sky blue shade trimmed in a darker blue lace, rustled as she came through the door.

From across the room, he smiled a diffident smile, conveying his contempt, but his gesture was wasted. Her bespectacled eyes were glued to the flowered carpet at her feet. Simon longed to shake her until her perfect white teeth rattled.

"Good day, Lord Glynden," she said in her whispery voice.

She was not going to get away with that mealymouthed act any longer. "Speak up," Simon said, a wicked light in his eyes.

Her head came up at the surprising tone. "Good day, Lord Glynden," she repeated, raising her voice a good notch. "Please be seated, my lord." She pointed toward a chair; she took the sofa. Simon ignored her direction and sat down beside her.

"I have tickets for tonight for us to see Edmund Kean in *King Lear* at Drury Lane," he said.

"You assume too much, my lord. I do not recall ever saying that I would attend the theater with you."

"Your grandfather gave me permission to escort you tonight."

"Lord Hamden does not speak for me," she replied.

Simon flicked his wrist. "*King Lear* is not to your liking?

Perhaps you would prefer some lighter entertainment. All the talk at the clubs is of a French songstress at Parker's, one Yvette la Roche. Rightly so. She is superb."

Simon heard her sharp intake of breath, before she said, "As I told you before, my lord, I am not attending any affairs after dark until my mother returns from abroad."

Simon raised an insolent brow. "I beg to differ. Lord Hamden expressly wishes you to acquire some town bronze." His lower jaw took on a stubborn jut. "Yes, I think we shall forgo Edmund Kean and see la Roche. In fact, I have heard that you, too, have an interest in music and a fine voice."

"My grandfather said that?" she asked, sounding amazed.

"No, I believe it was Boulton."

"The devil, you say!"

"Lady Brianna," Simon scolded, "your language!"

He felt her stiffen beside him. She neither apologized, nor commented further. He glanced at her lips, tightly pressed together to stifle speech.

Simon was immensely pleased by her discomfort, but he was not through baiting her. He motioned toward the pianoforte near the window, enjoying himself.

"Sing for me, my lady," he said, "so I can compare your voice with la Roche's."

Her lips came apart. "I fear, my lord, that I am not in good voice today. The inclement weather makes me sound raspy." She emitted a fake cough. "I cannot compete with a professional; moreover, I see no purpose in a contest between us. I will never sing in a public venue."

"Assuredly not, your reputation would be in shreds," Simon said dryly. "But we can still attend her performance at Parker's if you do not care for Shakespeare."

"I believe that Yvette la Roche has left Parker's," Brianna said. She had abandoned her throaty intonation, her voice now Yvette's melodious own without the French accent.

"Oh, I had not heard," Simon lied. "You are certainly au courant for someone who does not go into society."

"My maid is fond of gossip," she said. Simon smiled to himself. He had to give her credit for having a quick mind.

Brianna stood up, forcing Simon to follow. "I know you will excuse me, Lord Glynden. I have some letters to write."

Simon looked over at the clock on the mantel. "How very bad of me. I have overextended my time," he said aware that conformity demanded that morning calls should not exceed fifteen minutes. "But I shall take you up in my carriage at seven for our sojourn to Drury Lane, for, sadly, it appears we cannot have Yvette." His sigh was less than sincere. "However, I think you will enjoy Edmund Kean. He does tragedy so well. My bosom beau, Robinson Fitch, who is Lord Cragg, a baron, will share my box at Drury Lane with his friend Miss Norah Cunningham. Do you know her?"

"No?" he said when she shook her head of dark curls. "A jolly sort, Miss Cunningham. You do not need Lady Wisbach to chaperone. It is perfectly acceptable for your maid to stand in for your mother."

"I prefer to wait for Mama to come back from Europe."

"Nonsense," Simon said, dismissively. "I will not take no for an answer. Your grandfather thinks you should go into society and I have promised him to see that you do." Not quite the truth, but he was not going to let her wiggle out of the invitation. He brought her hand up and brushed his lips against her knuckles. "I can't let Lord Hamden down."

He dropped her hand and caught her chin with his fingers. "I want to see your eyes without these." He lifted her spectacles from her nose and set them on an end table. "Such a lovely violet color, a perfect complement to your dark curls."

Simon leaned over and kissed Brianna full on the mouth. He held the kiss a little longer than he meant, yet it was fairly brief. "Until seven," he said, surprised to find himself a bit shaken by the sweetness of so fleeting a kiss.

Brianna's heart raced as Simon left without a backward glance. She felt as if she were caught in a whirlwind. Her hands had gone to Simon's shoulders when his mouth had come down on hers. After all, it was hard to kiss someone without holding on. She should have objected. She should not have found the kiss one of the nicest sensations she had ever experienced. But, after all, she had admired Simon for some time and knew that he had feelings for her, well, for Yvette, yet he was kissing Brianna. Did he know that they were one and the same person? His mentioning Yvette seemed too convenient to be a coincidence. But she could not take a chance on coming right out and asking Simon if he was gammoning her. Lud, not knowing was dreadful.

Her hands pressed to her temples, Brianna knew she had to keep from going to Drury Lane with Simon tonight. She went to seek out Mary first, then her grandfather.

Mary agreed to feign illness. Brianna found Lord Hamden in the small parlor to tell him.

"Mary is feeling poorly, Grandfather. I fear I lack a chaperone and so must refuse Lord Glynden's invitation to attend *King Lear* tonight."

Lady Hamden, who had been leafing through the *Morning Post* while her husband wrote at his desk, put down the newspaper and said, "No need for you to forgo the entertainment, Brianna. Chiltern will be delighted to stand in for Mary. She has not been to the theater, which she loves above all things, since I gave up accepting evening engagements."

Surprising herself, Brianna felt no disposition to argue. In fact the unexplicable gloom into which she had sunk had vanished. She wished she could deny it, but she did care for Simon. She cared a great deal.

Norah Cunningham had flaming red hair, green eyes, and a pleasingly rounded figure, and she proved to be just as amiable as Simon had predicted. The two young women very quickly became friendly. But Brianna's heart beat a little faster when she was presented to Lord Cragg. She knew him as the young gentleman who had shared the box with Simon at Parker's, but she had never learned his name. She relaxed when Lord Cragg showed no sign of connecting her with Yvette, and all her tension melted away.

Many Drury Lane theatergoers arrived late and visited from box to box during the performance as well as at the intermission. People talked all through the acts. Going to the theater was as much an exercise in seeing and being seen as it was in taking pleasure in the play.

Brianna and Simon sat side by side in the front row with Lord Cragg and Miss Cunningham in the chairs beside them. Behind the young couples, Chiltern chatted with Norah's maid, a gray-haired lady her own age.

Commonplaces and questions and talk of this and that flowed among Brianna, Simon, Norah, and Robby. During a lull, all of them listened to Edmund Kean emoting as Lear.

Robby whispered something to Norah, and she blushed, and soon the couple had their heads together.

Left to their own devices, Simon and Brianna were flirting, too. Simon's laugh seemed warm and attractive to her. Her impish smile held magic for him.

Simon found it difficult to believe that this daughter raised in a very proper aristocratic family had compromised her reputation by singing on the stage of a second-rate theater. Yet her personality was more like Yvette's than the shy mouse identity she had taken on to hoax him.

Tonight Brianna was so alive and real that Simon knew he would be unable to stay away from her. He was more than halfway in love.

"I am glad to see you have come out of your shell, Lady Brianna. I feared that you would never show me this delightful side of yourself that I was certain was there."

Brianna's eyes rounded. "What an odd thing to say, my lord. How could you be certain?"

"I daresay I cannot explain it fully. Except, my dear, you are uncommonly pretty. Young ladies with your exceptional looks are never shy for long," he said, taking up her gloved hand and bringing it to his lips.

His startling statement left Brianna very much confused. She had begun to think that he might know that she was Yvette. Now she was not sure.

But, regardless, she found Simon irresistible, charming, and intelligent. He seemed to fancy her, but she still feared that her misguided stint on the stage would come to light and make it impossible for her to marry any worthy man.

At the intermission, Simon and Brianna were abandoned by Miss Cunningham and Lord Cragg, who visited with friends in another box, and Chiltern and her counterpart, who decided to stretch their legs.

Simon said, "I would be honored to escort you to Norah's rout," he said, leaning in close to her, his incredibly blue eyes staring at her lips as if he meant to kiss her.

Brianna turned her eyes to the stage's closed curtain. Earlier, Miss Cunningham had invited Brianna to a rout she was giving the next evening. Brianna had politely declined.

Simon put up a hand. "I know you are waiting for the countess to chaperone you. I heard you tell Norah."

"Not only that, but I cannot subject Chiltern to the mad crush. She is no longer a young woman."

Simon touched Brianna's bare shoulders lightly with his fingertips, sending sweet shivers through her.

"Can't I change your mind? Surely your maid will have recuperated by tomorrow. You could have her ride with us."

Oh, no I couldn't. Simon would recognize Mary Moore immediately. "I would be grateful to you, Lord Glynden, if you did not persist."

Simon stopped twitting her. He had a fierce desire to fold her in his arms. All thoughts of revenge had vanished.

Suddenly he was tempted to confess that he knew Brianna was Yvette and to assure her that her secret was safe with him. He almost owned up to it, but before he could, Chiltern and Norah's maid came through the curtains at the back of the box. He quickly realized this was neither the time nor the place for those particular revelations.

Instead, he said, "I shall press you no longer," and Brianna said, "Thank you, my lord."

In the darkness of the carriage on the way home, Chiltern soon dozed off, snoring softly. Brianna and Simon talked quietly, almost in whispers, their heads close together.

Long afterward, when Brianna played that night back in her mind, she would not remember exactly what their conversation had been about, only the effect that Simon had had on her in the dim light of the interior of the carriage. She had felt he was a kindred spirit, someone she could love for an eternity.

As Simon's driver approached her grandfather's house, Brianna leaned over and gently shook Chiltern's knee. The elderly woman blinked rapidly.

"Are we home?" she asked in a drowsy voice.

"Yes, Chiltern," Brianna said as the carriage came to a stop. Her voice became concerned. "Something seems to be amiss. There are lights in the windows all over the house, upstairs and down, and even in the servants' wing."

Simon bent around Brianna for a better view.

"You have the right of it," he said. The flickering snippets of soft yellow candlelight shone everywhere. "Is that unusual?"

"Unheard of this late in the evening," Brianna told him. "The sole lamp light comes through the vestibule transom above the front door. I do hope that neither Grandfather nor Grandmother has been taken ill."

Simon's footman jumped down from the seat beside the driver and unlatched the compartment's door from the outside and helped Brianna to the sidewalk. Chiltern followed and then Simon.

"I will see you to the door, ladies," he said. "Perhaps, I might be of help if there is an emergency."

But when the theater party walked through the front door, Boulton greeted them with a smile.

"The Earl and Countess of Wisbach are back from their tour of Europe, Lady Brianna," said the butler, whose gray hair was slightly mussed and his clothes not quite as neat as normal, a sign that he had dressed hurriedly to greet Lord Hamden's son and his employer's son's wife.

Brianna smiled brightly. "My mother and father are here at last. I must go to welcome them. Thank you for a delightful evening, Lord Glynden," she said.

Simon took her gloved fingers in his, but did not linger. "My pleasure, Lady Brianna." He released her hand, turned at the door, and said, "I shall call on you tomorrow," and was gone.

CHAPTER NINE

Brianna gave Chiltern her cloak, gloves, and reticule and rushed to the informal parlor, where Boulton said she would find her parents, while Chiltern went upstairs to see if Lady Hamden needed her, for she had been told that the elderly lady preferred to wait to greet her son and daughter-in-law in the morning.

Brianna walked into the parlor, where sunlight normally brightened the room, and over to her father. Now only blackness was beyond the windows, and her reflection stared back at her from the darkened glass.

"Here she is," Lord Wisbach said and pulled his daughter into his arms and kissed her cheek. Her mother sat on a sofa, smiling.

Her father was half a head shorter than his own distinguished male parent, who sat in a chair near the fireplace, shielded from the heat by a decorative Chinese screen.

Although Guy Mansfield's dark brown hair was free of gray, his hairline had receded, giving him a high forehead. He had a pleasant, rather than a handsome face. His large nose was knife-straight; his eyes a light brown.

Brianna asked about the trip, and he said, "It was grand. All that your mother and I expected and more. But there will be ample time to give you the details and relate our many delightful experiences. Greet your mama now and then we want to hear all about your admirer Lord Glynden."

Lady Wisbach rose from the sofa and opened her arms as

Brianna came to her. She hugged her only child before she put her daughter away from her a little and looked her up and down. "I adore the gown, so elegant. What is that color?"

"It's called woodrose, Mama. The modiste said the style is all the crack."

"I love the beading at the neck and hemline and the straight skirt. But only someone like you with a perfect figure can carry it off," Caroline Mansfield said to her daughter. "It is not a dress that hides flaws."

The countess was beautiful and had a fine figure herself. Her shiny black hair was pulled back from her face to highlight her perfect features. Her violet eyes were stunningly vivid. She looked far younger than her forty years. Brianna knew they could easily pass for sisters.

She took Brianna's hand and led her daughter to the sofa. "You haven't said anything about her hair, Guy," she said to her husband in a teasing tone.

"That, my dear, is because I rather like her mass of dark curls. The style suits her. I suppose the hairdo, too, is all the crack as you put it, Brie."

"But, of course, Papa," Brianna said, although she had adopted the short cut to make it simpler to hide her hair beneath Yvette's blond wig.

Lord Wisbach picked up the brandy snifter he had placed on a chairside table when Brianna came into the room. He inhaled the aroma of the liquor, warming the glass with his hands before he took a sip.

"Your grandfather says that Lord Glynden is quite taken with you. I have met the lad a few times at White's, and I can't say anything against him. Oliver Whitten, the Earl of Breede, is the viscount's father, you know, and there never has been even a breath of scandal associated with the family. I have known Breede for years and years. Glynden's parents have not neglected his manners or failed to teach him proper etiquette. Your grandfather agrees with me that his conduct is exemplary."

Guy Mansfield glanced at his father. The old gentleman

nodded his assent. "Glynden cuts quite a dash, although he seemed to be a little off on his perception of Brianna's true character. I do question just how well he knows her," Lord Hamden hedged.

"Not very well, Grandfather," Brianna put in. "After all, I have been in Lord Glynden's company but a few times." She frowned a little. "But, Papa, you make it sound as if he is a serious suitor."

The earl looked at the marquess again, his expression faintly irritated. "You did not say anything to Brianna about what we discussed earlier, Father?"

Lord Hamden shrugged. "I did not think that it was my place, my boy. I gave the lad permission to call. It is as far as I was prepared to go. Now that you are back, Guy, I am certain that Glynden will call again to clarify his position."

"Will someone please tell me what this is about," Brianna said, looking from one man to the other.

Her mother took Brianna's hand and wove her fingers through her daughter's. "Brie, Lord Glynden spoke to your grandfather with candor. He is taken with you and believes that you would make a perfect bride. But he has asked to court you in an informal manner to determine if you do indeed suit before he makes a formal declaration. Which, darling, is wise. It also means that you, too, can determine if you find him acceptable."

"Of course, she will find him acceptable, Caroline," Lord Wisbach said with some fervor. "Glynden is one of the most eligible bachelors in the *ton*. It would be a travesty to let him get away."

Brianna's moment of pure shock stilled her tongue. How could Simon Whitten want her for a wife? Granted, tonight he had seen her true self, but he had spoken to her grandfather when he thought her a missish ninny who had nothing to say for herself. She shook her head from side to side in confusion.

Her mother must have noticed, for she untwined their fingers and said, "No more of Glynden tonight, Guy. Let us seek our beds now. I am too fagged for a serious discussion."

Brianna took the cue and got up. She kissed her parents and grandfather on the cheek as her mother added, "Brie, I have so much to tell you about Paris and Rome and the quaint country pensiones where your papa and I stayed. We will talk tomorrow."

Brianna lay awake for a long time, remembering how as Yvette she had flirted with Simon from the stage and bantered with him in her dressing room. Yvette was much more her real self than the docile Brianna she had pretended to be.

He has asked to court you in an informal manner to determine if you do indeed suit before he makes a formal declaration. Simon had said that to her grandfather days ago before she had stopped playacting.

Yet tonight he had implied that he had always suspected that she had, what was it, yes, *a delightful side.* He had been sincerely attentive and charming. Put together with his avowals to her grandfather, Brianna was forced to conclude that Simon was truly considering proposing to her. The revelation left her crestfallen, for she could never marry him. Lord Glynden came from a family that would never tolerate a bride who had so forgotten herself that she had sung in a public theater. How lowering to be a fallen woman, ruined at eighteen. She fell asleep with tears trickling down her cheeks.

All the Mansfield clan slept late the following morning and rose at different times, drifting down to breakfast at their leisure. No one was in the sunny morning room when Brianna came down, and she picked at her eggs and toast in welcome solitude.

But shortly after she went back to her bedchamber, the Countess of Wisbach peeked in her room.

Brianna put away the unopened book that she had in her

lap and waved her mother inside. She had not been able to get Simon Whitten out of her mind and she gave the countess a sad little smile that plucked at Lady Wisbach's heart as she sat in a chair near to her daughter.

"Do you want to talk about what is bothering you, Brie?" Brianna gave a quick negative shake of her dark curls.

"All right," Caroline said. "But remember, dear heart, I am here to support you. I suspect something has happened between you and Lord Glynden to put you off him. Nothing could be too terrible for me to turn against you, my sweet. Nothing!"

Caroline resigned herself to her daughter's silence and changed the subject to her visit to Paris. For better than an hour, she talked about her tour of the Continent. Brianna's initial glumness gave way to questions and even giggles at the funny parts of her mother's narrative.

Although Brianna had had a nurse and a governess and teachers of dancing and singing, Caroline had been an involved mother, spending time with her daughter every day, regardless of her own social calendar.

Her daughter had many friends, both male and female, and an active, if narrow, social life at home in Somerset. Caroline planned to launch Brianna into London society, where she could broaden her horizons by meeting new people. In the countess's opinion she had made a good start to that end by catching the eye of Lord Glynden, a highly desirable young gentleman. But something was clearly bothering her darling girl about that association. Still Caroline kept her counsel, for she knew from experience that pressing Brianna would only cause her daughter to retreat even further. Despite her genial personality Brie could be exceedingly stubborn.

Shortly after the countess went back to her room to write a letter to a friend back home, Mary Moore came rushing into the bedroom, carrying Gilbert in her arms.

"Lady Brie, Lord Glynden is closeted with Lord Wisbach

in the library. Boulton says he has been there nigh onto an hour," she said, setting the black kitten down onto the rug.

Brianna felt the color drain from her face as Gilbert rubbed against her shins.

What could Simon have to say to her father?"

At that moment Boulton appeared at the door that Mary had left open.

"My lady," he said, "Lord Wisbach asks that you join him in the library."

"With Lord Glynden?" Brianna asked, her voice squeaking as it was wont to do when she was nervous.

"No, Lord Glynden has left. The earl wishes to see you and the countess immediately and said to convey to you and your mother that it is a matter of some import, and he must leave the house shortly for an appointment at his club."

"I will be there in a minute," Brianna said.

Boulton nodded and vanished through the doorway, turning in the direction of her mother's bedchamber.

Brianna remained as if glued to the window seat where she had been sitting until Mary said, "Aren't you going, Lady Brie? You know how impatient Lord Wisbach gets when he is kept waiting.

"Do you think Lord Glynden . . . do you think? Mary . . . ?"

"Do I think what, my lady?" the maid asked. "Oh, you fear his lordship might have guessed that you are Yvette."

Brianna nodded.

Mary shrugged. "You know him better than I do. I only saw him that one time in your dressing room at the theater." But she was not immune to giving an opinion. "His lordship was set on seducing you. I wouldn't put it past him to be angry enough to put a stick in your spokes and cause you trouble."

"But would he be so vindictive?"

Brianna glanced furtively toward the open door. Her lips snapped shut, for Lady Wisbach had appeared in the doorway.

The countess did not seem to be aware of the guilty expression on her daughter's face. She greeted Mary and smiled at Gilbert, who was curled up on his cushion in the corner.

"I have never seen such an amiable little cat. He came into my room and was as friendly as if he had known me for ages. Brie, did Boulton tell you Papa wants to see us in the library?"

"Yes, Mama," Brianna said and walked to the door. "Keep Gilbert here, Mary."

"Yes, my lady," the maid said and followed them to shut the door, for the black kitten was already rising from his soft bed to trot after his owner.

Mother and daughter walked silently down the stairs, keeping close together in the passageway to the library, but absorbed in their own thoughts. Brianna's pulse accelerated when she saw her father pacing in front of his desk.

He stopped when his wife and daughter came into the room, one hand on the back of the chair beside him.

"Please close the door, Caroline," he said, looking rather somber.

Her mother took Brianna's hand and led her to a leather couch. "Let's sit here, dear," she said. "Your papa looks serious. This may take a while."

To Brianna's surprise, her father chuckled. "Not at all, my dear. I do not think either of you will be displeased by what I have to tell you."

Brianna felt the air come back into her lungs, and she began to relax.

Lord Wisbach cleared his throat. "Brianna seems to have made a conquest of the Viscount Glynden, to put it mildly. He has sought and received my permission to propose to her."

"No, no," Brianna uttered and started to her feet. Her mother pulled her back down onto the sofa.

"Brie, calm down. Guy, Brianna does not appear to share Lord Glynden's feelings."

"I cannot believe what I am hearing," Lord Wisbach said, his back straightening. "You are not going to encourage the child to balk at this outstanding opportunity. Caroline, Glynden's mother was your friend, even long before she married Breede."

"Yes, Guy, and I do not have a word to say against her or Lord Breede. Frannie was a marvelous woman, a lady in every sense of the word. Oliver is a fine and honorable gentleman, but I am speaking of Brianna's desires. She has a right to refuse Glynden, Guy."

"Refuse him? Glynden and Brianna are a perfect match, in age, in looks, in lineage, in upbringing. Brianna is only eighteen. I know better what is in her best interest than she does."

Resentment toward her father rose up in Brianna's breast. Naively, she had believed that he would never force her to marry against her wishes. Now she wasn't so sure.

"Papa, I can't marry him," Brianna said, but her demurral was ignored. The earl had no intention of sparring with his daughter. He wanted only to get his wife on his side.

"Listen to me, Caroline," he said. "The viscount is everything in a bridegroom that you have always said you wanted for Brianna. How many times over the years have I heard you say that it would be wonderful if she were wed in St. George's as we were. I am sure Glynden would agree; after all Oliver and Frannie were married there, too."

Brianna was afraid that her mother would be persuaded.

"Guy," Caroline said, "I know you think you are doing what any good father would do. By the *ton's* standards you probably are, but I want Brianna to know a love like ours. But I see no harm in Lord Glynden tendering his proposal."

"Mama!" Brianna protested.

"Shh, Brie," Caroline said. "Just listen. It would be unseemly to dismiss Lord Glynden out of hand. I believe if you list the advantages of marrying him, you might come to a different conclusion than you have now." She paused a moment, pursing her lips. "Has the viscount trifled with you or used indelicate language or in some other manner insulted you?"

"No, Mama," Brianna admitted unhappily.

Caroline laughed. "Does he have a wart on his nose or is he in need of a bath?"

"Of course not, he is well enough in both looks and hygiene."

"Perhaps he is too handsome. I know men of his countenance can be the very devil with the ladies."

"I have nothing to say against his lordship personally," Brianna said. "But I just cannot wed him."

Her father threw up his hands. "Brianna, I have heard nothing to cause me to change my mind. You do not have a compelling reason for spurning Lord Glynden." He took out his gold pocket watch and flipped the lid. "Caroline, I do not have time to stand here bickering with the willful chit. I am already late for my meeting with my man of business at White's. Glynden is calling this afternoon. I trust you will do your best to change your daughter's mind. But whatever her bent, she will face Lord Glynden and treat him with all the respect that is due his position." He turned at the door and looked directly at his wife. "I fear, though, Caroline, that the Whitten clan will take a rejection as a clear slap in the face."

Brianna sat still, staring down at her hands folded in her lap. Caroline put a hand over her daughter's clasped fingers. She had not missed the warning in her husband's parting words. Lord Breede would be insulted on his son's behalf. Their families' long friendship could be irreparably damaged if Glynden took a refusal badly.

Caroline's gaze held affection when it rested on her daughter. "You are hiding something, Brie. Something which troubles you. I noticed it earlier today when we talked in your room." Life with Brianna had never been orderly or predictable. "But as I said then, I love you, dear, and nothing you have done can ever change that."

"I know, Mama, but I am old enough to take responsibility for solving the problems I create," Brianna said, bravely.

"Then there is a problem. It is not simply that you cannot abide Lord Glynden?"

Brianna sighed. "No, Mama."

Caroline did not let her relief show. Brianna's response just now said more than the two words. There was regret in the timbre of her daughter's voice. Brianna would solve the sticking point that was keeping her from accepting Glynden's proposal, or he might change her mind when she confronted him with whatever was bothering her.

Caroline got up. "I promised your grandmother that I would see Cook about tonight's dinner menu. So, I must leave you now, Brie. But I promise to support you in whatever you decide. We can weather the Whittens' rebuke, if it comes to that. But it would be rag-mannered of you to refuse Lord Glynden without a legitimate reason for turning down his proposal. Remember, he honors you by choosing you to be his wife. A young gentleman of his stature could have his pick of just about any marriageable young lady of the *ton*."

"I will talk to him, Mama," Brianna said, not able to promise more. Once she admitted to Simon that she was Yvette, it was he who would rescind the proposal, although Brianna was fully prepared to take the blame and save his honor.

CHAPTER TEN

Brianna was rehearsing in her mind the confession she would make to Simon when Boulton came to her room to tell her that Lord Glynden waited for her in the drawing room. She felt a twist of fear in her stomach that joined the general misery she had been feeling since she learned that Simon wanted to marry her.

Her misguided adventure was coming back to haunt her. How could she have not seen how irreparably wrong her flouting convention by singing in the theater would be? She had gained nothing, except a certainty that she was not meant to be on the stage. She did not have the temperament to stand before an audience of men who shouted and whistled and called indelicate suggestions to her.

Dread hung heavy on her when she thought of her parents and grandparents facing society's censure. She loved them so much. Her heart hurt, thinking of the pain that would be inflicted upon them if her total want of conduct reached the collective ears of the *ton*. No, she could not accept Simon's proposal.

Yet, once she confessed to being Yvette, Simon would, no doubt, be glad of her refusal and feel fortunate to have escaped a disastrous union.

The irony was that she loved Simon and under different circumstances would have been flying into his arms. Wrapped up in her own woes, Brianna wanted nothing so much as to have a good cry.

She realized, suddenly, that she had been standing still, staring at the door since Boulton had vanished through it some minutes ago. Simon was waiting below. She was shaking, inside and out, but there was no sense in prolonging the agony. She would cry later.

Simon stood beside a table in the drawing room of Lord Hamden's house, turning a small porcelain figurine of a Chinese lady in a red kimono around and around in his large hand. The myriad of tiny gold butterflies that decorated her robe equaled the number which gyrated in Simon's stomach.

His friend Robby Fitch would have sworn to anyone who asked him that the Viscount Glynden was the most self-assured, calm, and even-tempered gentleman that he knew. At the moment, Simon was anything but. He was jittery, emotional, and insecure.

He put down the knickknack and walked over to the fireplace and stared into the glowing coals that barely took the chill from the room. He picked up a poker and stoked the fire back to life, adding coals from the brass bucket with a small brass shovel.

Last night he had lain in his bed and stared at the shadows playing on his ceiling, amazed that he had fallen in love with Brianna Mansfield. In one of those rare moments of absolute clarity in one's life, he knew that he would never be happy unless she agreed to be his wife. He loved her beyond reason, common sense, or possible consequences. But suppose she would not have him?

Simon put down the coal scooper and turned away from the hearth, but remained where he was, facing into the room. His motives until last night had been less than honorable. What sort of man planned to be a philandering husband even before he took his marriage vows? One with a less than shiny soul, he answered himself bitterly.

What could he possibly have been thinking to consider the perfect bride to be a dull, unimaginative ninny, who would be nothing but a doormat for him? What a tedious marriage that would have sentenced him to!

His self-flagellation ceased as Brianna came through the door. A smile of relief formed on Simon's lips when she smiled.

"Lady Brianna," he said and sketched a bow. She said his name, but his euphoria faded when he saw that her smile was woefully weak and did not reach her doleful eyes.

Simon remained by the fireplace and watched her. Brianna seemed unsure of what to do with herself before she took a seat in a deeply stuffed chair.

Catching him unawares, she said, "I cannot marry you, my lord."

Only momentarily put off, Simon asked, "Can you give me a reason, my lady?"

The room took on an air of unhappiness that appeared to affect them both, neither knowing what the other was thinking.

Brianna looked directly at him, her gaze steady, but her voice cracked a little. "I know that you remember Yvette la Roche, the songstress at Parker's Theater. What you don't know is that I am she."

Brianna waited a moment, but when Simon did not react by word or deed, she went on. "I duped my family and took a position on the stage. My parents and grandparents know nothing of this lapse in propriety, and I intend for them never to find out, for it would devastate them. I believe you to be an honorable man, Lord Glynden. I beg you to keep my secret, not to protect myself, but to spare my family."

Brianna acted calm, but she was trembling inside, not as sure of Simon as she had just professed.

"I am curious, Brianna," he said, his arms crossed over his chest, "what makes you think that I do not already know that you are Yvette?"

She met his unreadable blue eyes, hers reflecting a moment of doubt. "Do you? No, you couldn't know." She shook her head rather vehemently. "My father said that you wished to propose to me."

"So?"

Faintly irritated by his nonchalance, Brianna said, "Gad, Simon, I would think it was obvious. You are a viscount and destined to be an earl someday. You would not choose a ruined woman as your future countess. Suppose my hapless adventure became common knowledge after we married? Not only my family would suffer, but yours as well. They and we would never live down the jokes. Society can be cruel in their scorn. Invitations would cease and doors would be closed to you. Your former friends would snub you and every important gentleman's club would reject you."

Brianna saw a faint smile tug at Simon's lips. "At least I have gotten you to call me Simon," he said.

Brianna's voice held a poignant smile. "Oh, my lord, in my thoughts you have been Simon ever since I have known you."

He looked pleased. "And, sweet Brianna, have you been thinking about me a lot?"

Brianna gave him the thinnest of smiles. "Let us stick to the original subject, Simon," she said. "I gather that you did know I was Yvette, but how?"

"I saw your cat in the hall one day. A black kitten with golden eyes might be common enough not to arouse my suspicions, but not a friendly one with a deformed hind leg, a curious gait, and the distinctive name of Gilbert. Boulton told me the kitten belonged to you." He smiled. "I asked him if you sang. 'Like an angel,' he said."

"I had wondered how that came about," Brianna mused. "My grandfather's butler is not one to give out unsolicited information. But you still asked my father for permission to propose to me?" She was truly confused. "It is my turn to ask why, Simon?"

"I should think *that* would be obvious. I love you, Brianna."

Brianna's jaw dropped.

"Close your mouth, my dear." His voice was soft and kind.

"You are too intelligent not to see that there were warm feelings between us right from the beginning. I felt that you sang directly to me when you performed at Parker's, speaking to me through your music. You must have sensed the rapport between us."

"Yes," Brianna admitted, "I did, Simon."

Giving in to him would be easy, but true love sometimes required sacrifices for the greater good, no matter how hard.

"Simon, come and sit here, please," she said, pointing to a chair that had been placed near the one in which she sat to form a conversational arrangement in the formal room.

He crossed over to her, but did not sit down. Instead, he pulled her up into his arms and kissed her, letting his mouth play against hers for a long time before he lifted his head.

Brianna snaked one hand behind the back of Simon's head. Despite her doubts, she kissed him back. She gazed up into his blue eyes and said, "I love you, too, Simon."

"I trust that means you will accept my proposal."

She did not answer. He put her away from him and studied her face. Her rueful expression touched his heart.

"All right, you still have reservations. Let us put them to rest," he said, respecting her caution. He pointed to the chairs. She sat down in one and he in the other.

"Fear of discovery," Simon said, ticking off what he supposed was holding her back. "By whom? Hugh Parker. Not likely. He is not the blackmailing sort. Besides, I got the impression that he admires you. Moreover, he is not going to be invited to any of the social affairs where you will be. Agreed?"

"Yes," Brianna said. "Mr. Parker was an ally. He could have taken advantage of my naïveté and caused me all sorts of grief, but he did not."

Simon nodded. "Next, Sean Cavendish, who is another creature entirely. He would resort to blackmail, but again he is not going to be popping up in the drawing rooms of the *ton*. Sean has too many enemies already to make one of me. He knows I could make trouble for him by revealing some of his shady deals and have him transported. Anyway, Sean would never connect you with the upper classes. He would be searching for Yvette among the mistresses of wealthy gentlemen to determine her protector."

Something uncomfortable crawled up Simon's spine. He had branded himself a seducer that night in Yvette's dressing room. Brianna was not stupid. A peer of the realm did not invite an unsuitable woman to have dinner with him unless his intentions were less than honorable, regardless of his lamentations at the time to the contrary. He could lie to her, but he could not lie to himself. His goal had been to make Yvette la Roche his mistress.

There was no comfort in knowing that he was no different in this respect from other young men of his class.

Even now Brianna might be thinking parallel thoughts. If not, sooner or later, she would wonder if he had a light-o'-love hidden away somewhere.

Simon sensed that his whole happiness hinged on how he handled this delicate matter. Yet he wanted her to know that he was ready to change. He reached out and touched Brianna's black curls.

"Brianna, I suppose it occurred to you that I was bent on making Yvette my mistress."

She inclined her head slightly.

Simon went on. "I could argue that taking a mistress is a way of our world, but I do not believe it. When it comes to matrimony, I think it depends on the man and his commitment to his marriage. In our imperfect world vows are not always kept. In truth, Brianna, the real you is more like Yvette, but, then, there has never been an Yvette, only Brianna playacting. We keep talking as if you and she were two different people. I love you, Brianna, with all my heart, and I promise you I will remain true to you all my life if you will have me. I have never meant anything more."

However, it was not Simon's words that convinced Brianna. She looked into his blue eyes and saw so much love there that she was rendered breathless.

Weakening, she said, "Still, there is always a chance that someone will guess that I posed as Yvette and start a rumor."

"Which we shall laugh at and deny with good humor. Rumors only take on a life of their own when the recipients object too strongly and give in to intimidation."

Brianna nudged aside all her doubts. "I will marry you, Simon," she said and plopped herself into his lap and kissed him deeply.

Simon thoroughly enjoyed her boldness and, prudently, did not bring up his original scheme to take both a biddable bride *and* a spirited mistress. After all, he wasn't a total fribble. Brianna did not have to know all of his past faults.

The engagement of Viscount Glynden and the Lady Brianna Mansfield was announced by her parents at a grand ball held at her grandparents' London home in early May.

The Earl of Wisbach and his countess were delighted that their daughter had come to her senses, particularly since it was obvious that the union was a love match.

Many of the gentlemen who had seen Yvette la Roche perform at Parker's Theater were in attendance that night. But not a single one of them suspected that the dark-haired beauty to whom they offered their felicitations was the blond songstress.

The marriage took place in June, one week before the viscount's twenty-seventh birthday, at St. George's Church in London. The nave was filled to capacity. The bride wore an exquisite ivory satin gown with panels of embroidered overlays while the groom was splendidly attired in dark blue.

After their vows, the happy couple left the church, their fingers entwined. The old-fashioned coach that carried them to the reception at Lord Hamden's was gilded and sparkled in the warm sunshine. Flowers decorated the reins and harnesses of the four white stallions that pulled the fairy-tale vehicle.

Inside the coach, Brianna and Simon gazed into each other's eyes. Their joyous smiles seemed to be permanently etched onto their radiant faces.

Simon's agent had found them a honeymoon cottage with modern amenities close to Brighton, but away from the hubbub of those on holiday, who were drawn to the resort by the Prince Regent's recently built Royal Pavilion. The house was staffed with discreet servants and close enough to Brighton for Simon and Brianna to take in the sights during their monthlong honeymoon.

Mary was to remain at Lord Hamden's town house with Gilbert until the happy couple returned to London and set up residence in a mansion in Mayfair.

"I would like you to sing for me when we are alone this evening, my dear," Simon said. "You have not done so since you were on stage at Parker's. I respected your fear that someone would come calling and inadvertently hear you."

"I did have a wealth of visitors wanting to offer their good wishes on our engagement," Brianna said, "but now that we shall be alone in our private cottage and no one would be so crass as to disturb us on our wedding trip, I shall sing to you all night if it be your pleasure, my lord." Her beautiful violet eyes sparkled. Her speaking voice was as musical as her singing voice.

Simon's chuckle was irreverent. "Not all night, my love. I have other pleasurable delights in mind such as making music of a very different sort."

Brianna pretended shyness and lowered her lashes. "My lord, you put me to the blush."

But Simon saw that Brianna's coyness was all playful. There was not a bit of nervousness about their wedding night, only bubbling anticipation. How could he have been so wrong as to what he had thought he wanted in a perfect bride?

He turned to her. "I love you so much, Brie," he said with feeling and kissed his beloved on the lips in full view of a crowd that had gathered on a street corner, drawn by the peal of the wedding bells from St. George's Church.

"And I you, Simon," Brianna said as the regal carriage passed by the cheering bystanders, who shouted their wishes for a long and happy life to the beautiful bride and the handsome groom.

UP TO SCRATCH

MELYNDA BETH
SKINNER

For David Andrews and for Hilary Sares,
who both grok cats,

and for Malachi Townsend Skinner,

much love
and many thanks.

CHAPTER ONE

Yarrowdale, England
June, 1819

The moment Malachi Townsend stepped from the carriage, he felt it. As his feet made contact with the ground in front of Yarrowdale Hall, he perceived a vibration or a sound, a faint stirring of something. He wasn't sure what it was, but he'd learned to trust his instincts. The cool night air brought the clean scent of the English countryside. Malachi inhaled deeply and took a few steps to stretch his legs.

"Do not stray too far, old boy," Max said, stepping down behind him. Max peered quizzically at the long, low building before them and gave a long, low whistle to match. "Our inheritance is a beauty, like the solicitor said. Should fetch a good price. What else can we do but sell it? Our worries are over, my friend."

Our inheritance. *Our* worries.

Malachi almost smiled. It had been that way between them since the day Malachi had rescued Max years before. They shared everything. Food, lodging, adventures . . . all but their females, of course. Max was a good man and a true friend.

Just now, he was also an uneasy friend.

Malachi watched as Max threw a wry glance up at the darkened windows. "Hell and blast," the tall man muttered, "I was not expecting a welcome home ball, but a footman with a light surely would not have been asking too much." He rubbed his whiskered chin. "This new moon leaves the countryside dark as the inside of a cow. We might have been better off back at The King's Breath, you and I."

Malachi gave him a look that clearly said Max was out of his mind.

"I know, I know." Max shook his head. "I liked the tavern master's daughter even less than you did. Grabby little thing. What else could we do but escape her? Still," he said on a sigh and nodded toward the house, "if *they* throw us out on our arses this night, we might end up wishing we had stopped. To be sure, it would not be the first night we have spent in a carriage, but with this fog gathering, the night promises to be devilishly damp and uncomfortable." He shook his head, and then, in spite of his gloomy words, he laughed and clapped Malachi upon the shoulders. "Go on, you check the grounds, while the new master of Yarrowdale Hall boldly takes possession of his domicile—assuming he is not shot first, of course."

He laughed again, but Malachi knew better than to be reassured. Life at Max's side was always exciting and quite often bordered on the dangerous—not that they didn't both love every madcap, carefree moment of it.

As Max strolled toward the enormous stone house, whistling softly to himself, Malachi flowed into the night and disappeared, moving silently, blending into the darkness as neatly as a shadow.

The long, straight lane they'd just driven down neatly bisected a wide, sloping lawn, almost completely devoid of vegetation, apart from a sprinkling of majestic old chestnut trees. Nothing to see there. Cautiously, Malachi made his way to the back of the house. No telling what he might encounter. When they were alone, Max usually shared his thoughts with Malachi, but as they'd driven north from London on this trip, Max had been uncharacteristically silent about their destination. Sensing his discomfort, Malachi hadn't pestered him. Instead, he'd claimed a corner of the carriage and slept most of the way, exhausted from their hasty trip back to England

and dreaming of a sleek and saucy little thing he'd encountered back in Morocco.

Malachi suppressed a sigh and peered around the back corner of the house, where a faint breeze carried the sweet smell of . . . *what?* He lifted his chin and inhaled. Orange blossoms? Impossible. This was England. Northern England. Cold England. No orange trees here.

The entire length of the back of the structure was planted with a wide parterre, which, even by starlight, Malachi could see was overgrown. Masses of perennial flowers tumbled over the low box hedges that should have penned them neatly in. The scent of the flowers and herbs tangled with that of common weeds. Malachi walked on, skirting the parterre, and came to a high hedge, taller even than Max. A cobbled path led through a gap in the hedge, and Malachi approached it, his heart beating hard, for he was suddenly aware that whatever had him on edge lay just beyond that opening.

Like a wraith, he slipped quickly through, instantly blending into the deeper shadow beyond, his eyes wild and searching, but he saw nothing, only another tall hedge a few yards away.

Concealing himself in the shadows long enough for his heart to slow, he walked to the new hedge wall and down its length. There had been little night sounds in the parterre, the squeaking of mice and the fluttering of birds' wings, the slithering of crawly things and the earthy rooting of moles and hedgehogs, but this hedge was silent, as though something had scared away all living things. And, as if that were not strange enough, the scent of orange blossoms was growing stronger.

The hedge formed a long rectangle, and Malachi had well nigh paced its entire perimeter when he finally found the portal that led to the enclosed space. An iron gate with spikes on the top blocked the path, but it was locked, so Malachi opted for squeezing beneath it, covering his coat with dirt in the process.

If he had a valet, the man would have had an apoplexy. Fortunately, though, neither he nor Max believed in such non-sense. They took care of themselves. Giving his coat a cur-sory shake, he stood—and froze. Before him lay a large glasshouse, softly illumined in one corner with lamplight, and someone was inside!

Moving carefully toward the lighted end, Malachi maneu-vered for a better look and was unsurprised when he saw that the only plants in the glasshouse were orange trees heavy with blossom. What did surprise him was that the glasshouse appeared to be occupied. Lived in! By a human! With furni-ture!

A small figure lay on a tidy bed a few feet from the glass wall. A book had fallen from her slack grasp, and her spec-tacles lay askew on her face. The lamp glowed atop a table at her bedside, illuminating her delicate features. Malachi watched for a few moments to be certain she was sound asleep before stepping up to within a few inches of the glass to survey the curious scene. A lady—and a beautiful one, if Malachi knew anything about such creatures—living in a glasshouse! It seemed like something out of a fairy story he'd heard a governess tell what seemed like a hundred lifetimes ago, at once whimsical and strange. Enchanting. Different from any place he'd ever been—and he'd thought he'd been everywhere with Max.

He had a sudden desire to find a way inside and curl up next to the beauty on the bed. She'd be warm. And she'd smell good. Not like the tavern keeper's daughter, who had smelled of lye and dog. *The King's Breath,* indeed! Malachi gave a snort. The place should have been named *The Dog's Breath*.

But as he peered inside the glasshouse, the memory of the tavern keeper's daughter's sweaty hands swirled and dissi-pated into the gathering mist. There were no dogs here. Just a lovely maiden with a lovely bed. Were those cotton sheets? It had been a long time since Malachi had slept on smooth cot-ton. He would lie across her bed in the luxuriant warmth of the glasshouse, and she would stroke him with lovely dry hands until he purred. . . .

Malachi closed his eyes and leaned forward, almost in a dream. But the pleasant fantasy didn't last long. His whiskered face rasped against the glass, and a sudden *something* brought him instantly alert. A sound, a vibration. Again, he wasn't sure what it was, but his eyes snapped open—and he found himself peering into the most beautiful pair of eyes he'd ever seen.

They were blue. He'd never seen their like. These eyes were the blue of the lake in Lucerne where he and Max had passed a pleasant summer—until they'd had to make a rather hasty exit. They were the deep, bright blue of a cloudless sky on a winter morning. Set against a canvas of long, fluffy white fur as pure as the snow on a mountaintop, they were mesmerizing—particularly since they stared back at him with the sort of expression females usually reserved for their paramours. Malachi had seen it before, many times, but this time it was different.

A spark of knowledge passed in that single, moving glance, the mutual recognition of a simple fact: They were in love. Mated for life, till nine deaths did them part. Well, fewer than that for Malachi, who was fairly certain he'd used up five or six of his nine lives.

CHAPTER TWO

Lady Moonbeam was shocked. This couldn't be happening. Why, just look at him! Missing a whisker. Ears notched from fighting. A scar running across his face. He wasn't white or even cream but a ghastly shade of orange the humans referred to as "marmalade." And—dear heavens!—did he have *seven toes*? Her mother would have been appalled. But, oh spit, he was handsome!

She turned her head, hoping he could not see her nose blushing even pinker than it must already be before realizing she must not appear timid. Hadn't Mother cautioned her that a lady must assert herself to remain in control of a virile tom? They were wild, impetuous, dangerous, she'd warned.

How delicious!

Moon quivered with excitement and pulled herself up to her full height before turning her most regal gaze back toward him—but he was gone! She panicked for a moment before a movement in the old oak caught her eye. He'd scaled it and was making his way swiftly along the very path Moon used in emergencies. She watched his progress quietly, marveling at his surefootedness. She was quite surefooted herself, and she'd traversed that way several dozen times, but she'd always been hesitant, while he looked as though he'd been born in that tree. He leapt effortlessly from the farthest-reaching branch to the roof of the glasshouse and, slipping soundlessly through the vent, instantly chose the correct rafter that sloped down to the largest of the orange trees and so down to the floor of the glasshouse.

Her mistress, short for a human, kept the tree branches trimmed almost high enough for her to walk beneath, exposing their green, velvety trunks, so the tom didn't have far to jump down, but after watching him, Moon was sure he'd have made it if it had been as high as the turret on Yarrowdale Hall.

She marveled at his skill, her heart pounding, as he approached. He stopped a tail's length away and allowed her to close the distance between them—a surprisingly polite gesture for a tom of his ilk. He was big. Big and powerful, and for a moment, she felt an urge to flee, yet something in his eyes compelled her to stretch toward him. Something more than a request and less than a command. A promise. Yes, that was it, she thought, almost in a dream, as they moved closer . . . closer . . . and closer still, until their noses touched, and Moon knew everything would be right. She'd found her mate at last. And not just any mate. A life mate.

Life mates were treasures so rare that most cats believed they were only a young queen's fantasy. Not Moon's mother, though. Lady Moonlight had believed, and late at night she'd whispered of it to Moonbeam.

"It does happen, Moon-kit," she'd say. "You must never give up hope."

And Moon had believed—at first. She wasn't a kitten anymore, though. She was long past her first Season, and she'd almost forgotten her mother's improbable tales. Moon was sensible—which was why she thought no more of it now. Instead, she nonchalantly licked her shoulder, demurely blinked at the large orange male before her, and simply accepted the startling fact of love at first sight without another twitch of her long, white tail.

"No other tom has ever discovered the way into the glasshouse," she purred.

"No other tom has ever loved you as I do," he replied.

CHAPTER THREE

Max emerged from Yarrowdale Hall frowning. Who the devil was Emmaline Rose? Whoever she was, she was the one calling the shots—and for some reason, the servants seemed to think Max could find her skulking about the gardens in the middle of the night.

Following the footman out the back door, Max could feel angry glares boring through the gathering fog and into his back. The footman on duty had awakened the butler and the housekeeper—*Max's* blasted butler and housekeeper!—and the three of them had held shoulder to shoulder, refusing to recognize his authority until "the mistress" approved, even though Max had the papers the solicitor had given him, which were supposed to prove his identity and his claim to Yarrowdale Hall.

Botheration! He and Malachi had been on the deuced jouncing, jostling road all the deuced day, and though the cat had slept—Malachi had been known to sleep through a hurricane at sea!—Max had not. He was sore and weary and not a little irritated at being shown to the back door rather than to a comfortable bed. Not that he expected bowing and scraping from his new staff. He was a plain mister and not some blasted duke, after all. But, dash it, his servants could have had a hearth warmed, couldn't they? It wasn't as though he'd been entirely unexpected. Certainly, they hadn't known his arrival was imminent, but they'd known someone would come to claim the estate sooner or later. Didn't they even keep a chamber ready for stranded travelers? He'd wager his boots they did, but they had no intention of letting him know about it.

He had two choices. He could ring a peal over their shoulders immediately, or he could go see this mistress of theirs and attempt to settle the matter amicably.

Well over six feet tall, dark, and broad of shoulder, and a commanding two-and-thirty, Max could instantly don a persona guaranteed to render the stiffest butler pliable—or to charm the primmest of young ladies. He knew he could have blustered and commanded his way through this mull, but he had not. Max didn't need a staff who would follow his orders unblinkingly. What he needed was information and goodwill for the short time he'd own the estate. It would be a tactical error to demand allegiance. He'd catch more flies with honey than with vinegar. Not to mention that he might be thrown out on his arse until he could return with a magistrate.

As he followed though the fog, he wondered just who this Emmaline Rose was and why the devil they referred to her as "the mistress?" Mistress of what? For it surely wasn't Yarrowdale. Max was the sole heir to the estate left to him by his great uncle, though he certainly did not deserve it. A pang of guilt stabbed him, but he shoved the feeling aside. What else could he do but accept the gift?

"What is Miss Rose like?" he probed. "Is she very old?"

The footman threw a steely glance over his shoulder. "I can give you no more information, sir. That will be up to Miss Rose."

The only thing that inspired that sort of loyalty was pure admiration. Or pure fear. Miss Rose must either be a saint or a harridan. In Max's experience, it was far safer to wager on the latter, and since she had the servants under her paw, Max prepared for the worst. Emmaline Rose. Even her name sounded starched-up. Probably some neighborhood spinster too cross and ugly to have snabbled herself a husband. Max had met odious harpies like her before. Termagants, crones . . . dragons. Whether they lived in grass huts on tropical beaches, in a

Bedouin's tent, or in a pasha's golden palace, inevitably they bent their attention to the affairs of those around them, gathering gossip until they knew everyone's secrets and could hold them all in thrall. The Yarrowdale villagers probably didn't breathe without the old dragon's prior approval.

Still, that didn't explain why she had the run of Yarrowdale Hall's garden at night. Softly, he whistled a bawdy tune he'd learnt from a sailor aboard his first ship as a boy. He'd find out soon enough.

Rounding a corner of the house's overgrown parterre, the footman stopped at an opening in a tall hedge and motioned toward the darkness beyond. "The glasshouse is through there. You'll find her there."

"Will you not announce me?"

The man shook his head. "Oh, no, sir. We don't any of us go in there, hardly ever."

"Why not?"

The footman gave him a look that suggested he was daft, stupid, or both. "Well, because she's in there."

"What, does she stay in there all the time?"

"Most of the time. Except when she doesn't." He pursed his lips. "That is, she comes up to the house for meals, most times—"

"Most times? You mean she dines at Yarrowdale Hall all of the time?"

The footman looked startled. "Why, yes sir. Though sometimes she takes her meals in the glasshouse, of course."

"Of course. Yes. Yes, I understand," Max said, not understanding at all. But he'd soon unravel the mystery, and the more he heard, the less he was inclined to use any sort of delicacy. The estate wouldn't be easy to sell if it came with a dragon haunting his kitchens and raiding his larders every blasted day. The thought occurred to him that she might be impoverished. He wondered if a small annuity would keep her away. Probably not. Dragons were rarely satisfied with mere gold. "Wonder if the village has sacrificed anyone lately," Max muttered.

"Sir?"

Max gave a wry smile and waved his hand. "Nothing. Thank you."

The footman shrugged. "We'll be waiting up at the house, sir." His Adam's apple bobbed, and he mopped at his brow, though the night was cool. "She'll want to see you alone. But . . ." he faltered and then took a deep breath. "But sound carries all the way to the house from down here. Even in this fog."

For whom was the man concerned, Max or the dragon? Max nearly laughed. Nearly. "See here, I appreciate the sentiment, old man, but I assure you there is no need to fret, for she, I gather, can handle herself as well as any gentleman—and so can I."

The footman gave a grim nod, clearly understanding Max's meaning, and Max went through the opening. "The brave knight hies hence to banish the dragon," he whispered. What else could he do? After traveling all the way from Morocco, he wasn't going to allow some meddling female to keep him from a warm, quiet, and blessedly still bed. "I am ready for anything."

But he wasn't ready at all. No, not at all.

CHAPTER FOUR

Emma awakened instantly. *Someone in the glasshouse!*

"Who?" she called, propelling herself to her feet and almost falling over. *Someone in the glasshouse!* "Who? What? What's the matter?" she called. As *Beowulf* fell from her fingers, images of chaos flashed through her mind: fire licking at the walls of Yarrowdale Hall. Enormous Viking marauders sailing up the river, demanding danegeld, pillaging, and—

She forced her heavy feet to still and put one hand to her forehead. "Viking marauders!" she scoffed. "Good Lord, Emma. Get hold of yourself." She'd been down deep. Grasping a chest of drawers for support with one hand and dabbing at the corner of her damp mouth with the back of the other, Emma willed herself to calm down. No one had invaded the glasshouse. It was only a dream. She was all—

"Hullo!

She whirled around and did stumble, then, but the man standing there reached out with one strong, startlingly masculine hand and saved her from an undignified sprawl across her own bed.

She uttered a syllable that sounded a bit like a cat's hiss, worked her cotton-filled mouth once, twice, and opened her lips to try again. *Introduction, introduction, how-do-you-do,* her mind whirred and clicked, but what came out was a blunt, "Who the devil are you?"

Evidently, the idiot didn't understand she was being intolerably rude, for he revealed a row of white, even teeth in a dazzlingly handsome smile, bowed, and said, "Good evening, Miss Rose. Mr. Maximillian Yar, at your service." He held out a small sheaf of folded papers. "My credentials, if you care to examine them. From my uncle's solicitor."

Emma's mind cleared as if by magic. "Yar?"

"Indeed."

"Not Smith or Jones or Han-*deuced*-over?"

"Afraid not."

She groaned. "The new master of Yarrowdale Hall come to claim the estate."

"Yes. I was expected?"

"Why, yes, but . . . but not so blasted soon!" Emma turned away, rubbing the bridge of her bowed forehead. "Good heavens, what a bumblebroth!"

"Is there some problem?"

"Well . . . yes! Yes, there is." She crossed her arms. "There is to be a wedding, you see."

"Yours?"

"You needn't look so incredulous. And no. Not mine." She sighed. "It is my friend Sophia, you see. She is to be married in a fortnight, right here in this glasshouse. Half the *ton* is set to attend. We were not expecting you to take up residence so soon, you see, and I did not see any harm in offering her mama the use of the—"

"There is to be a wedding? Here? In the glasshouse?"

"That is what I said."

"And half of the *ton* is set to attend?"

"Is there an echo in here?" Emma looked about them, her eyes deliberately wide.

He ignored her sarcasm. "Two questions."

"Go on."

"One: Which half of the *ton* would you say is coming here, the upper half or the lower half?"

Looking him deliberately up and down and obviously finding him lacking, she crossed her arms. "Oh, I believe *you* would judge it to be the upper half, I daresay."

"Good shot!" He grinned and gave her a salute.

"You deserve it, startling me as you did."

He nodded but didn't fall over himself to apologize at her rebuke. "I presume the guest list includes a baronet or two?"

"Three, actually, and two princes. Plus your assorted lesser peers—those insignificant dukes, marquesses, earls, and viscounts, you know."

"Oh-ho! Another good shot!"

"Thank you." Emma smiled. The people who knew her were always carefully subservient, while the people who did not were deliberately superior. This man was neither, and she found that refreshing.

"Right," he said. "Good. Perfect." He paced the dark gray flagstone floor, speaking as if to himself. "It is a perfect situation. Couldn't have planned it better myself. They will come, see the place, and we shall be free in a fortnight."

"What do you mean?" Emma demanded.

He ignored her. "I have a second question, but you are fatigued, and there must still be much to do before the wedding. You will wish to retire for the evening."

"I am awake and alert," she protested, stifling a yawn. "And the wedding preparations are nearly completed."

"What about the parterre?"

"What about it?"

"It is a complete mull!"

"Oh, that. Everyone in London knows the place has been derelict while your uncle's solicitors have been trying to track you down these many months. Do you know it is rumored that you were living as a harem master?"

She laughed—a little too gaily, evidently, as Mr. Yar scowled and said, "I fail to see why that is so unbelievable," which only made her laugh that much harder, particularly after a dimple in his cheek belied his stern expression, and his twinkling eyes gave way to an eruptive chuckle of his own.

With an effort, Emma straightened her expression. "In truth, Mr. Yar, the guests will understand the gardens being a bit overgrown, and they will not be here long enough to linger. They will arrive early for the ceremony and wedding breakfast and retire to their various lodgings by noon. The only rooms they will see inside the house are the public ones, and—"

"Why were they not invited to come early and stay at Yarrowdale Hall?"

"Over two hundred of them? We could not possibly hold them all. And how would I have fed them? I have the command of the servants but not of the purse strings. Your uncle's solicitor has had complete control of his assets. We could not spend one farthing of your money, so we could hardly hold a house party. But you need not fret. I daresay the guests' eyes shall be trained upon the bride and groom, rather than upon the sad condition of the grounds."

"No, no, no! I want their eyes trained upon the grounds!"

"What? Why on earth—"

"What the devil?" Suddenly Mr. Yar straightened, stilled, and looked about him for the first time. Emma saw his gaze light upon her rumpled bed, the chest of drawers, the clothespress, the lamp, the ewer, the little stove in the corner farthest away from her twin row of orange trees, where she heated water for morning tea or for a bath. Finally, his eyes found Emma's. "You live here!"

"Well, of course I do. I own this glasshouse. Did you not know?"

"You own it!"

"Why, yes. It was bequeathed to me by its former owner. I own it and a measure of ground that extends outward a hundred—"

"But the glasshouse is snugged up tight to the house! If you own the ground around it . . ." He groaned. "It cannot be! Uncle's solicitor said nothing of this. It—it is—it is a disaster!"

"Such high praise!" She smiled.

His eyes widened and focused upon her once more. "Oh! I am terribly sorry. Forgive me. I did not mean—"

"No, no." She waved her hand dismissively. "Not at all. Seeing as how you did not know of my existence, I will forgive your barging into a lady's home in the middle of the night, waking her from a sound sleep, scaring her half to death, and referring to her as a 'disaster.'"

"I am sorry for all of that, too," he said. "Your servants— or are they my servants?" He shook his head and grinned. "*The* servants would tell me nothing about you, and I thought you were some sort of neighborhood tyrant with the bizarre habit of skulking about the gardens at night. I am delighted to find that you are neither of those things and . . . um . . . who—whose servants are they . . . exactly?"

She chuckled. "Oh, my . . . you look so adorably confused and rumpled, I cannot possibly scold you further."

Max blinked. Adorable? Had the chit just used the word "adorable?" She was standing there regarding him with unconcealed amusement—as though she were watching a clumsy kitten or a callow lad trying to steal his first kiss. He needn't think she was referring to his masculinity, that was certain.

"I say, Miss Rose, are you always so outspoken?"

She nodded. "Mmm. Afraid so. Incorrigible. Quite impolite and not at all inclined to change."

He gave her an assessing stare, and she returned it measure for measure, surprising him even after her declaration of incorrigibility. She certainly didn't look the part. Dressed in a diaphanous pink concoction that looked more like a frothy syllabub than a night rail, she was small and blond and delicate. She looked quite a bit younger than his two-and-thirty years—call her twenty-five—and she'd probably never ventured more than six miles in any direction away from Yarrowdale Village. She was definitely not the sort to stand up to someone like him.

And yet there she was with her chin jutting out and her arms akimbo. He gave a satisfied nod. "Good, then. We are alike in that respect, and I daresay we shall bump along well together."

She gave a brief nod, more salute than curtsy. "Mr. Yar. Perhaps we should gather our wits and begin again—in a more civilized fashion this time."

"Indeed." He bowed for a second time. "Maximillian Yar, at your service."

She did curtsy then, the movement more graceful than any Max had ever seen. She made a simple curtsy seem more like a dance than a mere social pleasantry.

"I am Emmaline Rose, Mr. Yar. Would you care for tea?"

He nodded, and Miss Rose motioned to her small sofa, put on the copper kettle to heat, and began to assemble a tea tray. "So, Mr. Yar, I ask again. What precisely did you mean by 'We shall be free in a fortnight?'"

Looking over her shoulder, Emma watched indecision march across Mr. Yar's face as he obviously assessed her character and made a decision. "I plan to sell the place as quickly as possible," he said.

She whirled around. Nothing he could have said would have surprised her more. "You are not serious!"

"I am a traveler, Miss Rose. It is what I do, how I live."

"How you live?" she said with some surprise. "Can you mean that you have no permanent home?"

"None."

"What about your family?"

"I have none."

"Oh," she said, her voice tinged with what Max was sure was genuine sympathy. "I am sorry to hear it."

He waved his hand. "You needn't feel sorry. I lost them so long ago I do not remember their faces. One cannot miss what one has never had."

She nodded and poured out the tea. Max was grateful that she didn't pursue the matter. "You have no house, then?" she asked. "No apartments in Town?"

"None."

"A rolling stone."

"Indeed." He sipped his tea thoughtfully. "Once, years ago, in Spain, a Gypsy lass looked at the lines on my palm and proclaimed the Summer Solstice was a special and lucky day for me. She also said it was my destiny to roam, like her people."

"And you think she was right?"

One black eyebrow climbed high on his handsome face. "I must admit, her advice did give me pause. You see, I was born on the Solstice, and at the time she looked at my palm, I'd been traveling for three years already." He shrugged. "I took it as truth. What else could I think? I have been traveling ever since. Home is wherever I am. Greece, the Indies, South America, the Far East . . . what need have I of a cottage tucked away in some dreary corner of England? I would never see it. I certainly have no use for a grand estate such as Yarrowdale. The profit from its sale will allow us to travel in comfort for the rest of our lives."

"Us?"

He laughed then, an easy sound that told Emma he laughed often. "I refer to Malachi. My traveling companion. I rescued him on a wharf in Venice. Right after I had been thrown in," he added with a chuckle.

"And *you* rescued *him*?" she asked.

"He was starving," Mr. Yar said, as though that settled the matter. "We go everywhere together."

"Where is he now?"

He grinned and pointed. "Right over there. And it looks like he found a lovely, warm spot to sleep tonight."

Emma turned and gasped, for there, deep in shadow, lay two cats, one a long-white-haired beauty belonging to Emma, and the other a huge orange beast. "Heavens," she cried, "just how many thousands of miles have you two covered? Look at him!"

"Disreputable-looking, I know," Mr. Yar said with pride in his voice. "He is an adventurous sort."

"Like his master, I'll wager."

"Like his master," Mr. Yar conceded, bowing his head. "We have had many . . . adventures." He looked up at her then through a veil of thick, black eyelashes, one eyebrow crooked, and Emma's eyes widened. She was suddenly aware what sort of things a young man would include in any definition of "adventure." She looked away.

Max watched as Emmaline Rose blushed well nigh as pink as her gown, and he nearly laughed before good sense got the upper hand. It wouldn't do to embarrass the chit. He needed her goodwill as much as he needed his servants'. Hell and blast, he needed hers even more.

The estate was going to be impossible to sell with a dragon's den stuck right in the middle of it—even if she were a lovely, delicate little dragon. He'd have to vanquish her before he tried to sell. But how?

Max sipped his tea, assessing her over the rim of his cup. This particular dragon spit fire. She was forthright and outspoken. "Fight fire with fire," he muttered.

"Pardon?"

Max took a deep breath. "I want to sell Yarrowdale," he said, "but I cannot do it with you here."

Emma's heart skipped a beat. She blinked, once, twice, and then looked away, her hands shaking. Had he just said he wanted her to sell?

Mr. Yar cleared his throat. "This must all be very unsettling for you."

She turned. "On the contrary, Mr. Yar. This is a grand opportunity. I will take thirty thousand pounds for my glasshouse and the land upon which it sits."

"You will?" Mr. Yar sputtered, her easy capitulation obviously taking him by surprise. "Thirty thousand pounds?"

"I do not think it is too much to ask, Mr. Yar. My land extends to within a hundred feet of the house. I would like a partial payment in cash—say seven hundred pounds—and the balance can be transferred to—"

"I do not have thirty thousand pounds!" Max's temples throbbed.

She stilled. "You don't?"

"No."

"What do you travel on?"

"My wits, mostly. See here," Max said, "I don't suppose

you want to transfer ownership of the glasshouse to me out-right and trust me to pay you after the sale is complete."

"That would not be my first choice, no."

Max grinned. "Smart girl." He stood. "Well then, the only thing to do is to effect the sale in cooperation with each other, and then I can be off once more, and you can leave this drafty old conservatory for the comfort of some cozy little cottage tucked away somewhere here in merry old—"

He stopped short.

She was shaking her head.

"What?" Max asked. "You want to dicker over the price? I warn you, I will go no higher than thirty-three."

"No, no," she said. "I stand by my original offer. It is just that I will not be settling down in some cozy little cottage."

"Oh? Where will you live, then, if I may ask?"

"Greece, the Indies, the Far East."

It was Max's turn to be shocked. "You intend to travel?"

"I do. I had thought I would have to wait until my cat passed away, but you travel with yours successfully. Perhaps you will give me some pointers."

She wanted to travel! Alone! By herself. A woman.

Ha!

Max opened his mouth to protest, but long experience at thinking fast kept him from uttering a syllable. She wanted to sell, and that was that. He didn't want to say anything to dis-suade the chit, even if he did think she was completely mad.

"Very well," he said. "Good for you. Greece is particularly lovely in summer. You will enjoy it."

She dimpled and quivered, her eyes shining with uncon-cealed excitement. "I have always wanted to travel, but I thought—" She stilled. "Oh! You are right! The grounds are a terrible mull."

"What does that have to do with—"

"And the bedchambers will need to be aired, the house pro-visioned, invitations issued. We have much to do!"

"We do?"

"Well, yes! The cream of the *ton* is due to arrive here in

less than a fortnight. It is a perfect opportunity to find a buyer for Yarrowdale Hall—as you of course realized right away. Now you are here, a house party is possible. La, it is a necessity! We would be mad not to invite the guests to stay at least a night or two. Do you think a week is too long? Dear me . . ." Hastily, she yanked open a drawer in her dressing table and scribbled a note. "Here, give this to any of the servants, and you will be shown the proper respect." She glanced at a clock sitting on a high shelf over the foot of her bed. "Good heavens! It is past one in the morning! Best snabble some rest while you are able. Good night!"

Max raked his fingers through his hair. "There are a dozen questions I wish to ask, but devil a bit if I am not too tired to ask them."

Emma watched in amusement as Mr. Yar yawned. "Well then," she said, "I shall expect an interrogation at breakfast—which I eat promptly at seven."

"Seven! Ugh! An uncouth hour." He bowed. "Miss Rose. Until tomorrow." He walked to the ornate, leaded glass door of the enormous conservatory. "Come, Malachi." He gave a small whistle and patted his thigh, but his cat sat blinking at him. "Malachi! Come!" he tried again, but the enormous tom only nuzzled Lady Moonbeam before flopping on his side and turning his head upside down. "Ah. So that's how it is, is it?" Mr. Yar said. He grinned at Emma lopsidedly, looking for all the world like his tom. "Would you mind if he stayed?"

"Certainly," she answered. "Lady Moonbeam and I should be delighted."

"Lady Moonbeam. A perfect name for her," Mr. Yar said, his green eyes giving Emma's cat an appreciative survey. "An exotic creature. Not unlike some of the cats we encountered in China. Wherever did you find her?"

"She was bequeathed to me, along with the glasshouse." Emma gestured around her. "My benefactor brought them back from China, as you said. There were seven of them, at first. I was left the entire clowder, but I lost most of them to a fever."

"Will there be no others?"

"Moon is the last of her kind. And she is eleven. Much too old to . . . ah."

"I see. Well, good night, then."

"Good night." Emma watched him go, thankful for his polite delicacy and wondering how he'd been orphaned and how he'd acquired such refined manners, for Maximillian Yar looked and behaved like a gentleman. He was a tall man, broad of shoulder, lean, and muscular. Were it not for the condition of his clothing, which had obviously seen better days, he might have been some handsome duke or marquess. His bearing was almost regal, if a little rough around the edges, as though he'd been in a fight or two.

And he looked ready for another, any time.

A tom cat, her head warned, *someone dangerous. Someone to steer clear of.*

"Oh, Mr. Yar, one more thing," she called after him.

He turned. "Yes?"

"No one comes inside the glasshouse but me. Not ever."

He cocked his head at a rakish angle. "I do." Clicking his heels together, he tugged his forelock and threw her a mischievous grin. "Good night, Miss Rose."

Lady Moonbeam and Malachi watched him go with mirrored expressions of disbelief. "Why is he leaving?" Moon asked.

"I do not know," Malachi said.

"They didn't even touch noses or—or do that thing they do with their mouths!"

"No. And there were no soft words. No stroking. Not even a nuzzle."

"Do they not know they are life mates?"

"I have learned human males are almost as resistant to the idea as toms, dearest. Still, when one's life mate does appear, it is impossible to just swish one's tail and walk away."

"It looks as though your human isn't having any trouble."

"It does look that way," Malachi admitted, "but something was different about him—his smell or maybe the way he moved, I don't know. His heart knows he has found her, even if his mind does not."

"Yes. Well, if his mind sells the house before his heart realizes he has found his life mate, you shall both be going away." Her beautiful voice came out in a wail, earning her a baleful glare from her mistress.

Malachi licked her soothingly. "Not to worry. They will realize what they are, I am certain. Perhaps it will just take a day or two. Humans are not like us, beloved."

Lady Moonbeam sighed. "I wish humans were as sensible as cats."

CHAPTER FIVE

Max awakened refreshed and feeling as though he could eat the leg of a running bull. Brilliant summer sun shone through the mullioned windows of his opulent blue and gold bedchamber, and he guessed that it was well past noon. He had missed breakfast. And luncheon. He swore and then stopped himself, midcurse. He was the master here, which meant he could order a meal any time of the day.

He smiled into his mirror as he dressed. For once, the threadbare condition of his waistcoat and the thinness of his cravat didn't bother him. The master of Yarrowdale Hall could dress any deuced way he felt like. And, anyway, as soon as he sold the place, he'd buy new clothing. Coats, cravats, hats, everything.

But before he could accomplish that miracle, he had a house party to arrange. He chuckled. Max Yar giving a house party for the *ton*! The very idea was ludicrous.

Ludicrous or not, though, it was fact, and there were a thousand things to do. Uncle had been dead nearly a year, and the enormous house was musty. The once-beautiful gardens were hideously overgrown. The footman who had escorted Max to his chamber last night had said some of the staff had drifted away or been dismissed and that the stables lacked mounts, the larders food, and the cellars wine. Max didn't know the first thing about any of that, but someone around here would. The butler, he supposed. That was the man's job, wasn't it? To know of such things? And what about a steward? Was there a steward here? Max hadn't seen one. But didn't such people usually live in a separate cottage on an estate this size?

And there was one more thing. The tiny dragon. Max couldn't let her continue to believe she could just spread her wings and go flying off by herself into the unknown. She wasn't in truth a dragon. She was more like a butterfly. Small and delicate, she'd be blown over by the first squall she sailed into. There weren't many women traveling alone, and those who did looked more like Amazons than butterflies. Max sighed. She was a feisty thing in spite of her diminutive size, and he suspected she'd put up a fight when he told her she couldn't go traipsing off alone. Not that he cared. It wasn't his problem, after all. She could do what she wanted to. She wasn't his responsibility. No, sir!

He started downstairs to find his butler while humming a bawdy song he'd learned from a certain ancient senora in Spain and thinking. He shouldn't have encouraged her last night. *I should have pinched that butterfly's wings right then and there. I should have put my foot down and told her she couldn't—*

Max froze and stared. His little butterfly was standing in the cavernous front hall with her hands fisted at her sides, ringing a peal over two men three times her size. Before he could react, she grasped each of them by one ear and twisted, walked to the open front door, and then none-too-gently shoved them both onto the front stoop.

"Candlesticks up your sleeves! You should be ashamed. You are lucky you do not have a noose around your necks! Go find honest work, gentlemen. In this country, we do not suffer thieves. If you are seen in this neighborhood again, I shall have the magistrate arrest you!" she said, ending with a flourish as she firmly closed the door behind them.

The hall erupted into applause, and Max realized that dozens of eyes had been peeking silently from behind doorways. Gamely, the butterfly smiled and bowed low in the manner of an actor, and the crowd dispersed—all but one bent old man, who timidly walked up to Miss Rose and inclined his head in Max's direction.

Miss Rose looked up at Max, who was still on the stairs.

"Good morning." She reached for a bell rope and gave five sharp tugs. Almost instantly, a cry went up, and an army of servants surged past Max and up the stairs, stopping only long enough to curtsy or bow and murmur a hasty "Good morning, sir."

"Good afternoon more like," he said, after they'd passed.

"I instructed them that it would be impolite for them to say so," Miss Rose said. "This is Mr. Underwood"—she winked surreptitiously—"the village tailor you asked me to send for?" She winked once more for good measure. "He is not well known, but I assure you his work rivals anything London has to offer, and he graciously agreed to work on short notice."

The man smiled gratefully and tugged at his forelock. "We are all pleased you've come at last, sir." The tailor pulled from his pocket a piece of string. "Raise your arm, please."

Bemused, Max stepped down to the floor and complied. What else could he do?

Miss Rose continued, "You'll find the lower two floors and the cellars in order. They were not in bad shape to begin with, but the upper floors will take more time, I am afraid. I've sent your head groom to Town to secure five new mounts, and Mr. Balance and Mrs. Trews—they are your butler and housekeeper—to Town to buy wine and provisions. I've also addressed supplemental invitations for the wedding guests to stay the week in Yarrowdale Hall and composed an advertisement for the London newspapers announcing the sale of the house. Thomas, the youngest of the grooms, is standing ready to deliver them in London. When Mr. Underwood is finished, you have only to sign the invitations and approve the wording of the advertisement, and all will be in order. The rest of the workers are outside."

Max walked to the window. The tailor followed without a

protest, measuring all the while. Out on the lawn, a crew of four raked the gravel drive while six others trimmed hedges and perhaps a dozen worked with scythes.

She tapped the windowpane. "They will gather the trimmings of course, the perennials will be thinned along the drive and planted elsewhere, and there will be fresh flower arrangements here in the house before your guests arrive. I had to procure the flowers elsewhere," she said apologetically. "I only grow orange blossoms in the glasshouse. Oh, and I've penned an advertisement for a new aviary master—your uncle was fond of hawks, not hounds—sent for twelve new decks of cards, and hired an orchestra to stay for the duration of the party. Five pieces should be enough, shouldn't they?"

In response, Max could only chuckle.

Her blond brows slammed together. "What is so amusing?"

"You."

"Me?"

Max stood still as the tailor measured his shoulders. "Here I was worried about you traveling alone. I should worry more about the poor cabin boy who leaves your bed unmade or your perfume bottles undusted."

She smiled. "No, no. I shall leave the poor cabin boy unmolested. It is the captain who will be dusting my perfume bottles."

Max laughed.

"Are you hungry?" she asked. Not waiting for his answer, she bustled off toward what Max hoped was the kitchen or dining room. "I vow I am starving, though luncheon was only two hours ago!"

"I'm finished, sir," the tailor said. "Would you care to choose fabric and styles now?"

Max shook his head. "I trust you."

"Very well, sir." The man beamed and bowed, and Max strode off after the dragon. He'd been wrong. Terribly wrong. She was definitely not a butterfly.

CHAPTER SIX

"Thank goodness we did not lose Cook," Emma said, sopping up the last delectable bit of turtle soup from her red china bowl with her last delectable morsel of bread. "Delicious!"

Across from her, Maximillan Yar shook his head. "I do not understand how you can sit there so tranquilly with a typhoon raging about you."

"I told you! Everything is taken care of. The house and grounds will be beautiful. The *ton* will descend and find a grand estate situated conveniently near the road to London and be falling over themselves to bid. You will be a rich man in a month. Stop worrying."

Emma looked up from her bowl to find that the deep lines Mr. Yar had worn between his eyebrows for the past half hour hadn't smoothed any. "Tell me."

"What?"

"Come now, out with it. What is bothering you?"

Stirring his tea, he considered a moment before answering. "I am worried about Miss Emmaline Rose."

"Emmaline Rose?"

"Is there an echo in here?" he asked with a grin. "Yes, you. See here, after we sell this place, Malachi and I will travel in first-class cabins, not in dank sailor's quarters. We shall dine on oysters and pineapples, sleep on cotton, and awaken whenever we please. But you . . . you shall have to economize, which is much harder for a woman alone than it is for a man.

Thirty thousand pounds sounds like an enormous sum, and if you stayed here in England on dry land, it would be. But trust me when I say that on the high seas thirty thousand will dwindle to nothing before you know it, and then you will be—"

Emma couldn't help laughing.

"What?" he asked.

"Mr. Yar, I know very well how much thirty thousand pounds will and will not buy."

He set down his cup and steepled his fingers. "I will own that you have performed adequately here since my uncle's death, but—"

"Adequately!" Emma set her teacup down with a plunk. "The estate has had no steward for nearly a year, but the fields are planted, the sheep were shorn, and the accounts are all perfectly balanced, including this morning's expenditures. Adequately, my eyes!"

Over near the door, someone cleared his throat. "Excuse me, miss . . . and, uh, sir . . . but Mr. and Mrs. Henry have just arrived to pick up the weekly shipment. They brought this." The footman placed an envelope on the table.

"Of course," Emma said. "Tell them the shipment is ready."

"What shipment?" Mr. Yar asked as Emma carried her dishes to the dry sink.

"Orange blossoms," Emma said, trying to keep from smiling. "I grow orange blossoms and sell them."

"Oh. How very enterprising."

Emma could tell by his tone that Mr. Yar did not understand, and so could the footman, evidently, for he piped up proudly, "Miss Rose here sells orange blossoms to all the brides in England. Scotland and Spain, too. She even smuggled some out to France, one time!"

Mr. Yar raised one dark eyebrow and looked to Emma for confirmation. "Oh?"

Emma changed the subject. "I inherited the business from my mentor, the woman who owned the glasshouse before me."

"How did she come to own the glasshouse?"

Emma shrugged. "She would not say. She was given it long ago by your great uncle. It is said they met in some foreign land and they fell in love. She followed him here from somewhere far away, and he either could not or would not marry her, but he did not have the heart to banish her. I cannot confirm the story, as there are none left alive from that time. She was very old when she took me in."

"You were an orphan?"

Mr. Yar had a knack for making it necessary for her to change the subject. She nodded. "She was a kind woman. She made a tidy living from selling her orange blossoms, and she taught me everything she knew. The blossoms have allowed me to be financially independent."

"The blossoms and the smuggling, I presume?"

Emma laughed and turned to the footman. "The candlewicks need trimming, Thomas. Please see to that, and I will go speak to Mr. and Mrs. Henry myself."

Max watched her quit the room, feeling a little out of balance. So his little dragon wasn't just an accomplished steward, she was also a merchant!

His eyes lit upon the envelope on the table. It was completely unmarked on the outside, which in Max's experience was a sure sign that it contained money.

So, of course, he opened it—what else could he do?—and gave a long, low, appreciative whistle. Emmaline Rose wasn't going to be sleeping in musty third-class cabins. No, she'd deuced well buy her own ship!

CHAPTER SEVEN

"Are you sure they went this way?" Moon asked. Two days had passed, and the cats had hardly left Emmaline and Maximillian's side, but today, while the humans had taken luncheon, the cats had curled up to take a nap in the sun, and when they awoke, the humans had disappeared. Fortunately, tracking them wasn't difficult.

"Yes," Malachi purred. "I can hear them."

Moon listened but could only hear the warm summer wind sifting through the chestnut trees and the bees browsing among the bluebells. "You have good ears," she said.

"Thank you, beloved."

The morning and early afternoon had been a busy one for the humans, and Moon suspected her mistress had come to her usual place to sun herself and rest. Perhaps Malachi's master really was with Emmaline. Moon quivered happily at the thought of the two of them curled up together on the sunning rock.

They continued to pad a little-used footpath that wound up the side of a steep hill not far from the house. Finally reaching the summit, Malachi nudged Moon under a rhododendron, and Moon meowed softly, for her mistress was standing on a familiar rocky promontory a few feet away, staring down at the valley far below. "She is alone."

"I do not think so," Malachi breathed, sniffing the air. "He is here somewhere."

Emmaline stretched her arms above her head and bent at the

waist in a very feline way that Moon liked to think she'd taught her.

"Do not do that!" shouted an anguished voice.

Moon and Malachi both jumped as Max leapt out from where he'd been hidden from their view behind a second rock outcropping and jumped over onto Emmaline's high perch, nearly losing his footing in the process.

"No tail," Malachi whispered. "No balance."

"Poor darlings," Moon agreed.

"And *you* are scolding *me*!" Emmaline cried, clutching for Max's hand. "If I sit down, will you stop capering about and scaring me half to death?"

"Yes. Absolutely. Yes. Please. Sit. Please."

Emmaline laughed, and they both sat.

Malachi nudged Moon with his shoulder. "They are sitting together," he purred softly.

"But they are not even touching," Moon qualified.

Emmaline scooted toward the edge of the rock and sat swinging her legs over the side, while Max sat well back, frowning. She glanced back at him and laughed. "If you are so afraid of heights, why did you come up here?"

He shrugged. "I saw the footpath."

"And you climbed it even though you are afraid of heights?"

"Are you implying that I followed you up here for some nefarious purpose?"

"You did, did you not?"

"It looked dangerous."

"So you came up here to keep me from falling?"

"Yes," Max said stubbornly. "What else could I do?"

"Would you stop saying that?"

"Saying what?"

" 'What else can I do.' It is annoying. And I do not need saving. The very idea!" Emmaline laughed. "I have climbed to this very spot thousands of times. I can find it on a moonless night. I assure you I am quite safe."

"You come here that often?" Max asked.

"It is my favorite spot on the whole estate. You can see the entire valley from here. Is Yarrowdale not lovely?"

"Indeed. And the people here seem very amiable, too."

"Yes. I love Yarrowdale."

They fell silent for a time, watching a falcon gliding in swirling circles on the cliff's updraft. They'd fallen into an easy camaraderie these past two days. *Too easy,* Max thought. He'd begun to feel a little selfish, a little dastardly.

"If you love your home so much," he said suddenly, "then why do you want to leave it?"

Emmaline sighed. "I grew up listening to my mentor's tales. I want to cross a desert on a camel as she did, trek through the jungle, climb mountains. You are a traveler, Mr. Yar. Surely you understand such desires."

He nodded. "I do, but . . . Miss Rose, I confess I did not come here for the view or the solitude, nor to prevent you from falling. It is your desire to travel that has me worried. You may travel for a month or two, maybe six, and then tire of it, and you will regret that you sold your glasshouse."

Shaking her head in denial, she opened her mouth, but Max held up his palm. "I do not wish to discourage you from selling," he said. "On the contrary, I want to sell Yarrowdale Hall quite badly, and I doubt I can do that if you retain ownership of your part of it. But I do not wish to be the cause of a lifetime of regret, either. I simply want you to be certain of your desires before you rush into an irrevocable decision."

"We might not have another opportunity like this, Mr. Yar. The wedding will see the arrival of the cream of the *ton*. It is the ideal time to sell. The ideal time to win a top price."

"Why do you need a top price?"

"What makes you think I do not?"

Maximillian laughed. "You needn't play games with me, Miss Rose. You see, I am as incorrigible as you are. I looked inside the envelope your footman gave you, the one from Mr. and Mrs. Henry?"

"Why, you scoundrel," Emma said, not really meaning it. "I wondered why it was open."

"That was a tidy banknote."

"Did you read the statement from my solicitor, as well."

"Of course."

She looked down at her hands. "It is not all my own doing. My mentor saved every farthing she made for years and invested wisely through her uncle. I inherited a great deal of the sum you saw on the statement."

"And made it grow, I'll wager."

She offered no denials.

"You can be in no hurry to sell your glasshouse. I am the one who needs to take advantage of the house party to bring the best possible offer. But I can wait. After a time, income from the estate will allow me to return to the seas."

"You do not have to wait, Mr. Yar."

Moon watched Emmaline's face soften as it always did when her mistress reached down to stroke her. "You are kind," Emmaline said, "and I appreciate your honesty and concern, but I am quite set on leaving before the Winter S—before the winter." She stood up. "It is late, and there is still much to do. If you will excuse me?"

"What else can I do?" Max said with a grin, but he wondered what she'd been about to say. The winter what? Something that started with an "S." One thing was certain: She wasn't going to tell him even if he asked. But what could a spinster's secrets matter to Maximillian Yar?

It did not signify.

Dismissing the matter from his mind and standing carefully, he silently followed Emmaline back down the footpath.

The cats followed long enough to watch the two of them part, Maximillian heading for the stables and Emmaline heading for the house.

Moon's ears twitched in annoyance. "It has been nearly three days."

Malachi sat beside her and licked his paw. "I know. Be patient, beloved. Humans are stubborn. Or blind." He gave the equivalent of a cat chuckle, a throaty sound that any human would mistake as a purr.

"And deaf, apparently. They did not notice us."

Malachi batted at a leaf. "I do not think they noticed much but each other."

"I suppose that is good," Moon sighed and said again, and not for the last time, "I wish humans were as sensible as cats!"

CHAPTER EIGHT

The next day dawned rainy and cool, and Emmaline was glad to have an excuse to stay inside the glasshouse. At first, she told herself she was staying inside because was tired. She hadn't slept well. And, indeed, after she'd breakfasted and dressed in her favorite work gown, a soft, faded blue calico, Emma did something she never did. She lay down again. But she didn't sleep. Instead, she spent an hour staring at her beautiful green orange trees and listening to the rain pattering against the crystalline walls of her home.

How many other ladies lived in a glasshouse? Surely she was the only one. And soon, there would be none.

"Unpleasant thoughts?"

She gasped and sprang to her feet. "Mr. Yar! Do you not respect the privacy of others?"

"You live in a glasshouse," he said dryly. "You have no true privacy."

"I do if people stay on the other side of my hedges."

He padded over to her sofa, looking for all the world like a smug and unrecalcitrant tom cat. "Why are you hiding?"

"I am not hiding! It is raining."

"Hardly a sprinkle. Not enough to keep you from coming to the house for breakfast. I arose early for the occasion and was quite vexed when you did not show."

"Sorry."

"Liar."

She grinned. "Correct."

He put his feet up. "Come now. Tell me what hideous thoughts were shaping your lovely face into such worrisome lines just now."

Lovely? She looked down at her hands. "I . . . ah . . ."

"Yes . . . ?"

Say something, Emma! her mind shouted. "I . . . ah . . . realized you were correct. I am going to miss this place. Terribly."

"Why sell, then?"

"Because I must.

"That is hardly an answer."

"Would you care for tea?" she averred, not waiting for his response before reaching for her kettle.

"I love your tea," he said, allowing her to change the subject. "Flavored with orange zest. Delicious. It reminds me of the West Indies."

She smiled and busied herself with the tray.

"It is cozy here in the glasshouse in the rain," he said, looking up at the cloudy sky. "You take care of the place beautifully. How do you keep the glass so clean?"

They chatted amiably about the care of the glasshouse while she made the tea and poured it out, and Emma was grateful they'd stepped away from the subject of her finances, but her relief was short-lived, for as soon as the tea was finished, Mr. Yar leaned forward and said, "I have been going over the accounts this morning. You spent an enormous sum of your own money to keep the estate running over the past year."

She offered no denials.

It hadn't been long after the old man's death that his solicitor had discovered some discrepancies in the accounts, and the Yarrowdale steward had suddenly disappeared along with all of the estate's petty funds. The solicitor immediately froze all of the estate's accounts, pending the arrival of the new master, but the village depended upon Yarrowdale Hall, and someone had to step in. In the end, Emma spent her own money on everything from medicine for the cottagers to seed for planting the fields.

"I do not regret the money," she said "I love Yarrowdale. It is an extraordinary place with extraordinary people. You've not been to the village yet, so you cannot possibly know—"

"Yes, yes. But, *now*—blast it!—I am indebted to you."

"It was my money, Mr. Yar. I had a right to spend it, and I did."

"Why would you spend that much money on an estate you intended to leave all along?"

"The village depends upon the Hall, Mr. Yar. It was the village I was concerned for, not the estate." She sipped her tea. "I was found wandering there as a small child, and the whole village took me in."

"The whole village? I do not understand."

"One cottage provided a blanket, another a cup of milk. A shirt here, a pair of used shoes there. I was even given a doll." Emma bent down to pick up the old, faded rag doll that lived on her bed. "I was passed from one family to another, until my beloved Miss Thatcher adopted me."

"Your mentor?"

Emma nodded. "She said she fell in love with me at first sight. I do not remember living anywhere else but right here in the glasshouse."

"An unconventional childhood."

Emma nodded. "And a happy one. I am grateful to Yarrowdale. It has given me so much."

Suddenly, Emma couldn't sit still. Setting down her teacup a little too hard, she rose and wandered to her worktable. "But I am sure there are a hundred places—a thousand!—that are just as pleasant."

Absentmindedly, she picked up her garden shears and moved to the nearest of her orange trees. "I am certain I will never miss it." She lopped off a wayward branch. "I am certain I will meet many people just as wonderful as those in Yarrowdale." *Lop!* "And I am certain that the new owner of Yarrowdale Hall will take fine care of the orange trees." *Lop-Lop!* "And even if he does not—even if he forgets to water—*Lop!*—or forgets to fertilize or check for insects—*Lop-Lop-Lop!*—or deadhead or trim—"

"Or if he savages them with his shears as you are doing now, perhaps?" Mr. Yar came beside her and laid his hand over Emma's. His touch was warm, his skin tanned and smooth, and Emma realized her hands were shaking.

"Do not be afraid," he said.

"Of what?"

"The unknown," he whispered.

She watched, unable to think, as his eyes shuttered, and he flicked his gaze down to her lips. In a moment of perfect clarity, and in spite of not having any sort of experience with that sort of thing, she realized he intended to kiss her. Tilting his head, he leaned ever so slightly toward her, and—

And at the last possible second, he reached to take her shears from her hand. "I think I would do a better job, even if I know nothing about it."

Emma danced away. Dear heavens, he'd nearly kissed her. Hadn't he? Or was Emma just telling herself stories? "I—have a birthday present for you!" she blurted.

"A what?"

"A present. In honor of the day you were born." Emma retrieved a small parcel from her workbench. It was wrapped simply in a square of white lawn and tied with bleached cotton twine. Handing the little package to him, her fingers tingled and felt warm where they brushed his. She gasped at the amazing sensation, and then, to cover her reaction, she whirled around, put her hand to her mouth, and pretended a nasty cough. *Fly, fly,* her mind shouted. *Flee the glasshouse! Now!*

"I say, are you quite well?"

She meant to say "Fine," she truly did, but what came out was quite different. "Fly!" she said.

"Ugh!" A pained expression blossomed on his face. "You swallowed a fly? I hate it when that happens."

Somehow, Emma held back a nervous giggle. "Disgusting," she agreed, mirroring his expression. "Pray, let us forget it forthwith. Open your present." She turned away and busied herself with oiling her shears. "It isn't much," she said over her shoulder. "Just a trifle, really."

"Seeds!" he said, behind her. "Orange seeds. From your trees, I presume?"

Emma nodded. "Miss Thatcher brought back the original seeds from China." She strode over to one of her trees and stroked its shining green leaves lovingly. "They blossom well nigh all year, even when they are bearing fruit. They are the only ones of their kind in all England. Perhaps all the world."

"This is not a trifle!" he said. "These are a precious gift!"

"And a foolish one, for you have nowhere to plant them," she said.

"I might . . . someday. In the meantime, I shall keep them right here in my pocket. They will remind me of you. Small and full of life. Unique . . . and valuable. Thank you, Emmaline."

Full of life? Unique? Valuable? And he had used her given name!

Her heart beat a warning as she finished oiling the shears and polished them dry with a cotton cloth reserved for that purpose. Over the years, Emma had oiled those shears so many times her hands knew what do even if her mind did not—which was fortunate, as this time her entire focus was upon the man behind her. What was he doing? He was quiet as a cat. And as predatory.

She laughed at the stray thought. Predatory? *Yes,* her mind answered, *predatory.* He'd almost kissed her, hadn't he? And, heaven help her, she'd almost let him!

And why not? He was handsome and wealthy and amiable in every way, and she was twenty-and-nine years old and had never so much as held a man's hand. Why not kiss this one? Did she not long for adventure? Kissing a man would be a delicious adventure. Kissing a man like Maximillian Yar would be—

What?

Folly. Sheer folly.

He was too handsome. Too intelligent. Too *manly*. Too dev-ilishly attractive. Emma liked him. She liked him a lot. What if she began liking him too much? What if she fell in love with him? What then? They might kiss and . . . and . . .

Her rational mind went a-begging as the more visceral, feminine part sifted through images of what she and Max-imillian might do together, until she suddenly realized that she had said nothing for what must be several minutes.

Finishing with the polishing cloth, she replaced the shears on her worktable but did not turn around. "I am not afraid," she said, and the seconds stretched into a minute before she realized she was alone in the glasshouse. He had gone!

Emma's face burned with mortification, and she buried it in her hands. Men like Maximillian Yar did not ask permis-sion to kiss a woman. They just did it. He hadn't wanted to kiss her. If he had, he would have done it, and that was that. The sad truth was that she'd imagined it.

"Did you see that?" Malachi purred to Moon. They were lying together on the warm flagstones near the glasshouse stove. "They almost did that mouth thing they do."

"Almost." Moon gave a worried sigh.

"They want each other."

"I see that, but they still do not."

Malachi licked his paw. "They will if they have enough time. We shall have to be certain that they do. For now, let us just watch."

Moon sighed again. "I do wish humans were as sensible as cats."

CHAPTER NINE

When Max returned to the glasshouse late that afternoon, Emmaline was sitting alone, picking at the remains of the meal she'd sent for. She'd been alone all day, which was unusual, so the servants said. A stab of guilt pricked his conscience.

She'd known he was about to kiss her that morning. And she'd wanted him to. There was no mistaking the signs. She'd blushed softly. Her lovely bosom had risen and fallen a little higher, a little faster. Her pupils had become great, liquid pools of desire. Oh, yes, she'd wanted him to kiss her. Her attraction for him was running rampant. But she wasn't prepared for it.

He'd sensed that this afternoon and deloped a split second before his lips made contact with hers. And then she'd neatly pretended it hadn't almost happened. She'd probably deny it now, if he pressed her about it. He'd probably lost his chance.

Not that it mattered to Max. Not really. She was pleasant enough to look at. A beauty, really. And she was good company. Intelligent and funny, she never failed to know when he was being serious and when he was deliberately affecting the guise of a sarcastic blackguard for comic effect. It was easy to spend time with Emmaline. And she seemed to enjoy spending time with him, too.

But Max knew a dozen young ladies in every port who were quite willing to spend time with him. Many were as pretty as Emmaline Rose, and some were as pleasant. And all were more than willing to kiss him.

No, it did not matter to him in the least if he never kissed Miss Rose. In fact, it could be damnably inconvenient. She was too . . . nice. She might have expectations.

Expectations were bad. Max always tried to steer clear of them, both his own and others'. If a man sailed as the winds blew, if he had no expectations, he couldn't be disappointed. Trying to sail into a wind was a good way to end up on the rocks.

Very well. He would not make the mistake of almost kissing her again. Which meant he'd better stay away from her, because she was too deuced tempting!

All at once, she reached to pull the rope that hung beside her table, and the high, clear sound of a good-sized bell mounted atop the glasshouse rent the air as Emmaline sighed and pushed her plate away. She hadn't taken more than a few bites.

Guilt stabbed Max again and gave a savage twist. He just couldn't leave her there. "Mmm . . . salmon and lemon sauce," he said. "It is my favorite dish."

She didn't even flinch at the sound of his voice but sat up a little straighter. "I know," she said, without turning around. "You mentioned it a day or two after you arrived—and do you never ask permission before you enter someone's home?"

"A day or two after I arrived! Upon my word, you are devilishly observant and remember everything! I must be careful what I say around you. And I do not knock on glasshouses because that would be ridiculous since I can see the occupant clearly as I stand there." He took off his gloves and tossed them onto the table and sat opposite her. "I suppose I gave some clue about today being my birthday—though I'll be hanged if I remember what it was."

She nodded. "When you told me about the Gypsy who read your palm, you said you were born on the Summer Solstice, remember?"

"So I did."

"And today is Midsummer," she said.

"Well, bless me, so it is! Say, Mr. Balance mentioned some pagan ceremony they are holding down in the village tonight."

She laughed. It is not a pagan ceremony. It is the Midsummer celebration. It is held every year."

"Have you ever attended?"

A worry line appeared on her brow. "I never miss it."

"What time does it begin?"

"At sundown. It starts with the lighting of a bonfire. The villagers gather round and play music. It is quite a cacophony. You will hear it up here. Anyone with an instrument of any sort plays, while the children bang along with makeshift drums, and those who do not have an instrument sing. After that, there are dancing, contests, games, and feasting. It lasts until dawn."

"It sounds exhausting!"

"It is." She smiled softly. "It takes stamina to last all night. I think that must be why they hold it on the shortest night of the year."

"Or perhaps they chose the Solstice so that they have the longest day of the year to sleep it off afterward?"

She smiled, and Max stood up. "Sounds like good fun. Mind if I join you?"

"Oh, I . . . I will not be going."

"Why not?"

She stood and, walking to her worktable, she picked up her shears again. She was clearly closing him out of her world. "There is too much to do."

"Have your trees not endured enough torture for one day?" His footsteps echoed across the glass as he approached her once more. He wanted to touch her. Reassure her. But he couldn't. Not in the way that came most naturally to him, the way he wanted to, with a warm embrace and a warmer kiss. Suddenly, he realized he was close enough to smell her starched cotton gown and her hair, which always managed to smell of orange blossoms, and Max stepped back. "Do you feel you must travel because Miss Thatcher did? You do not have to live up to her example, you know. You can find your own path—even if you discover that path begins and ends right here in Yarrowdale."

"No . . . no. That isn't it. I want to travel. I need it."

"Need?"

Her eyes widened.

"Why do you need it, Emmaline? Why do you need to leave Yarrowdale now . . . before the winter?"

Her wispy, blond brows slammed together, and Max knew he'd struck gold.

"You are impertinent," she said.

"Why, thank you, my lady. Mr. Impertinent at your service." He bowed low and then looked up at her with a wink. "I have been called worse."

"I wager you have."

At that moment, a servant appeared at the ornate door of the glasshouse, and Emmaline moved to let her in. It was the housekeeper.

"You rang, miss? Are you finished with your supper? May I clear it away for you?"

"Yes. Thank you, Mrs. Trews."

The plump young woman bustled over to the table and gave a disapproving click of her tongue at the nearly full plate. "Was there something wrong with it, miss?" she asked, shooting daggers at Max.

"No, Mrs. Trews. It was delicious. I am just a little . . . dyspeptic tonight."

"That's too bad," Mrs. Trews said. "You'll have to be careful down at the village tonight and stay away from the sweets."

"I am not going."

Mrs. Trews whirled around. "Not going? But you always go, miss! You haven't missed it since you come. The villagers need you there. Especially since this will be your last." She shot Max some more daggers, these jagged and dipped in poison. "She's the reason they have the celebration to begin with," she told him. "I don't suppose she told you that, though."

"No, Mrs. Trews, she did not. Is there anything else about the Midsummer celebration I should know but which *she* will not tell?"

"Oh, for heaven's sake!" Emmaline cried.

The housekeeper's scowl melted into a conspiratorial grin. "Indeed, sir."

Emmaline stalked to the corner, growling, and Max laughed. "Go on."

"Well, sir, it ain't a 'Midsummer' celebration at all. It's to celebrate her coming. She arrived on Midsummer's Day, you see. Toddled into the village and right into their hearts. Came out of nowhere. Dropped off some carriage."

"Do you mean she was left here?"

"Yes sir. It had been raining, and her little feet left tracks— her feet and the carriage's wheels. She was left, sure as anything. I saw the tracks myself!" She addressed Emmaline, "I ain't telling him anything that ain't common knowledge." She turned back to Max. "You'd find it all out in the village tonight, anyhow. You are going, ain't you?"

"I wouldn't miss it."

"Good! Everyone is expecting you to be there, sir. 'Tis a special occasion, having the squire at Midsummer's Eve once again. Just like in the old days." She smiled wistfully. "Well, I'd best finish here"—she flashed a glance at Emmaline's turned back, winked at Max, and finished in a whisper—"so you two can make ready to leave."

Max winked back.

The housekeeper put the dishes on a small tray, turned down Emmaline's bed, laid out a night rail, and lit two lamps. "There, now, miss," she said, "everything will be ready for you to fall into bed when you return from the village. Perhaps you can lay in a wink or two before the guests start arriving." She turned to Max. "Usually, everyone sleeps past noon the day after Winter Solstice and Midsummer. 'Cept for her.

"The Winter Solstice?"

"That's when we reckon her birthday. Not that it matters. She's always up at dawn, Midsummer, Winter Solstice, or no. I reckon it's hard to sleep until noon with the sun beating down through the glass. But 'tis no matter, for tomorrow everyone will have to be up and about before the wedding guests arrive. Thank goodness they're Town folk who keep Town hours. They won't start arriving until midafternoon, I should think. The celebration ends at dawn, when the sun peeks over the mountains, call it six-o'-the-clock, near enough. Mr. Balance and I have given everyone leave to sleep until ten. It's the best we can do."

"I'll see you at the celebration, Mrs. Trews," Max said. "Will you save a dance for me?"

She dimpled. "That I will, sir." She left with a whimsical expression on her face.

"Well," Max said, to Emmaline. "You had better change your clothes."

"I beg your pardon!"

"You are not attending your own celebration in your work dress, are you?"

"I told you. I am not going."

"Why not?"

Their eyes met and he held her gaze for a few moments before the stubborn look faded from her lovely blue eyes. She sighed and sank onto the sofa with her hand rubbing her forehead. "I cannot bear to go. It will probably be my last."

Max sighed sadly, knowing her words for unvarnished truth. "Miss Rose . . . Emmaline. I am invited to a thousand such events by dear friends all over the globe. Pig roasts in Bali, coming-of-age ceremonies in Africa, weddings in the fjord lands. Most times, I am embraced by the villagers, treated as one of them. I eat their food, dance their dances. And each celebration is always my last. Good-byes are a traveler's constant. If you travel, you shall have to get used to that. And you may as well start now." He bent down to take her hand and pulled her to her feet. "This week, I am the master of Yarrowdale Hall. Next week, I will be just plain Mr. Yar, lost in a sea of faces on some lonely wharf far away, but right now, in this instant, I belong here. I want to attend this celebration. It may be the only time I ever attend such an event as anything but a stranger. Tonight, I am one of the villagers."

"You are more than that," she said. "You are the master of Yarrowdale Hall. You are a pillar of the community."

"Exactly. And it is a position I will never hold again. Please, Emmaline, make my one evening of glory complete." He smiled. "Attend the celebration upon my arm. I am new here, and most of the villagers do not even know what I look like, but with you beside me, I know I will be accepted unconditionally. I will truly belong, just this once. Please, Emmaline. Please attend. I ask you as a fellow traveler . . . and as a friend. Nothing would please me more." He took her hand in his and bowed over her trembling fingers before delivering what he knew would be the *coup de grace*.

"Besides," he said, "you owe them a chance to say good-bye."

CHAPTER TEN

A rousing, galloping country dance had just ended when the sun peeked over the horizon at last, and a cheer rent the air. Everyone still present—perhaps two-thirds of the villagers—applauded and whistled, while a few groaned to others' delight, and within moments, good-byes echoed across the green as people started for home. Emma stood in the green and watched them scatter, a smile on her face.

"Thank you for comin', Emmaline! Many happy returns," an old man called, and another cheer echoed over the valley. Emma's smile faded along with the night.

Beside her, Maximillian chuckled, oblivious to her distress. "What a night!" he said with a sigh. "I'll go get the trap, shall I?"

Emma nodded and gestured toward Lady Moonbeam and Maximillian's cat, who had appeared on the village green around midnight. "I hope the furry celebrants will tolerate a ride in a wagon."

"Oh, Malachi will hardly notice. He is quite used to any form of conveyance—anything from barges to camels."

"I suppose Lady Moonbeam will have to learn to tolerate such things, too. And a trap is a good start, not as wild as a camel. Not as bumpy, I imagine."

"Yes, and much better-smelling."

Emma laughed in spite of her melancholy mood. Maximillian had kept her laughing all night, hardly leaving her side. "Thank you, Maximillian," she said.

"For what?"

"You turned what could have been a morbidly unhappy occasion into something pleasant I will always remember. I am deeply grateful." Expecting some tomfool witticism, Emma was surprised when he took her hand and brushed his lips across it instead.

"I am so glad to have been here for you," he said simply. And then, taking up the reins with one hand, he helped Emma into the trap with the other. His hand felt warm and comfortable, and Emma felt a silly sort of loss when she had to settle into her seat, and he let go.

Did he feel the same way?

Nonsense! She was telling herself stories. He hadn't wanted to kiss her this morning. He'd had ample opportunity all night, and he hadn't so much as kissed her hand until now. He hadn't lingered even then.

As the four of them wound up on the side of the valley toward Yarrowdale Hall's high perch halfway up the tall hill, Maximillian kept up a steady stream of laughing commentary. Emma smiled and nodded and answered where she ought, but her heart wasn't in it. After a while, the daisies and bluebells at the side of the road became a blur as her eyes and mind unfocused, and she was a little girl once more, coming home that first time with Miss Thatcher.

". . . and then I danced with Mrs. Purdy's apple pie," Maximillian said, "and flew up into the tree with the vicar."

"Mmm . . ." Emma nodded absently.

At his bark of laughter, Emma's mind sifted through what he'd just said, and she covered her mouth. "So sorry."

"No, no. I understand. Your thoughts are far away."

She nodded.

"As *you* will be, quite soon." He clucked to the sleepy horse and twitched the reins, and they drove on in silence for a time, watching the rising sun melt the fog from the hollows below. "I had fun tonight, Emmaline. Thank you."

Emma smiled, and he turned his eyes to the valley, his face full of alert curiosity. He looked ready for anything, sitting straight and tall, the morning sun glinting on his halo of dark curls and his green eyes roving hungrily over the landscape.

"Thank you for remembering my birthday," he said suddenly. "No one has ever done that."

"It was nothing. A few seeds and a request to the cook."

"Yes," he said, "but"—he looked over at her with an intense expression—"*no one has ever done that.*"

"Why not?" she asked softly.

He swallowed and gripped the reins harder, eliciting a whicker from the horse. "I know nothing else but traveling. My parents died suddenly when I was very small, and I was passed so often from one relative to another that I never felt settled anywhere. Not even in Yarrowdale."

"You spent time in Yarrowdale?" Emma cried. "When? How do I not remember you?"

He sighed. "I wasn't here for long, and I was kept inside. My other relatives had not been kind, you see," he said, his face lined with the bitter memory, "and I expected no better from Uncle. What else could I do? I ran away two days after I arrived, the first time I was let outside."

"But your uncle was a kind and decent man!"

"So I have learned." His soft voice was tinged with a sweet sadness that made Emma's heart ache. His only family was now gone. He sat staring at the road, lost in unhappy thought, judging by the expression on his face.

Emma touched his hand briefly, bringing him out of whatever dark place he dwelt. "Did we meet?" she asked.

"Oh, yes," he said, a grin appearing on his handsome face. "I watched you sneak into the glasshouse to steal a piece of pie."

"Oh!" Emma cried. "I remember that! I remember *you*! You took the rest of the whole pie," she accused, "and I got blamed for it."

"For which I am profoundly sorry, but that pie got me halfway to Bristol."

"Oh, dear. What did you do then?"

He smiled. "It is a long story. For now, let us say I was extraordinarily lucky."

"To live?"

"To not be caught!" He grinned, and Emma smiled too. She loved his optimism and his laughing eyes.

"Wait a minute! How old were you?"

"Nine."

"Nine!" Emma gasped. "So young."

"Mmm," he agreed with a nod. "And you must have been about . . . what? Two?"

"Do you remember nothing of your parents?" she averred.

Max took note. He knew very well that she'd been seven, not two. He'd learned down in the village that she was older than she appeared—almost thirty. Now he knew that she was sensitive about turning thirty. That fact, coupled with her admission that she was in a hurry to leave before the Winter Solstice—her birthday—had led him to form a theory about why she was in such a hurry to leave Yarrowdale behind. "I have no memory of my parents," he said.

"Then you have never truly had a home."

"What?" He glanced her way. "Oh! No . . . no, I don't suppose I have. But you needn't feel sorry for me. I like it that way. Nothing to keep me from traveling as I please. When my ship leaves the harbor, I never have second thoughts."

Unlike you, Max thought. He'd never met a person who was so much a part of her home. She'd sent down roots just like her orange trees. She hadn't been adopted by Miss Thatcher only; it was as though Emmaline had been adopted by the entire village. And she them.

During his long absence, Emmaline had provided everything from a physician during a fever to extra fodder for the village cows last winter. But the villagers' regard wasn't restricted to her largesse. They spoke of her with genuine love and admiration in their voices as well as gratitude. They would miss her when she left.

She was staring out across the wide valley to the ridge of mountains in the distance.

"How far away is that ridge?" He asked

"Miles as the crow flies, perhaps thirty on foot. Why?"

"The mountains are lovely," he said. "So green. They look full of life. Have you ever been?"

She shook her head and alighted, and Max followed her, handing the reins to the footman on duty.

"Why not?" Max asked. "I thought you craved adventure."

"There is no adventure in these hills, Mr. Yar. Good day." Giving a demure curtsy, she plowed through the sunshine and around to the back of the house.

"Heh!"

Max looked over at the footman, who had made the sound. "Is there something you need to add to the discussion?" Max asked.

The footman pulled at his forelock. "I beg your pardon, sir."

"Not at all. I am interested in what you have to say."

"Well . . ." The footman hesitated. "I was just a little surprised she said there is no excitement here, sir, what with the robbers and all."

"Robbers?"

"Yes sir. Only last month, during the full of the moon. They carried off the silver in the dead of night, but she heard them as they stole past the glasshouse and sounded the alarm with her bell. Roused the whole village, she did, and they were caught red-handed. And then there was that runaway earl and his young bride on their way to Gretna Green." He bent toward Max and lowered his voice. "She hid them, you see, their parents but two seconds behind. And I suppose you know about the flood down in the valley last spring?"

"I am not aware of it."

"Oh, it was terrible, sir. The rain wouldn't stop, and the brook became a tempest in the valley. And our Emmaline," he said proudly, "she saved the Smith children!"

"She saved them?"

"Well, they weren't drowning or the like, but they might have, if the river had climbed any higher, and she led them to safety, sure enough. Risked her life to do it, too. Don't let her tell you there's no excitement hereabouts, sir."

"Thank you."

"Thank *you,* sir," the footman said proudly and led the horse away, a spring in his step.

"Hm!" Clearly, Emmaline's little adventures had left her wanting more, and she believed there was more to be had out there somewhere.

She was right.

Max paused to think of all the wonders he'd have missed if he'd stayed at Yarrowdale as a boy. He loved his wanderer's life, unconventional though it was. Perhaps Emmaline would love it too. But, oh deuced, devilish hell, what if she did not? Should he do more to stop her? Had he any right? And what made him believe he was more qualified to decide than Emmaline was herself?

Because, said a voice, coming from somewhere deep inside his soul, *you know what traveling is really like.* "And it isn't anything like Yarrowdale," Max murmured to himself.

At that moment, a carriage turned off the road and rolled up the drive. The first of his guests. They were early by four hours, but it was no matter; Emmaline had had the estate completely prepared for the house party two days before. "Here we go," Max said, pasting on a smile and dismissing his concerns about Emmaline's future from his mind.

It did not matter what he thought Emmaline should do. She was a woman grown, not a green girl, and she did not need his protection or his direction. He thought back to the morning after he arrived, when she'd marshaled half the population of England to ready Yarrowdale for this moment. She was a dragon, not a butterfly, and woe to the man who forgot that. For a moment, Max almost had.

The occupants of the carriage alighted, an older, distinguished-looking gentleman, a beautiful young woman—clearly his daughter, as they shared the same inquisitive dark eyes and classical features—and a matron, once a beauty herself. A stepmother, Max decided.

"Oh, Papa, it is just as I remember. I cannot wait to see her! May I run along to the glasshouse and surprise her?"

"You are well nigh a married lady now, Sophia, I suppose you may do as you please," her father said indulgently. "Do try to stay out of mischief—though with you and Miss Rose together again, I expect that will be a strain on both of you. You two were always up to your pretty little eyebrows in one bumblebroth or another."

"Oh, Papa!" The bride-to-be looked on her father with laughing, intelligent eyes before kissing him on the cheek and dashing away without even noticing Max standing there. Max decided he liked her and her father. The stepmother, on the other hand . . .

Spying Max with eyes that missed nothing, the older woman marched forward, waving a newspaper—folded open to the advertisements section, Max saw. "Good morning, my good man. I am Mrs. Charlotte Browning, and this is my husband, Reginald Browning."

"Maximillian Yar," Max said with a bow. "At your service."

"Oh! My, my!" The woman tittered. "I did not realize." Remembering herself, she curtsied.

"I see you have seen my advertisement," Max observed.

"Indeed," Mr. Browning said. "My wife has a notion that she would like to purchase the place as a wedding present for our daughter."

"Oh . . . it is just a silly whim. Nothing serious, in truth," Charlotte Browning said, even as her eyes appraised each stone and mullion with an assessing gleam.

Max smiled to himself and led them inside.

As the footman led the horse and trap away, Malachi and Moon leapt down, arched their backs, and sidestepped away from the large carriage, which followed the trap. Something in the newcomer's tone of voice had Malachi's fur standing on end.

"I do not like her," Moon grumbled, uneasy.

"Neither do I. And neither does Max."

"Clearly," Moon agreed. "Did you see the way he bristled? If he'd had a tail, it would have been puffed out as big and wide as that woman's thick, clumsy, hairless ankles!"

With a cat laugh, Malachi batted at a leaf stirred by the first breeze of what promised to be a beautifully warm and dry summer day.

"Why did he smile and lead them into the house?" Moon asked. "Why did he not simply send them away?"

Malachi sighed. "I do not know."

"And he made Emmaline cross," Moon accused.

Malachi padded off in the direction of the house. "You go see what your lady is doing, and I shall keep watch on Max." He slipped in through the front door just as the butler closed it behind Max and the newcomers.

A few seconds later, a shriek rent the air of the rather austere entry hall, which hadn't a carpet or soft cushion anywhere, Malachi noted with some irritation.

"What is that?" the woman cried, pointing at Malachi.

"That is my cat, madam," Max said with a touch of ironic amusement in his voice that the lady evidently missed.

"Keep it away!" she cried.

"Oh . . . not to worry," Max assured her, picking Malachi up, cradling him in his arms, and ruffling his ears. It probably wasn't the most diplomatic thing, but what else could he do? His friend was being maligned. The cat purred and closed his eyes. "See? He is quite harmless. He is my best friend," Max crooned, "aren't you, old boy?"

"Ahh . . . ahhh . . . ah-*choo*!"

"Bless you, my dear," her husband said.

"Dust," the woman said quickly. "From the road."

"Of course," Max said. "You will wish to refresh yourselves after your journey. Mr. Balance, please show Mr. and Mrs. Browning to their bedchambers at once. I will have a tea tray sent up straightaway, and we shall speak again at luncheon. Perhaps you would like to tour the estate. Until then, please make yourselves at home. Yarrowdale Hall is yours to enjoy."

"Thank you, Mr. Yar," Mr. Browning said. "May I ask for one small favor?"

"Anything."

"Will you inform me before you accept another offer?"

"Of course." Max bowed and watched the Brownings climb the stairs behind Mr. Balance, taking note of the way Mrs. Browning ran her fingers appreciatively over the intricately carved oak balusters. He almost laughed out loud. So the bride's mother was eyeing the place! "Perfect," he told Malachi. "We shall have Yarrowdale sold before the happy couple says, 'I do.'"

CHAPTER ELEVEN

"It is perfectly hideous," Sophia said. The wedding gown was waiting there in a large box on the bed. "You open it, Emma. I fear that if I do it, the thing will leap out and attack me."

"It cannot be that bad."

"All those flounces and furbelows—it is far too ornate. I wanted something more simple, but Mother—"

"Oh, Sophia!" Emma cried as she pulled the pearl-encrusted creation free. Yards and yards of white silk spilled from the box. "Beautiful!" She held it up to her friend, admiring the effect. "You shall be the loveliest bride ever."

"Do you think so?" Sophia asked, wrinkling up her nose.

"Can you not imagine what you shall look like with this lovely train trailing behind you in the glasshouse? Oh, the white silk against that dark stone floor! The morning sun shining through the glass! The orange trees in full blossom!"

"Oh! Certainly! The trees! *If* my mother does not have them cut down because they might obscure the guests' view of the ostrich feathers in my hair or some such."

Emma ignored her friend's remark about her trees, knowing it to be an exaggeration. "Ostrich feathers? I thought you wanted a wreath of orange blossoms," she said, stroking Lady Moonbeam's fluffy back soothingly. The cat had hardly left Emma's side these past two weeks, and Emma supposed it was because of all the upheaval. She didn't mind. Truth to tell, she needed a little soothing herself, and it was calming to pet Moon.

"I did want a simple wreath of orange blossoms." Sophia sighed. "But that is too simple for Mother. She is out of control! Do you know she has ordered one thousand yellow roses? And a wagonload of huge yellow satin bows and swags to go with them. I have always dreamed of being wed in the glasshouse. I have admired its simplicity, its natural beauty, but now I fear the place won't be recognizable—or even visible under all that yellow rubbish. It is all too fancy, and she has invited too many people. The glasshouse will be obscured under a mountain of yellow ribbons and spectators. Oh, Emma, Arthur and I are both quiet, private people. We want to live very simply. We do not need—or want—all of this." She waved her hand vaguely in the air.

"All of this?" Emma asked.

Sophia frowned. "Mother discovered the advertisement in the *Post* as we drove here this morning. It is all she could talk about. I fear she wishes to buy Yarrowdale Hall for a wedding present. La, Emma, she will expect us to live here instead of in Cornwall, and she will be visiting us every fortnight! And . . . and—oh!—I *hate* the color yellow!" She buried her face in her hands. "What am I going to do?" she sobbed.

"There, there." Emma comforted Sophia as her tears subsided. As miserable as Sophia was, Emma was certain her friend would be even more miserable living in Cornwall. Sophia loved the social whirl of London. Emma suspected her desire to live in Cornwall had more to do with Sophia's desire to be rid of her stepmother's influence than with a desire for a "simple" life. "Sophia, doesn't your dear Arthur keep a small house in Town?"

"Yes . . ."

Emma smiled. "Has it occurred to you that, as a married woman and mistress of your own house, you can tell your butler that if certain people come to call you are not *at home*?"

Instantly, Sophia brightened.

"Now then," Emma said, handing Sophia a handkerchief. "I have an idea. Help me into your gown."

"Why?" Sophia sniffled.

"You have never seen anyone but yourself in it. If you see it on me, you will know it isn't as terrible as you think. You will even be able to see the back of it. The veil and train are particularly lovely, but if you still do not like all the furbelows, there is a wonderful tailor in the village, who would be only too happy to remove them."

"Remove them?" Sophia cried. "But Mother would—"

"Whose wedding is this?" Emma asked. "Hers?"

Sophia bit her lip.

"It is *your* wedding gown. You are almost a married woman. It is time you started to act like it."

Sophia reacted as though she'd been struck, but after a moment, her face smoothed into a placid, relaxed resolve. "You are right. Thank you." She hugged Emma. "Go on, then," she urged. "Please do try on the gown!"

As Max strode around the corner and into the gallery a few minutes later, he froze. Two young ladies, one tall and dark and one small and blond stood in front of the large mirror there, their backs to him. Though he knew instantly who they must be, he shook his head in disbelief. Miss Browning looked the same as she had only a scant hour before, but Emmaline . . .

"Beautiful," he said without thinking. "Stunning."

At the sound of his voice, Miss Browning turned around. "Do you think it so, Mr. Yar?"

"Indeed," Max said, finding it interesting that Emmaline *hadn't* turned. And was that a blush he saw infusing her nape with a delicate pink?

It was, and Sophia Browning had noticed, too, for her large brown eyes grew even larger, and she looked from Emmaline to Max and back several times, the silence stretching awkwardly, before speaking. "I . . . just remembered something I forgot," she said. "But of course you know I forgot it, since one cannot remember a thing unless one forgets it first, can one?" She laughed nervously. "It is in my . . . elsewhere."

Emma tried not to roll her eyes uncharitably skyward and failed miserably. Sophia was her dearest friend, and she meant well. How was she to know that Emma didn't wish to be left alone with the man she'd almost kissed like a strumpet at twilight only the day before? She'd probably looked ridiculous to him, with her face up and her eyes all moony and her lips all puckered. Well, she hadn't looked quite that obvious, she conceded—but, man that he was, he'd probably been able to tell she was willing enough—and he'd probably been appalled, and now here she was in his house dressed in a blasted wedding gown! Where was a cataclysmic volcanic eruption when one needed it?

"Whatever it is," Emma told Sophia, fervently wishing the Earth would open up and swallow her, "I am sure we do not need it. We have your gown, your veil, your fan, your reticule, and your slippers—even your flowers." She pointed to the wreath and nosegay of orange blossoms that lay on a table nearby. Had she said "your" enough to make it clear to Maximillian that she wasn't trying to entrap him? Or entice him? Or something equally disastrous?

Emma turned just enough for a quick glance at Maximillian. It was a mistake, for then she couldn't look away. Where she'd expected amusement or sardonic irony or horror, she found none. Instead, the man was staring at her with what appeared to be unabashed masculine fascination. She told herself that was rubbish. She was just telling herself another story—but she still couldn't look away. Their eyes met and held.

Sophia fidgeted with her sleeve. "Yes . . . well, I shall return in a—"

Emmaline blinked. "No!"

"—moment."

"Sophia, you mustn't go!"

"Yes, yes . . . I . . . hear my mother calling! Yes, Mama!"

And with a raised eyebrow and a not-very-covert nod of the head in Maximillian's direction, Miss Browning fled the gallery.

Emma shivered, though the breeze wafting through the open house was warm. *Fool!* she admonished herself. Mr. Yar didn't want to kiss her. All he wanted from her was her help in selling the estate. He was pleasant enough, of course, but that did not mean he wanted to . . . to . . . to have an *adventure* with her! She suppressed a sigh as he approached, sat in a nearby chair, and regarded her lazily.

"Catching robbers, Emmaline? Hiding an eloping earl and his would-be bride? Saving children from a flood?"

Emma blinked. "Trying on Sophia's wedding gown. For her," she added. "So she can see how it looks."

He didn't give the gown another glance. Emma might as well have been wearing her tattiest morning dress. "Why did you not tell me about the adventures you have had here in Yarrowdale?" He asked

"Adventures?" Emma shook her head. "I call them misfortunes. Any sane person would. An adventure is trekking through a jungle on an elephant or riding a camel over a desert. Adventure is sailing through a hurricane or meeting Pygmies in the wilds of Who-Knows-Where."

"Hurricanes can sink ships—misfortune enough—and I have heard some Pygmies like to have foreign guests. In their soup pots," he added. "The line between misfortune and adventure is frightfully thin indeed, Emmaline."

"Perhaps, but I do not see any jungles or elephants here in England. Adventure, Mr. Yar, is out there."

"Adventure is everywhere. Life is everywhere, Emmaline! You just have to open your eyes to see it. Your robbers and your flood were adventures! And helping those two people who were so desperately in love! Glorious!"

"All of those things happened in my own backyard."

"Adventure always happens in *someone's* yard."

"Yes, but I could wait the rest of my life before anything like those things you've mentioned ever happens again."

"Sometimes, Emmaline, one has to make one's own adventures. *Carpe diem*." Suddenly, he stilled, tilted his head, and gave her a wicked grin.

"What?" she asked warily.

Without another word, he stood, took her hand, and pulled her along the gallery and out into the hall, the wedding gown's long, white train following them.

"Where are we going?" Emma cried.

"Shh!" He stopped, looked up and down the empty hall, and opened the door to a little-used parlor. Drawing her inside, he swished the train out of the way, closed the door soundlessly, and turned with a triumphant expression.

"What are you doing?"

"Seizing the day, Emmaline, seizing the day."

And then, before she could say another word, he drew her into his arms and kissed her!

Suddenly, it was as though Emma were someone else entirely. There was no awkwardness, no ineptitude. She wound her arms around Maximillian Yar and kissed him back with all the expertise of a strumpet. Now, *this*—this was glorious!

The kiss went on and on, and when his questing hand strayed a little beyond what was strictly proper, she made no protest. In truth, she matched his movements, and did a little questing of her own, winding one hand into his silky black hair and the other over his—

"Emmaline!"

Emma couldn't tell if his voice was a growl or a groan, but she meant to find out. With a half smile and a deliberately cocked eyebrow, she took a step closer. "*Carpe diem*."

CHAPTER TWELVE

Pulling back, Max raked his fingers through his hair and, forcing himself to turn away from her, he walked to the door.

From behind him, Emma's voice came to him on a whisper. "What have I done?"

He stopped and closed his eyes. "Nothing I did not want you to do, Emmaline," he said over his shoulder, "but I . . . I have to leave—now. Now, before I do something we will both regret."

He left without another word, without even looking her in the eye, feeling like a coward, a dastard, a . . . a man in love.

Closing the door behind him, he strode down the hall as though pursued. A man in love? Where had that absurd thought come from? What the hell was wrong with him? He was no more in love with Emmaline Rose than a cat with a dog. What he was was in lust. And she was a beautiful, willing, intelligent woman, but here he was running down the hall like a striped ass. Seize the day indeed! He wasn't heeding his own advice.

Why not?

What was happening to him?

From the day he'd turned fourteen, Max had had at least one girl waiting for him in every port! Emmaline Rose was just another port of call. She was no different than the others, not really. He'd got to know her more than he had the others, that was all. He certainly wasn't in love with her! No. And when he left, he'd hardly be able to remember her face, much less her name.

An image of her face a moment before he'd kissed her flashed into his mind, and he knew it for a lie. She'd been trusting, eager. There was no way he could ever forget her.

But he was definitely not forming a *tendre* for her. No. She was pleasant enough, intelligent, and kind, and she had a pretty face, but it wasn't as though he'd miss her when they parted. . . .

An image of her standing in the gallery in that deuced wedding gown and veil assailed him. Small, pale, and utterly beautiful. A second image flashed into his mind, an image of himself, standing beside Emmaline in the glasshouse, pledging his undying love. . . .

Ha!

Even if he were willing to settle in one place this young— which he wasn't—the blasted woman was set on traveling, on being independent, free. He understood that, didn't he? That's what he wanted, too. He didn't want to be lashed down, trapped in some dreary English backwater, any more than she did.

Max surged outside into the sunshine and took a deep breath. Shaking off the image of Emmaline in a wedding gown, he made for the stables, but his eyes strayed over the valley and down toward the village. Yarrowdale wasn't dreary, his conscience defended. It was a cheerful little place with decent, hardworking people. People with frank words and ready smiles, as prone to spout wisdom as they were a jest. It was unfair to call Yarrowdale dreary. As Max waited for a horse to be saddled, he thought of Midsummer Night. The celebration had been quite merry indeed. Almost wild. Definitely not dreary.

The villagers had called him "squire." Squire Yar, by the devil!

A sudden idea seized Max. What if he and Emmaline traveled together? They could stay here for now, build funds, travel for a time and return home to Yarrowdale together.

Home? Together? Max scoffed.

The whole world was his home. And if he traveled with Emmaline, they wouldn't be able to keep their relationship anchored. Oh, no, not with the way she'd kissed him back. Emmaline approached kissing as she did everything else—nothing halfway.

And he couldn't give her the other half—not without marrying the miserable chit! And marriage would lead to children . . . who deuced devilish well did not belong on a ship. Max knew that from experience.

"Wait!" he told the groom. "Have we a saddle for that one?" Max pointed to a great black roan stallion in the corner stall, who was watching him with the whites of his intelligent eyes showing.

"That one, sir? He's one of the new mounts. A wee tad skittish still. Untried but for the ring at Tattersall's, truth to tell, and we been too busy to gentle 'im down. Best take this 'un, sir. I'll tell the stablemaster to gentle the roan right quick."

"No need," Max said. "I will be leaving Yarrowdale before long."

"Yes, sir," the groom said with a downward twitch of his mouth. "It's a shame, if you don't mind me saying so, sir. You're well liked, here, and it'll be odd not having a Squire Yar up to the Hall.

Squire Yar.

"The roan, if you please." A hard ride on an untried stallion was just what Max needed.

A few minutes later, he and the roan thundered across the stable yard and over a stone fence. What else could he do? He had demons to flee, demons more fearsome than the wildest stallion.

From a windowsill high above, the cats watched in dismay. They'd been in the gallery when the humans kissed. They'd watched Maximillian leave, watched Emmaline run from the room, crying, and now Maximillian was gone.

"This is terrible!" Moon moaned.

"Yes." Malachi twitched his tail. "We are running out of time."

"I caught that wretched bird woman"—for so the cats called Mrs. Browning, who always wore a profusion of ostrich feathers on whatever headdress she chose—"in the morning room, measuring the window!"

"Why?"

"She intends to have it bricked up! She says she cannot abide the morning light!"

"But she does not awaken before noon!"

"Oh, Malachi, what are we going to do? If Maximillian and Emmaline sell Yarrowdale Hall, you and I will have to part!"

"Or part with them."

"We have to do something." Moon's tail lashed furiously.

"But we have had no opportunity to—"

At that moment, opportunity arrived in the form of one old man, whose carriage rolled into the stable yard below. "Oh, no, Sir Basil!" Moon wailed.

"Who is that?"

"Who are *they,* more like," Moon said, her back arching and her tail growing puffy as seven wiggling bitches spilled from the carriage in a barking, yapping, whining mass of canine chaos. "Sir Basil's 'ladies,'" Moon growled. "Named for the patronesses of Almack's. A more haughty pack of impudent mongrels you will never find. Sir Basil and Squire Yar the elder were great friends. The ladies have chased me more times than I can count."

Suddenly, Malachi rolled onto his back and batted at Moon's tail.

"This is no time for play!" she growled.

"Indeed it is!" Malachi cat-laughed. "For you've just given me the most delicious idea. Better than a warm hearth. Better than fat mice. Better than cream!" He leapt from the windowsill and waited for Moon to follow. "Come down, my beloved! We have a plan to concoct."

CHAPTER THIRTEEN

Mrs. Trews knocked on the door of Emma's private salon and entered without waiting for a reply. "We can't hold dinner much longer, miss. The syllabub has already lost its froth, and the poached eels are now stewed eels. Much longer, and the dinner rolls will be cannonballs."

Emma sighed. "Just a few more minutes. He knows what time the meal was to be served. I am sure he will be home soon."

She gave Emma an understanding pat. "I'm that worried for him, too, miss. Everyone is. The menfolk are out in the stable yard organizing a search, should it be needed. You just give the word."

Emma nodded, and the housekeeper left. With the two cats curled sound asleep on her lap, Emma forced herself to sit still, though her feet wanted to pace the floor. Maximillian had ridden out on an untried stallion six hours ago. Outside, the sky was beginning to darken. The mantel clock chimed half past eight and then ticked loudly on, boring into Emma's dwindling reserve of calm. What if he'd been thrown and broken a leg or hit his head or—

She sobbed. What if he were dead?

It was her fault. If she hadn't kissed him like some Drury Lane Aphrodite, he wouldn't have fled as though his boots were on fire.

Burying her face in her hands, Emma gave in to tears, barely registering the cats' gentle protests, the re-entry and subsequent hasty, silent exit of the housekeeper, the barking of Sir Basil's dogs, the crunching of gravel on the drive, the soft click of the front door lock, the sound of heavy footsteps coming down the hall.

"Good evening, Emmaline."

Emma's head snapped up. There he stood, the answer to her prayers. "Maximillian!" Pushing the cats from her lap none too gently, she jumped up and flew toward him. He was muddy, and she'd known better-smelling pigs, but she didn't care. "You're home! You're home!" Somehow, she stopped short of careening into him for a long, crushing hug. Somehow, decorum won over relief and happiness and . . . and *love*?

She froze, eyes and fingers wide. Dear God, had she fallen in love with Maximillian Yar? Backing up, she shoved her quaking hands behind her back and said with an evenness she did not feel, "I am so glad you have decided to return home."

Seemingly oblivious to her distress, he busied himself with removing his gloves and coat. He was a perceptive and intelligent man, awake on all suits. Why would he ignore her feelings, so?

"Home, Emmaline? Yarrowdale is not my home, and soon it shall not be yours, either." Turning, he spied the half-finished snifter of amber liquid on the table at Emma's side. "Brandy, Emmaline?" He peered closely at her face. "And you have been crying. I say, is something bothering you? Did something dreadful happen?"

All at once, Emma's anxiety evaporated like a fog at midday, only to be replaced by a white-hot anger. "Yes. Something dreadful did happen—you came back."

"Well, of course I came back. What else could I do? Did you expect that I would simply kiss you and flee, never to return and—"

"I care not one whit about that silly kiss, you buffleheaded jinglebrains!" she cried, though she cared very much indeed.

"Then why are you shouting?"

"I am not shouting!" she shouted. "I am merely expressing

my displeasure that you are late for dinner. You are the host, for pity's sake! It is most improper—to say nothing of imprudent. Do you not want to sell the estate?"

"Who said anything about not selling?"

"If you wish to make a good impression, ruining dinner is not the way to begin."

"You held dinner for me?" Unaccountably, Maximillian smiled.

Over on the sofa, the cats quivered with hope. "Look at them!" Malachi licked his paw. "I'll wager my last ball—"

"Malachi!"

"Uh . . . *fur*ball! I'll wager my last *fur* ball that they will do that mouth thing again."

Moon sighed happily. "And then they will probably mate at last!"

But things did not progress as the cats hoped, alas.

"How dare you grin?" Emmaline cried.

"You were worried."

"You are deuced right, I was worried!"

"You are relieved."

"I am annoyed," she shot back.

"No, you aren't." He laughed. "What you are is cross as crabs. Mad as hops. Vexed, testy, and snappish!" He laughed again.

"Ohhh . . . !" Emmaline whirled around and stomped to the door. "And what *you* are is a . . . a *man*!" she cried, quitting the room and slamming the door behind her.

Seconds later, Max heard the butler ringing the dinner chimes. The hellcat was going to dinner without him! Taking up Emmaline's brandy snifter, he swallowed the contents in one gulp, surprised to find that it wasn't brandy at all. She'd been drinking whiskey. Smooth, burning, arse-kicking whiskey!

Sitting in her spot on the couch, Max absently stroked the cats and tried to dredge up some irritation with Emmaline, but instead of finding himself in high dudgeon, he found himself feeling . . . well, *pleased*!

What the devil?

And why had he laughed?

Because you could not help it, old boy, his mind answered. *Because you quite liked the idea that she was waiting up for you, worried that you might not come home.*

Quitting the salon, he made for his bedchamber, rang for cold water, and washed hastily. He didn't want to miss dinner. He shouldn't have laughed at her. He hadn't meant to be gone so long, but, by Jove, he just wasn't used to having to contort his own desires to match others' schedules. No one ever waited for him to come home. No one ever worried about him.

Emmaline was the first.

He started to ask himself what right she had to be angry with him, but pulled himself up short. Great galleons! He knew exactly why she was angry. Wouldn't he feel the same way if *she* disappeared for an entire afternoon? She'd been worried about him because she cared for him.

A sudden thought occurred to Max: Was that all she felt? Was it possible that Emmaline was falling in love?

Max frowned. He didn't want to be the object of a sad memory in Emmaline's life. He was a rolling stone and probably always would be. He certainly wasn't ready to settle down yet, and even if he were, he couldn't—wouldn't!—become the stone that anchored her, pulled her down, trapped her, stole her dreams.

"Watch yourself, lad." He addressed Malachi, who was lounging on the windowsill with Emmaline's cat. "Females are trouble—begging your pardon, madam!" he told Lady Moonbeam. He considered the delicate white creature before him. So like Emmaline. Pale and small—deceptively so, for she meant big trouble. "I shouldn't have kissed your mistress," he said, heading for the door. "It won't happen again." He sighed and left the door ajar behind him so the cats could depart at their leisure.

"A kiss!" Moon exclaimed. "Yes, that is what they call it!" Malachi nuzzled her shoulder. "Beloved, I do not wish to frighten you, but he means what he says. He will not kiss her again."

"Oh? Was he not merely clawing at the wind?"

"No. I recognize that tone of voice, and he was not jesting. It is time to chase our plan down the mouse hole."

Moon leapt down from the sill. "I am ready."

"Are you certain you can handle all seven of them?"

"I am frightened," Moon admitted, "but I will do what must be done."

Malachi bumped his head lovingly down the length of her, perfuming her with the scent of affection and worshipful possession. "When this is over, I shall climb to the very top of Yarrowdale Hall and sing a long, loud song of my brave Lady Moonbeam."

Moon stilled suddenly. "Dearest," she said, "you have just given me the most splendid idea. Two of them, in fact. Additions to our plan. Come, I shall tell you about them on the way to the dining room."

Emma was resolved to stay angry with him. Everything would be so much easier that way. They'd sell the Hall and the glasshouse, move on, and never see or think of each other again.

She stifled a laugh, garnering curious glances from several of the guests seated at the dining table, before clearing her throat and fixing her gaze firmly on her plate. Creamed onions had never looked more appealing. The only way they could look more appealing was if the entire plate of them were placed squarely on top of Maximillian Yar's overly masculine head. Another giggle tried to bubble forth, but she tamed the hysterical beast and cut an onion in half for revenge.

Oh, she was mad, a lunatic, a Bedlamite.

I am in love, that is what.

A sigh escaped her, earning her more covert glances, but Emmaline didn't care. Let them look. They couldn't know her feelings for Maximillian. She would conceal them, even from him—especially from him!—and make a tidy end to what had become a horrible mull. How could she have allowed herself to fall in love with someone so unsuitable?

They were destined along different paths, just as Miss Thatcher and the elder Squire Yar had been. But it did not signify. He was not the only fish in the sea. She was going to see the world as Miss Thatcher had done. Elephants and their mahouts, volcanoes and those who worshiped them, fiords and the descendants of Vikings. It was her dream, her destiny. She'd repaid the village for their kindness tenfold. She had every right to leave them. And if she didn't do it now, before the Winter Solstice, she feared she never would.

All she had to do was keep *him* at arm's length, avoid looking him in the eye, and conclude their business transaction as quickly as possible. Then they *would* stay angry with one another, sell the Hall and the glasshouse, move on, and never see or think of each other again.

Simple!

And then, at that moment, Maximillian stepped into the dining room, and Emmaline knew nothing would ever be simple again. Their gazes met, and an apology flowed soundlessly between them.

She was lost.

Relief and alarm, uncertainty and love tumbled inside her, but Emmaline had no time to sort out her emotions, for at that moment, Lady Moonbeam appeared in the doorway.

"Meow!"

Instantly, Sir Basil's ladies, who were lounging variously under and around the dining table, whirled into a yapping, yelping, growling mass of canine wrath and bolted for the doorway.

"No!" Emma and Maximillian shouted simultaneously and launched themselves to block the pack, to no avail. The dogs leapt over, wiggled through, or pushed past them, and Moon darted down the hall, the dogs a split second behind her. Maximillian ran after them, leaving Emma sprawled on the floor, her skirts immodestly higher than they should be.

"I say!" Sir Basil exclaimed.

"They will kill her, Max!" Emma cried. "Run!"

"Max?" Mrs. Browning sniffed.

Emma didn't have time to let fly with the insult that sprang to her lips before Moon, having escaped her pursuers, doubled back, bounding into the dining hall and sailing over Emma in a blur of white. Moon flew across the table lengthwise as though her tail were on fire, and the entire pack pursued her.

Right across the table.

Furry paws landed in plates, platters, and tureens. Tails sent goblets flying. Chairs clattered to the floor as the guests dodged the melee. Syllabub and creamed onions flew everywhere.

Lady Moonbeam, meanwhile, leapt from the far corner of the table and from there to Prince Frederick's shoulder and onto the wide, marble windowsill. As the night was fine with warm weather and no draft, the windows had been left open, and Moon made use of the portal to escape.

Emmaline wished she could follow her.

Mrs. Cowper, the little white poodle mix, had had a hard time scrambling onto the table, and when she did, she decided that baked ham was much better than the prospect of too-rare cat. She was happily gnawing on the large ham bone, while Mrs. Drummund-Burrell, a wolfhound, had clearly determined that one of the guests was concealing her prey. She was running up and down the table, peering into laps, snuffling loudly, and growling until one of her large, black feet landed on the edge of the blackberry tart, flipping it into the air and landing it squarely on the bridegroom's lap.

A feminine giggle rent the air.

"Sophia!" Mrs. Browning scolded. "This is not funny! It is—"

Thwack! An apple tart followed its confectionery sister,

Arthur ducked, and the tart neatly plastered itself just above Mrs. Browning's plump décolletage.

Everyone froze except Sir Basil, who opined, "Well, at least there is no elephant here, trying to drink everyone's syllabub," and everyone burst out laughing at the old man's absurd statement.

Maximillian came into the room as everyone was standing up and dashing at their ruined clothing. "Yarrowdale Hall is a happy place where people are accustomed to turning wizened apples into applesauce," he said. "And so it shall be tonight! After we have all refreshed ourselves, we shall serve an early supper on the garden terrace *à la flambeaux* and dance until the moon is high in the sky."

"A splendid idea!" The Duke of Bedford exclaimed. "Applesauce, indeed. I was wondering how I could possibly make a decision without seeing the place turned out at night."

"Are you thinking of acquiring Yarrowdale Hall, Your Grace?" Mr. Browning asked.

"It is situated nicely between London and one of my northern estates," the duke said. "And," he added with a laugh, "I presume Mr. Yar and Miss Rose will be taking their feline companions with them when they leave."

Apart from Mrs. Browning, whose eyes flashed her annoyance, the guests joined the duke in laughter. Everyone melted away to their chambers, leaving Emma alone with Maximillian once more.

"Well," Max said.

"Well," Emma echoed.

"Good news about the duke."

"Yes."

"And did you see Mrs. Browning's expression when he announced he was interested in buying?" Max asked.

"She was unhappy."

"The price just doubled, for she is stubborn and proud, and he is rich as Croesus."

"Yes. Well, I shall speak to the servants about supper on the terrace. The poor things. This"—she gestured about her—"is a terrible mull for them to clear."

"A mull attributable to cats and dogs, rather than to some lack in the house, grounds, or staff, thank goodness."

"Indeed," Emma agreed. "Nothing to discourage bidders."

"Speaking of whom," Max said, dabbing at a blob of onion clinging to his waistcoat, "I should hurry. A proper host never leaves his guests unaccompanied, I hear. I should be the first to reappear downstairs."

Emmaline recognized his words for what they were: an apology.

"Thank you, Maximillian."

"I rather preferred it when you called me Max," he said on a bow and quit the room.

Outside, in the garden, Moon and Malachi met under a rhododendron bush. "Were you successful?" Moon asked.

"I was," Malachi said. "A liberal dousing, all over his cravats. She is going to be terribly angry."

"Let us hope so," Moon said. "Did you hear what Max said? The chase didn't discourage the duke or that bird woman."

"This next horrible scene might. And if it does not, then we have other options."

Moon's tail beat against the ground. "It feels so . . . so wrong to do such things!"

"It is for their own good, beloved."

"I know." Moon sighed. "But I wish humans were as sensible as cats!"

CHAPTER FOURTEEN

Out on the terrace, the guests shifted nervously in their chairs and pretended not to notice the speaking looks, glares, and impassioned pledges of innocence that were silently passing between the bride-to-be, her fiancé, the bride's stepmother, and a certain lady seated on the periphery, a young widow known in White's and Brooks's as The Butterfly, for her tendency to gaily flit from one man to another and for her distinctive carnation perfume. Every London blood knew she was *vastly* beautiful, *frightfully* elegant, *devilishly* rich, and *terribly* discreet. And she was welcome in the highest of circles, which was why she was at Yarrowdale Hall that night, her signature scent wafting delicately around her corner of the terrace.

Unfortunately, it was also wafting in the groom's corner of the terrace—and none too delicately. It seemed as if the poor man had bathed in it.

Fortunately, the bride was more sensible than her mother. As one of the resident cats sauntered past her table, Sophia noticed that the enormous orange beast smelled faintly of carnations, and she realized what must have happened. Immediately, she sent a look of apology to her dearest Arthur, sitting miserably across the candlelit table. They were deeply in love. How could she have thought, even for a moment, that he had been unfaithful? A loving glance from her dear Arthur that she had been forgiven unconditionally, and the rift between them was healed.

Too bad it could not be healed for her stepmother, who was as allergic to carnations as she was to cats. The poor woman was sneezing quite violently.

Malachi walked to the middle of the terrace and into the large space that had been kept clear for impromptu musical performances during and after dinner. Sitting down in a pool of light from the dozen flambeaux, he blinked once, twice.

"Oh, Malachi," Moon meowed softly from the terrace wall. "Are you sure this is necessary? It is so . . . so *ungentlemanly*."

"Yes, beloved. I must do what must be done. Look away."

But Moon bravely watched—along with everyone else on the terrace—as Malachi, to the tune of a gentle Bach concerto, loudly brought up an enormous hair ball and deposited it prominently on the shiny marble floor in the center of the terrace and then lay down to wash himself. Down there.

It was a performance not to be forgotten.

Supper was over soon after—a little sooner than it should have been—and everyone retired to the ballroom for a change of scenery and some dancing. By the time the evening was over, it was quite late, and everyone, guests and servants, were happy to retire for the night.

But Malachi and Moon were just getting started.

The bell ropes in Yarrowdale Hall were a fairly new addition, having been installed for the elder Squire Yar. Confined to a wheeled chair for the last year of his life, he'd had the ropes hung quite low, and they had been installed in places that might have seemed odd in other houses: at the foot and head of each staircase, at the front door, out on the terrace, and in long hallways, as well as in all of the first-floor public rooms and in the bedchambers.

It was a great convenience, and it had had the added benefit of entertaining Lady Moonbeam, who had delighted in batting at the ropes' long, red tassels. Squire Yar had been fond of the cats.

He would perhaps have been less fond of them this night, however, for his dear little Moon and her new beau spent what was left of the night, creeping from room to room, pulling at the ropes and dashing off to hide before the servants saw them. The bells rang at odd intervals all night in the garret rooms, and none of the staff slept.

In the servants' hall the next morning, some blamed the mischief on one or another of the guests, while others blamed the ghost of the old squire, who, they claimed, was registering his displeasure that his heir was selling the Hall. Privately, a few of the servants decided to retaliate covertly against the guests they deemed responsible, while others were just plain terrified, and everyone was weary and cross.

The day began with spilt breakfast trays, tepid bathwater, and wrinkled cravats, and went downhill from there, and Yarrowdale Hall gained an indelible reputation among the *ton* as having an inept, aloof, and recalcitrant staff.

Things were coming along splendidly. At least from the cats' perspective.

Mrs. Browning, on the other hand, looked on the verge of an apoplexy all morning. Most of the servants had laid blame for the bell-ringing squarely at her feet. A less-than-perfect wedding would be a small price to pay in order to discourage the Duke of Bedford from bidding on Yarrowdale Hall, they reasoned. The old hag would probably discharge all of the servants and start fresh, whether they were to blame or not, went the whispers.

The angst and ire among the servants were running high, and Maximillian and Emmaline spent the morning attempting to cool tempers and smooth ruffles—both the servants' and the guests'. It was exhausting, and they were both ready for a little solitude, a little peace.

They got neither.

CHAPTER FIFTEEN

Max looked out over the valley from the rocky knoll where he'd followed Emma what seemed like weeks ago. He loved the summer. Especially in Yarrowdale.

The sun peeked out from behind a cloud, limning the patch-work valley below in rich, golden light. In spite of his fear of heights, he loved high places such as the knoll. It felt anonymous, alone. Good, and yet not good.

He sighed. He did not understand himself.

Yarrowdale wasn't the most beautiful place he'd seen. It didn't even come close to some of the wonders he'd witnessed—towering blue mountains, thundering white waterfalls, crystalline seas filled with brilliantly colored fish flitting here and there, hypnotizing him with their beauty.

"Will you miss it?" Emmaline's soft voice came from behind.

More than any other place I have ever been. "A little," he said. "Are you part tigress? I did not hear you approach," he said.

She sat down companionably beside him.

"I have been thinking of planting roses along that wall, just over there, beside the ice house." She pointed.

"That will be nice."

"It would have been."

The seconds stretched on, and they watched the hawks—a pair of them, this time—soaring over the valley. "What is it like to see a place through a change of seasons?" Max asked suddenly.

She turned to him, her face a mask of disbelief. "Have you never lived in one place for a whole year?"

He shook his head. "Never."

"How very . . . sad." She looked down at her hands. "Listen, I . . . I behaved badly last night and I—"

"You were not the only one."

"Will you close your mouth and let me apologize?" She laughed.

"There is no need. It was nice to have someone worry about me like that." *And frightening.* "I am sorry I handled it so badly."

"My pleasure."

"Liar." Max leaned back as she laughed again. "You should stay in Yarrowdale, Emmaline. Your heart is here."

"If I do not leave now, I never will."

"Why must you sell?"

"If I do not sell, I shall come home," she said simply. "I am not as strong as Miss Thatcher was. I will not find what she found."

"What did she find, Emmaline? What are you searching for?"

Emmaline stood up. "This is your home, too," she said simply. "Why will you not stay? You already know what the rest of the world is like. You don't have any idea what it's like to stay in one place."

Max was saved from forming a reply by the appearance of a coach on the horizon. In a moment, it was apparent that there were more than one. They watched until the number grew to a dozen. And all of them were rolling toward Yarrowdale Hall.

"We had better get down there," Emmaline said.

The wagons and coaches made it to the Hall before Emma and Maximillian did. All twelve wagons were carefully covered in canvas and oilcloth save one—which was honking.

"Swans?" Maximillian wondered.

"Seventeen of them." Sophia sniffled, coming toward them across the lawn. "Seventeen! Oh, Emmaline!" she wailed. "Everything is ruined!"

"There, there," Emmaline soothed, throwing an alarmed look at Maximillian. "What is wrong, dearest? What is in all those wagons?"

" 'Surprises.' " Sophia sobbed. "From Mother. A thousand yellow roses, a thousand yellow swags, a thousand beeswax candles, a twenty-piece orchestra, and five hundred fireworks. Oh, Emmaline! It is too much. Too much! Arthur and I wanted a simple wedding, not a circus!"

There was nothing Emma could say. Sophia was right. It *was* too much. And there was nothing Emma could do about it. It was up to Sophia to rein in Mrs. Browning. "She is *your* stepmother," Emma said at last, hugging her friend. "And it is *your* wedding."

That evening, Sophia took to her bed, claiming a megrim. Emma worried about her excessively until Arthur came to her in the parlor after supper.

"Do not worry," he whispered. "Sophia and I spoke at length just before supper. She is fine, and everything will be made right." Briefly, he pressed her hand and looked intently into her eyes. "I promise." Giving a nervous glance at Mr. and Mrs. Browning, Arthur moved off, leaving Emmaline wondering what his odd behavior meant, but she had no time to contemplate the matter, for a knot of people was forming around the Brownings, who were engaged in what appeared to be a spirited discussion with the Duke of Bedford and Maximillian. Emma moved to investigate.

"Ninety thousand," the duke said calmly.

"One hundred," Mr. Browning said.

They were both looking from each other to Maximillian. Mrs. Browning looked as though she might burst at any moment.

"One hundred and fifty," Bedford offered. The gathering crowd gave an awed murmur.

The seconds ticked by. Mr. Browning bit his lip.

"Two hundred thousand!" Mrs. Browning erupted. "I shall pledge my own fortune."

The duke bowed stiffly and withdrew from the circle, and the crowd melted away, leaving Maximillian and Emma alone with the Brownings.

"I shall have my solicitor draw up the documents," Mr. Browning said. "Come, my dear. Let us waltz."

"With pleasure, Mr. Browning," she trilled, her skin florid with triumph.

Maximillian watched them walk away. "A little overconfident, is she not?" he said softly, so that Emma was the only one who could hear him.

"What do you mean?"

"I did not yet accept her offer."

"It is an outrageously high price. You would be mad not to accept it."

"Mmm . . . you are right, of course." He stared after the Brownings for a moment, appearing lost in thought, and then he suddenly offered Emmaline his arm. "Would you care to dance? I am quite a good dancer."

"I am not."

They laughed then, a brittle sound, it seemed to them both, and they danced twice that night, including the Sir Roger de Coverley, a merry dance indeed, but their hearts were not in it. When the night was over, they each went to their beds gratefully and fell into a fitful sleep, both dreaming of cats. Dozens and dozens of cats.

CHAPTER SIXTEEN

"Mornin' Sir," Mrs. Trews called to Max as he walked down the stairs the next morning. "Don't worry, the mistress is already up, trying to shoo them off."

"Them?"

"Why the cats, sir! Didn't you hear them last night?"

"Cats?" Max exclaimed. "Where is she?"

"Somewhere outside," the housekeeper said, waving her hand.

Max surged outside. The day had dawned sunny and dry. A warm breeze blew in from the north, bringing just a hint of a crisp chill. It was perfect weather for the wedding tomorrow. It was also, Max realized before he'd got halfway around the Hall, perfect weather for cats.

They were all over the place.

The most battered-looking assemblage of toms he'd ever seen skulked about the grounds, stiff-legged and hissing. He'd counted thirty of them before he reached the glasshouse, where Emma was writing a message to one of the local gentry, asking for the use of his pack of hunting dogs for the morning.

"Isn't that a little severe?" Max asked.

"What else can I do?" Emma shrugged. "I can't think of another way to discourage them, and Mrs. Browning is in a perpetual state of near swoon." She gestured to the roof of the glasshouse, where Lady Moonbeam was curled up, sleeping in the sunshine. "She was up on the roof of the glasshouse all night, calling out to them. Singing to them."

"Singing?"

"Lovelorn," she said.

"I thought she was too old!"

"I did too." Emmaline buried her face in her hands. "I cannot believe it."

Maximillian looked up at the roof of the glasshouse. "Perhaps Moon cannot, either. She probably did not know the response she would have. But she is a wise old girl. I wager she knows not to come down with all of these toms about." He regarded Moon a moment. "Finish your letter. I shall return."

After a few minutes, he did return, with a plate full of fish and a parade of meowing tom cats behind him.

"Playing the Pied Piper of Hamlin, are we?" Emma asked when he was safely inside the glasshouse *sans* cats. "What will you do when the fish runs out?"

"It isn't for them," Max said, laughing. "It is for her." He held the bowl up to Lady Moonbeam and called to her, to no avail.

"Here, let me have a go," Emma said, taking the bowl. Crooning to Moon, she coaxed the cat down from her high perch.

"I can't figure it out," Maximillian said.

"What?" she asked over her shoulder.

"Where is Malachi this morning? It isn't like him to be left out of the romantic fray."

Emma laughed. He isn't left out. He is guarding his interests. She pointed up at the oak tree, where Malachi lay, calmly keeping watch over the scene. "None of the other toms have dared climb that tree while he is there." She finished writing her letter and, sealing it, handed it to Maximillian. "Will you see this is delivered?"

He nodded. "I wonder how long the toms will stay around?"

"They will leave in two days."

"Two days? How can you be certain?"

"That is when Moon and I are leaving. I have booked passage on a ship bound for Greece. I wish to see the Parthenon. I did not think you would mind concluding my business for me, and I detest long good-byes."

"When have you ever said good-bye, Emmaline?" Maximillian held her gaze for a moment and then, without another word, quit the glasshouse. Emmaline lowered her forehead to the top of her writing desk and wept.

Maximillian and Emma both came to breakfast too late to avoid each other, but not late enough to avoid Mrs. Browning, who sailed into the room sneezing and filled her plate to the brim with kidneys and eggs.

"What is the meaning of this?" she demanded between fits, waving her fork.

"I believe," Max drawled, "that it is a fork, madam. I am unaware of any special meaning attached to the silver."

"The cats!" she cried. "I mean the cats. A-*choo*!"

"Ah, yes," Emmaline said. "The cats. I believe Malachi and Lady Moonbeam are out in the glasshouse. Is that not correct, Mr. Yar?"

"Not dose cats," Mrs. Browning said in a nasal voice. "De odders! I heard theb caterwaulink all night." Pulling her handkerchief from her reticule, she blew her nose none too discreetly and went on. "Disturbing creatures. I do not know how you stand them. I will be glad when you take them away. Especially that female," she said with a shiver. "She is the one responsible for gathering those demons outside, but that tom of yours, Mr. Yar, is no better. They both make me sneeze."

Maximillian folded his napkin and set it aside. "It is perhaps fortunate, then, that this will not be your home, Mrs. Browning, but your daughter's. She does not appear afflicted, as you are." Sparing a glance at Emma, laugh lines appeared about his eyes.

Catching on, Emma brightened. "Indeed, Mr. Yar. You are correct. Our cats' essence has permeated the whole place. You will have to persuade Sophia to visit you when you are in Town, Mrs. Browning, rather than coming here. The road down to London is quite fine after all, so she should be able to visit you quite often. You would be uncomfortable here. There are always cats around. Cats, cats, cats."

"Humph!" Mrs. Browning scowled. "We will have to find a way to exorcise them. Perhaps a pack of hunting dogs. Vicious ones."

Emma gave a guilty flinch and narrowing her eyes at Max-imillian, gave an almost imperceptible shake of her head. He understood her meaning. Standing, he walked to the fireplace, slipped her letter from his pocket, and tossed it into the flames.

Max was almost finished with a task he'd set for himself when Emmaline appeared. He was standing in the middle of Mrs. Browning's bedchamber. There was no escape, but Max was not contrite, and he watched with growing amusement as Emmaline soundlessly opened the door and carefully backed into the room before slowly closing the door once more.

"Hullo," he said.

She whirled around. "What are you doing here?" she asked.

"I could ask you the same."

"Why, I . . . I am checking to see that Mrs. Browning has fresh candles."

"And your portmanteau?" he asked, gesturing toward the bag she carried.

"Candles," she said. "Naturally. The servants are a little short-handed today. Mrs. Browning has them all downstairs hanging yellow ribbons and arranging yellow roses."

"I see," Max said, though he didn't believe her for a second. "Then why were you sneaking into the room?"

"I will tell you why!" an arch voice boomed from the doorway. "Because, like you, Mr. Yar, she has—has—ah-*choo!*—has heard about Sophia and that dreadful beast who stole her away.

"What?" Emmaline cried.

"Do not pretend ignorance of my ungrateful s—s—s—*achoo!*—stepdaughter's elopement. I found this on your counterpane," she said.

"You had no right to invade my bedchamber!"

"It is not *your* bedchamber. And neither is this one," she said, pointedly.

Emma snatched the letter from her hand and scanned it.

> *My dearest Emmaline,*
>
> *I know you will understand why I am doing this, and I know you will not worry, as Arthur told me he spoke to you last night. Thank you for everything. We will see you on our way south to Cornwall, and I remain*
>
> > *Your devoted friend,*
> > *Sophia, a Gretna Bride*

"I knew nothing of this," Emma said.

"Nor I," Max said.

"Liars *and* thieves," Mrs. Browning said. "I confess that I am not surprised."

"Thieves?" Max asked, not really caring what she thought, but needing to know in order to avoid any of her mischief-making later.

"Clearly, Mr. Yar, you and your . . . *houseguest,* here, were already aware of Sophia's elopement and realized that no—a-choo! a-choo!—no one of good breeding or deep pockets will buy Yarrowdale Hall now. Not after such a scandal has occurred on its grounds. And with your incompetent staff and infestation of dreadful cats"—the mere mention of the word brought on a spate of violent sneezing—"I daresay no one of *ill* breeding or *shallow* pockets will consider a purchase, either. But skulking about in our chambers will do you no good, for my jewelry is safely locked away."

At that moment, Malachi emerged from beneath her bed and, hopping up onto the counterpane, loudly announced his presence. "Meow!"

"Malachi?" Emmaline wondered aloud.

"Meow?" her portmanteau chimed in, and a fluff of white poked out of the top.

"Lady Moonbeam!" Max exchanged speaking glances with Emmaline.

"Humph!" Mrs. Browning scoffed. "How dare you bring those creatures into my chamber."

"As you pointed out," Maximillian said, "this is not your chamber."

"Humph!" Mrs. Browning huffed again. "I would not buy the place now for a tenth of what I have offered."

"Madam," Max said, smiling broadly, "I would not sell it to you for double."

Mrs. Browning's eyes filled with rage, and she turned on her heel. "My servants will come for our things. I hope you have enjoyed your taste of the *ton,* Mr. Yar, for it will undoubtedly be your last."

"One can hope," Max drawled.

Her footsteps were still echoing down the hall when Max and Emmaline turned to each other, words and laughter tumbling from their mouths.

"Why is Lady Moonbeam in that bag?"

"What are you doing here with Malachi?"

In answer, Maximillian pulled from his watch pocket a large sheaf of fresh catnip. "I rubbed it onto the counterpane," he admitted, "and Malachi did the rest."

Emmaline raised one delicate blond eyebrow. "We were targeting her gowns."

Two seconds passed before they both dissolved into laughter. Emmaline placed the portmanteau on the bed and sat down, clutching her stomach, while Max sat heavily near the fireplace, his eyes dancing. But soon their laughter subsided, and their grins shaped into worry lines.

"I should have asked you," Emmaline said. "It was wrong to take action without you."

Max waved his hand dismissively. "We are both guilty of that transgression. I should have asked you."

"But you are the master of Yarrowdale Hall!"

"And you are the mistress of the glasshouse," Max said. "I refuse to share the guilt unequally."

Emmaline smiled. "Very well." She looked down at her hands. "Thank you."

"And," Maximillian said, as though she had not spoken, "I will forgive your share of the guilt if you will but answer me one question." Standing, he came to the bed and, pulling Emmaline to her feet, placed his fingers under her chin and drew her gaze to his.

"Yes?"

"Why did you do it?"

"Because, I—I could not bear to sell Yarrowdale Hall to one such as her," Emma said.

"Is that the only reason?"

Looking away, Emma nodded. Maximillian lowered his hand, and she moved to the window. "So," she said. "It is decided. We sell to Bedford. He is not the encroaching mushroom that Mrs. Browning is, and he will not pale at the thought of scandal. I am certain he will be only too happy to—"

"Emma."

"—acquire so fine a—"

"Emma!"

"Yes?"

"I am not going to sell to Bedford."

"You aren't?"

"No," Max said, stepping closer. "I am not."

"Why not?" Emma whispered.

"I have had enough traveling. I like to travel, but I did it at first because I had no choice, and I continued doing it because I did not know anything else. I did not know what having a home was like until I came here. It made me feel good to be called 'Squire' and be looked up to. But even more than that, to have someone worry over me, to have someone remember my birthday, my favorite meal—it was *wonderful!*" He took another step closer. "My dear Emmaline, I have been happier here than I have ever been, and I would be a damned fool to give it all up. I will stay in Yarrowdale. This is where I belong."

"Oh, Max! *That* is why I did not want to sell!"

He took another step, closing the gap between them, and placed his finger over her lips. "Shh . . . let me finish." He took her hand and kissed it and looked into her eyes once more. "I have informed Bedford that I do not wish to sell and I asked him for a loan of thirty thousand pounds. You can still go, if you wish; I will buy the glasshouse and try to be happy for you. But my home, like my heart, will always be at your side, and if you will have me, Emmaline, I will follow you to the ends of the earth. As your husband."

Kneeling before her, Maximillian took her hand in his again, his eyes full of love. "Please say you will marry me, beloved."

Throwing her arms around him, Emmaline sent them both tumbling to the floor. "Yes! Yes, I will! What else can I do?" She laughed.

And what else could Max do but kiss her?

After a long while, Max cradled her against his chest, closed his eyes, and breathed in the warm, sweet fragrance of orange blossoms that always clung to her shiny hair.

"Where shall we be married? Venice? Athens? India?"

"Why not here in Yarrowdale?"

Max gave her a quizzical look.

Emmaline shrugged. "You were right; adventure is everywhere. I realize now that what I craved wasn't lions and hurricanes and jungles and elephants. No. What I wanted—needed!—was someone with whom to share the everyday adventures."

"And you were afraid that if you did not begin your search by your thirtieth birthday—by the Winter Solstice—that you would never find that someone, because Miss Thatcher had already completed her adventures the year she turned thirty."

She sat up and peered searchingly into his eyes. "You are so wise." She took his hand and gently kissed each of his fingers. "I would like to travel someday, but I do not wish to miss a day of your first autumn in Yarrowdale. The leaves are beautiful here. Crimson and yellow and flaming orange. And our harvest festival is always such fun!"

"Christmas in Italy, then?"

She shook her head. "We would miss the first snowfall, and I confess a childish delight in decking the halls with green. We could not have our own Yule log in some drafty Roman hotel.

And what Italian cook can make a proper Twelfth Night pudding?"

"I have never had a Christmas pudding."

"There. You see? We must stay through Christmas."

"I suppose spring in Yarrowdale is on our itinerary as well?"

"Indeed. The hills burst into color, all green and fragrant and—oh Maximillian!—what an adventure it will be to share it all with you! You are seeing it all for the first time, and I feel like I am too. I cannot wait to leap into it!" Grasping his hand, she pulled him toward the door. "Come. Let us go plant those roses! Right now."

As they walked out the door, Max asked, "No wedding journey?"

Emmaline stopped and stared out across the valley, a soft smile on her face. "A short one," she murmured and then gifted him with a brilliant smile. "I should like very much to climb those mountains across the valley—with you."

Behind them, Moon and Malachi purred happily.

"So, we brought him up to scratch," Malachi said on a satisfied sigh.

Moon blinked at him. "I do not imagine we had much to do with it."

Malachi licked his paw and rubbed his ear thoughtfully. "You are right, beloved. They were life-mated, after all. They would have found each other eventually."

"Eventually," Moon agreed, "but I am glad it happened before they sold Yarrowdale Hall. This will be a lovely place for our kittens to grow up."

Malachi froze, his paw in midair. "Kittens?"

Moon gave a soft smile, tucked her white paws contentedly under her, and curled her tail around Malachi. "Three of them, I think."

EPILOGUE

Harvest was over, and the air outside was chilly and crisp. The weather had been unseasonably cool, and the trees were already barren outside, but inside the glasshouse it was eternally summer, and Emmaline's orange trees remained lush with green and heavy with blossoms. The morning sun shone through the beveled glass, sending rainbows skittering over the dark gray flagstones, which were deliciously warm—especially near the little stove, where Moon and Malachi waited in an inviting pool of morning sunlight.

They, like everyone else in the glasshouse, were watching for Emmaline, who was due to arrive any moment.

Turned out in their Sunday best, the Yarrowdale villagers had all crowded inside. Many had small gifts perched proudly on their laps—homemade scarves, candies, or carved wooden boxes. Their pet was wedding this day—by special license!—and not to just anyone but to none other than the squire of Yarrowdale Hall. Which, they all agreed, was as it should be.

Their smiles seemed to bounce off the glass along with excited murmurs, laughter, and the intermingled strains of a lively Mozart concerto. The air was thick with the scent of soap and starch and orange blossoms and joy.

Malachi sighed and gave a contented swat at the tip of Moon's lazy tail. "Where are the kittens?"

"Locked safely away in the Hall. I wanted them to be here, but they are so young; they cannot possibly understand. And here there are so many feet," she said, glancing nervously at the assembled crowd.

Malachi's eyes filled with love. "Is it not strange, beloved, how everything works out in the end?"

"No, dearest. It isn't strange at all. Some things are meant to be. Every stray has his home. Every heart has its mate."

At that moment, the ornate glass door opened, the orchestra stilled, Maximillian took his place at the opposite end of the glasshouse, and everyone stood. Malachi and Moon watched happily as Emma walked serenely between the twin rows of orange trees, wearing Sophia's beautiful, abandoned wedding gown and a simple circle of orange blossoms in her blond hair.

Malachi's chest swelled with pride. She was his mistress. Lady Moonbeam was his mate. And Max was still his friend. Everything was perfect. This was his home. His family. His life.

But then, all at once, as Emmaline passed, Moon gave a cry of alarm. A trio of perplexed kittens hung with their forelegs outstretched and their tiny claws embedded into the back of the bride's gown.

"The kittens!" Malachi sprang to his feet. If they fell, they'd probably roll onto Emmaline's long, white train, but if not, the flagstone floor was hard and jagged, and their three-week-old bones were yet tiny, and—tooth and claw!—there were so many feet around them!

"I'll get Sun!" Moon cried. "You take Star!"

"What about Jewel?"

Moon wailed in answer, her eyes full of misery.

Yet the cats weren't the only ones who had noticed the kittens. The villagers tried to keep straight faces, but inevitably giggles erupted amongst the children, and the adults weren't far behind. Emmaline's steps faltered as Moon's pupils dilated and her hindquarters wriggled in preparation for a spring.

At the last moment, Max reached down with his strong hands and gently plucked all three orange-and-white fluff balls from Emmaline's train. Handing one to Emmaline, Max held out his crooked arm to her, a kitten in each hand snuggled against his chest. Emmaline tossed her flowers aside and cradled her furry burden with a warm smile. The wedding couple laughed, and Malachi and Moon fell into step beside them. They all walked the rest of the way together as the villagers looked on with a smile.

Lady Moonbeam exchanged fond glances with Malachi. "I am glad humans are so sensible!"

About the Author

Melynda Beth Skinner lives in Florida with her own true love, their two dear daughters, and one spectacular orange troublemaker, Malachi

She invites you to visit her at www.melyndabethskinner. com, where you can e-mail her or chat with her online.